WHITEFIRE

At Tyuratam, red flashes warning of systems failure in the test missile began in turn on each of the monitoring consoles, the Soviet technicians becoming increasingly frantic as each electronic function within the sophisticated weapon began to die. Then, like all its predecessors on the NE-04 test programme, the giant missile plunged downward, out of control.

In a mad rage the programme director slammed his fist onto the master control console. 'No!' he bawled, his total frustration overwhelming him. 'It cannot be! There is nothing wrong! *Nothing!*'

In a glass booth overlooking the centre a Red Army (Rocket Forces) general lifted a telephone linked directly to the Kremlin and reported the latest failure, visualizing, as he spoke, his own bleak future.

Also in Arrow by Glover Wright

THE TORCH

WHITEFIRE

Glover Wright

ARROW BOOKS

Arrow Books Limited
17-21 Conway Street, London W1P 6JD

An imprint of the Hutchinson Publishing Group

London Melbourne Sydney Auckland
Johannesburg and agencies throughout
the world

First published by Hutchinson 1983
Arrow edition 1984

© Geoffrey Glover-Wright 1983

Printed and bound in Great Britain by
Anchor Brendon Limited, Tiptree, Essex

ISBN 0 09 934740 7

*To Reginald Charles and Doreen Emily Glover-Wright,
my parents, with love*

ACKNOWLEDGEMENTS

I am indebted to the following people for their invaluable assistance in the research and writing of this book: Lt-Commander O. M. de las Casas, MVO, OBE; Lt-Colonel M. E. Kreisel, Assistant Army Attaché at the United States Embassy in London; Lt-Colonel Edward O. Yaugo, Commander 1st Battalion (Ranger) US 75th Infantry (otherwise known as the Black Berets), whose awards and decorations are too numerous to list here; Viscount Villiers, for allowing me to pick his inventive, scientific mind; Lord Bethel, for information on Kremlin personalities; two long-standing friends in the 'Annexe' who would prefer to remain nameless; Mrs J. Griggs of Jersey; Miss Caroline Griggs, also of Jersey, for her long, uncomplaining hours spent on the typescript; Mr Andrew Nurnberg, my own personal 'Russia-watcher'; and last, but certainly not least, fellow author and friend Jack Higgins, for allowing me the use of his excellent and extensive research library and for offering me his completely unselfish advice.

'I am become death, the destroyer
of worlds'

> Incantation –
> The Hindu god Vishnu

PART ONE

The Board

Berlin 1945
The Führer-Bunker

'Seal them in!' Hitler roared. 'Let the traitors rot for all eternity!'

Above, Berlin crumbled under Russian hammer blows, but deep below ground the only effect they had was to shake more fine dust off the massive reinforced concrete walls and ceilings.

Karl Muller let his pitiless, blue eyes fall briefly from the ravaged face of his Führer and onto the sleeve of his own immaculate black SS uniform. The dust was like some creeping disease: it lay on clothes and worked itself into hair; it filled creases in skin like mortar so that the men who lived in the bunker had faces networked by fine white lines, making even the young seem aged.

Fools! thought Muller. Only crazy men could stay in this concrete trap. The time had come – as much as he admired the past achievements of the Führer – to direct his loyalties in another direction. And to Muller there was only one other loyalty: himself. 'It will be difficult to get to the island, my Führer,' he said, but his handsome face had that bland expectancy of a man who knew his problem would be solved.

Adolf Hitler scribbled a note on personalized notepaper and held it out, his hand shaking so badly that Muller found it impossible to read what had been written. He reached out with slim manicured hands and steadied it, and only then did Hitler release it. It was a carte blanche directive giving Muller immediate access to any form of transport or facility he might need. Life for Karl Muller was suddenly going to be much easier.

Hitler was talking again and Muller jerked his mind back to the reality of the doomed underground fortress and the madman before him.

'When you have executed them, bring me the results of

their work.' Without warning an unnatural fire exploded in Hitler's piercing blue eyes and Muller understood why men stayed loyal to the drug-ridden, half-crazed mortal they placed higher than any god. 'I will find out where their failure lies! I shall seek out their treachery!'

'You have a great instinct in these matters, my Führer,' Muller agreed, filling his words with admiration.

But Adolf Hitler was no longer listening; he was speaking and it was the duty – the privilege – of others to listen. The tirade continued and nobody – least of all Karl Muller – would dare to stop him. Muller stood completely still, waiting, every bone in his body, every muscle, screaming for release.

Hitler shuddered and let out a sigh, then slumped against his chair. 'Aah!' he breathed as if seeing his past glories sweeping once more before him, then slipping hopelessly away: irretrievable memories of a Golden Age. '*Der flüsternde Tod!*' he whispered hoarsely and with a certain sad regret. The whispering death.

He lifted his eyes to Muller, and a hand, still trembling, index finger and thumb a fraction from touching. 'We were this far – *this far* – from being Masters of the World! Even now, if those traitors had not failed me, the Reich could rise from the ashes like the Phoenix and destroy its enemies in their farthest cities. Nothing could have stopped us. Nothing! Why should the future have the fruits of our genius? *Why?*'

Muller thought that Hitler was building himself up for another hysterical outburst but there was no strength left.

Softly, almost pleading, he said: 'Bring everything back. Kill them all and seal them in forever, then return to me.'

Muller cracked the heels of his high, gleaming jackboots together, then snapped a perfect Nazi salute in the air. 'It will be an honour to return to your side, my Führer. My greatest privilege would be to die with you.'

Hitler nodded and waved him away. Foolishly he did not look into the lying, ice-blue eyes of the SS executioner.

The Arctic Circle
1945

The U-boat surfaced close to the grey concrete jetty hacked out of the base of the cliff. Above it, the black-rock island smashed like a fist through the Arctic waters; a tilted plateau which offered no shelter – save the stone needle of the lighthouse and its two huts – to any wretched soul who might have survived the marrow-freezing waters.

Winter, like the Third Reich, was dying and ice floes floated like smashed white china on the whipped grey surface of the sea. On the plateau itself, patches of snow hid in crannies between the rocks while moss and lichen – which survived everything – clung yellow and green to whatever surface gave them succour.

The U-boat commander trained his glasses on the cliffs, experiencing a wave of loneliness that only a place so bleak and hopeless could inspire.

'Men have gone mad here,' he said to Karl Muller. 'The Norwegians call it the Fist of Thor, the Russians the Devil's Claw. How our people can work here is impossible to understand.'

Muller said nothing. He raised the fur-lined hood of his parka over his high-fronted black cap, drawing the cord tight so that only half of his face and the silver SS death's-head badge was visible. The commander glanced at him from the corner of his eye. This place suits you, he thought.

'How close can you get?' Muller asked.

'Right up to the jetty. They've blown the rock projections away beneath the surface. You won't even get your boots wet.'

Muller barked an order down the steel hatch at his feet. Below him, in the hull, the SS death squad formed themselves into a line, the leading man ready with one boot on the rung of the vertical ladder.

The U-boat grated metallically alongside the jetty and Muller climbed down onto the hull, then jumped for the slimy concrete, grasping the corroded railing for safety. Then he reached under his hood to both ears. As his men followed, he took a nickel-silver Walther automatic pistol from its holster beneath his parka and screwed a plated silencer onto the barrel.

On the bridge of the submarine, the commander watched him expressionlessly; only the defeat in his eyes gave away his inner feelings. If anyone had to kill me, he thought, I would choose you. You would do it well.

The death squad began to move up the wet zigzag path cut into the rock, stumbling occasionally on the dangerous surface. At the summit, Muller directed them toward a clump of rocks and ordered them to wait. 'If anyone comes to the surface before I'm ready,' he said, 'kill them.'

Taking a pack from one of the men he ran toward the lighthouse, entered it and made his way down a circular iron stairway to a basement. There sat three bearded figures, bundled in heavy winter clothing, feet up on a pot-bellied stove, chairs tilted back, their rough hands filled with playing cards. Despite the stove their noses and cheeks were blue and ill-looking from the cold. All three saw Muller at once and scrambled to their feet, the chairs crashing backward as they sprang rigidly to attention. He shot them immediately, one bullet for each. There was no sound bar a sharp *phut* preceding each muffled *thump* as the heavily clothed bodies dropped to the stone-flagged floor.

He found a heavy key in one of the dead men's pockets, then pushed aside a large but surprisingly light wood packing case to reveal a solid steel door. He opened it and stood cautiously on an iron grating above a vertical ladder which plunged deep into the rock. Quickly, he began placing explosive charges from the pack at strategic points on the walls, connected them to a timer, then stepped out again into the circular well at the base of the lighthouse.

His men waited for him impatiently at the clump of rocks, stamping their feet against the cold. As he ran up to them he snapped an order and they began removing camouflage netting from a low black steel door, its riveted surface already a home for the creeping patches of moss. The door was operated by a lever which gave way easily to pressure, allowing the heavy panel to swing outward smoothly on well-oiled hinges.

Clammy, stale air filled their nostrils as the death squad ran, heads ducked, down the low-ceilinged emergency escape tunnel, the crash of their boots accompanied by a fierce metallic *clack* as their Schmeisser machine pistols were cocked for firing. At the end of the sloping tunnel, Muller swung the wheel on a circular gas lock, then pushed his men through, following himself at their rear.

As they entered the control centre, the faces of the white-coated scientists inside jerked around in surprise. The Schmeissers flamed and roared without warning, allowing neither appeals nor protest, flinging the bloodied bodies against the rough concrete walls.

Muller waved his men on towards the corridors leading off the control centre, then, moving quickly, placed a single bullet in the brain of any of the bodies that showed signs of life. From one he snatched a key hung on a neck chain, then darted to a small office where the safe was located. Opening it, he gathered up the contents and swept them into a yellow oilcloth sack taken from his parka pocket. Somewhere behind him he heard long raking bursts of fire from the machine pistols, then silence. He kicked the safe closed with his boot, then sprinted back toward the gas lock and the emergency tunnel. Breathing in short, quick gasps, and sweating despite the intense cold, he moulded a tiny amount of plastic explosive on the inner clamp of the steel door, then jammed in the detonator and stepped outside into the freezing air. He swung the door shut and pulled the lever up, feeling at that moment a deep vibration under his feet as the charge in the bowels of the lighthouse detonated. Working faster now, his breath coming in rasps, he placed six metal wedges in the rim of the door, then used his remaining explosives on the rocks around it. This done, and ignoring the sudden thumps from inside the door, he dashed for the zigzag path down the cliff to the waiting submarine, the yellow sack bouncing on his back as he scrambled down the dangerous descent. Above him, he heard the flat crack of an explosion.

At the bottom, the commander called out to him but Muller did not answer. He jumped for the boat's rail, then mounted the conning tower.

The commander said: 'The Führer is dead. Berlin has just announced it.'

Muller stared at him incomprehendingly, then reached up to his ears and pulled out two wax plugs. He dropped them to the deck.

'The Führer is dead,' the commander repeated. 'Confirmed. Berlin radio.'

Muller pulled back his hood and threw his black SS cap far out to sea. He smiled at the commander's astonishment. 'The war is lost, Kapitän. How long do you think I will last if the Allies catch me?' He jammed a hand into an inner pocket and came out with a leather wallet. 'Here are my new papers. I shall need seaman's clothing – your lowest rank if you will.'

The commander turned his face to the sea, breathing in the pure, frozen air.

'We all want to survive, Kapitän,' said Muller quietly. 'It has been a long war.'

'Yes,' the commander agreed, wearily. 'It has been a long war. What about your men?' His eyes lifted to the clifftop.

Muller smiled and stepped down the ladder. 'They're staying,' he said.

Underground, on the island, the SS death squad screamed until the linings of their throats bled, but no one would ever hear them.

On the surface the dark island was silent, and beyond, on the sea – and farther still, on the land – the guns of war too fell silent as the last remaining forces of the 'master race' bowed to inevitable defeat.

Summer came, then winter snows which covered the black hostile face of the island as if concealing its dreadful secret.

The Arctic Circle Today

The nose cone of the missile iced up as it cleaved through the freezing, thin air over the Russian outer islands of Novaya Zemlya. The fine skin of ice slithered backwards until it touched the nearest point of the red Communist star emblazoned on the black titanium hull. Farther back along its great length the thrusting ion-propulsion motors blasted a trail of white-hot flame and condensation as the ICBM screamed on toward the Arctic Circle. Quite suddenly, the rocket flamed out and the huge nose dipped sharply toward the white wastes below.

In the underground headquarters of the Soviet Missile Test Centre at Tyuratum, frustrations exploded as yet another unexplained failure of their new NE-04 missile was registered. Frustrations which turned quickly to fear as recriminations began.

'I hate this place!' Jemma Elliot complained as she sat astride Matthew Jordan, letting her pubis scratch along the skin over his hard-muscled stomach before pushing herself onto him. She breathed in sharply with intense pleasure, moving slowly, bringing him to orgasm in her own time. For a while she lay beside him in the narrow bunk, smoking – to his displeasure – then got up and began washing herself in the handbasin.

Jordan had heard her comment but had chosen to ignore it; he had heard the same complaint from her too many times before. He watched her at the basin and felt desire moving in him again. Leaning over, he crushed out the still smouldering remnant of her cigarette, then stood up and clasped her swaying breasts from behind, watching his hands work on them in the mirror.

She extricated herself. 'No!' she said. 'Not just because *you* want to. I won't be used!'

'Who's using who?' Jordan retorted, then, shaking his head wearily, began pulling on his clothes.

'Christ, you give up easily!' she sneered. 'What's the matter – this place sucking the guts out of you at last?' Her voice had the sharp nasal bite of New York, though by birth she was British.

Jordan faced her, then ran a large hand through his sandy crew-cut. 'You were recruited like the rest of us,' he pointed out. 'You had a free choice. No one forced you to work on the project. *Your* decision.'

'All right! So I'm finding it difficult to adjust. Just leave me be. Hear me?'

'Why don't you go topside? I think you need the air.'

'And freeze my ass off? I may suffer from claustrophobia but I like my warmth – I'll stick it out, thanks!'

'Suit yourself.' Jordan clicked the door shut behind him and walked the length of the corridor, shaking his head once more in exasperation and silently cursing his involvement with her. He should have known better. Never involve yourself emotionally when there's no escape route, he advised himself pointlessly. And certainly there was no escape, sealed in under tons of rock!

He entered the sophisticated communications room, raised a hand in greeting to Simpson, the chief duty operator, and poured himself coffee from the ever-hot percolator.

Simpson dragged the headphones off his head and rubbed his ears roughly to increase the circulation.

'So what's new in the world, Ray?' Jordan asked. 'Wall Street up or down?'

Simpson looked up from his rubbing. 'Never take any notice, Dr Jordan. Share prices aren't my thing.'

Jordan let his arm swing out, taking in the banks of complex, highly expensive equipment. 'They should be. What do you think pays for all this hardware?'

'I just work it, sir. I'll leave that side to you.'

'Not me. I just drive the bus. I can't count past six zeros. So what *was* on the news?'

'The usual: recession, depression, unemployment up, East-West relations down; world chess championships in

Geneva – Tavrin winning of course, England bombed out again in the test match. The Russians are mopping up in Poland but they've got more trouble in East Germany – same pattern, strikes, factory takeovers, food queues, the lot. Washington's sanctions are beginning to bite and the Kremlin's making angry noises. Can I cheer you up some more?'

'Did you pick up AFN for the ball game?'

'Sorry, missed it. You were a big college star, weren't you? Rough game Yank football.'

'Another lifetime,' Jordan murmured with a rueful grin, and fingered his slightly misshapen nose.

Simpson surveyed the solid frame of the man, taking in the wide shoulders and heavy forearms, bared by the short-sleeved shirt and brushed with a matt of blond hair. Jordan's head too was large, with a strong sunlamp-browned face – his nose once Roman but now distinctly broken and reset. His warm – almost tan-coloured – eyes were gentle, belying the enormous strength of his body. It was a face men admired without jealousy – and women found more than a little interesting. Matthew Jordan, coming from a privileged Southern background, could have entered the American political arena with ease – his image and credentials were perfect – but all politics, he knew, involved compromise; the wrong kind of compromise – and Jordan had too much of the sharp cut of the idealist about him to enter that blurred world.

He stood up to his full six feet five inches. 'You monitored the Soviet military frequency in the last two hours?'

Simpson slid a long report sheet along the console. 'All there.'

Jordan glanced at it but did not read the details. 'Well?' he asked, instead.

'No problems,' said Simpson. 'We didn't get a mention.'

'Let's keep it that way,' Jordan murmured and slid the report back.

London

'What we are looking for', said the interviewer, 'is a special type of man. Someone who would work independently of all other personnel. Someone who could stand being totally isolated. Isolated in both the geographical sense and also cut off from the normal close companionship of his fellows. Such a man could not share – would not feel the *need* to share if you see my point. He must be willing to be disliked; possibly even hated.'

Simon Howard crossed his short legs, his small feet shod in polished leather shoes which gleamed at the toes like a guardsman's boots. 'You're talking to him!' he stated with a smirk, his accent London but shaded with odd multi-national nuances which emerged unexpectedly, then faded abruptly. Now American, now South African; a touch there of Australasia; a hint of upper-crust English. His voice had a shifting quality which, to a listener, was bewildering. The interviewer wondered whether – though this was the third and final interview – he really was talking to the same man.

'You prefer isolation?' he asked.

Howard pointed a brown finger at the desk. 'Read my curriculum vitae,' he said, proud of his use of Latin. 'It's all there – everything I've done.'

'And in your earlier life? Your childhood?'

Simon Howard had nothing to say about his childhood.

'Yes, well . . . the rest is all here . . . now this business of your leaving the British Army? I wonder could we broach that subject once more. Just to get it straight.'

'Nothing more to say. I don't take orders that are stupid.'

'Orders that *you* believe to be stupid!'

But Simon Howard considered the matter closed. He crossed his hands over his knees and looked at the interviewer.

The interviewer, in turn, studied the hands. They were very brown – so much so that he wondered if, in the distant past, Howard's family had not welcomed a touch of colour into their lives. The cutting edges were ridged with hard, yellowed callouses and the tips of the fingers, too, had that same peculiar dead look to them. The nails were cut back and extraordinarily pink and the interviewer knew they had not been chewed. He blinked as the hands were splayed.

Howard said: 'Look, I like special duties, OK? Working on my own. That way I don't get to die for no one else. My mistake? OK, *I* get the chop. No one else.' He leaned back in the straight-backed, uncomfortable chair. *'Actually,* I quite enjoy a touch of isolation – it gives one a chance to improve one's mind.'

The interviewer glanced at his face, searching for any hint of mockery. But there was none; Howard had simply assimilated his accent and manner quite unconsciously.

'So you joined the Australian Army to fight in Vietnam, then transferred to the Americans. Long Range Patrol Unit, I see.'

'LURPS. They call 'em LURPS. Great outfit. Kill-a-gook-a-day, that's their motto.'

'Yes, I see. Then on to South Africa and Rhodesia . . . anti-terrorist units were your speciality. You seemed to have supplied the best body count they'd had . . . the – er, LURPS, I mean.'

Howard nodded, fingering his ears.

The interviewer fell silent, then said: 'INTERSAT is not looking for a killer, Mr Howard. We need a watcher – someone to keep an eye on the way things are going. Really, it is essentially an undercover position . . . though outwardly you will assume security duties. Initially it would be up to you to look after the personal safety of two of our directors who are at present in – shall we say – *delicate* positions due to certain highly important – even crucial – negotiations. INTERSAT, as you probably know already, is the largest company in the weather/communications satellite business. Our techniques are well in advance of the competition, and therefore secret. As this is a comparatively new field our scientists and technicians must be employed on a long-term basis, otherwise they might be tempted away, taking with them our latest techniques. Nevertheless the danger is always there ... the isolated conditions our people sometimes have to work in are not always accepted readily. Often employees believe they can handle it but ....'

'They do a runner,' Howard offered.

'Precisely – they do a "runner". Now our weather satellite research station on Beacon Island is a case in point. We lease it from the Russians for quite a considerable sum in foreign exchange and also a certain amount of high-technology information. This is our normal policy, you understand; there is nothing sinister in this. By this method we are, perfectly legally, able to declare a location neutral, and thereby enjoy certain international privileges. We have such operations in South America, Africa and, as I mentioned, with the Russians.'

Howard shifted uncomfortably and drew his black eyebrows together, giving his already elfin face the look of a malevolent black imp. His quick eyes were quite black and cunning. 'Don't like Russians,' he said.

'Oh, they have no physical contact with the island. Our neutral status ensures that.'

Howard removed a white handkerchief from the top pocket of his blazer and wiped non-existent dust from the shiny toe of his shoe. 'Troublemakers,' he continued, as if the interviewer had not spoken. 'Always sticking their oars in other people's business – know what I mean?'

'As I said *if* INTERSAT offers you an employment contract you will have no contact with them.'

'Suits me.'

'Actually, to be honest, you have already been accepted. You know the terms already – so if you are willing to join us ... ah ... when could you start? To leave in fact. We need you to fly to Frankfurt and meet two of our directors right away.'

'I've always got my bag packed,' Howard said with an air of indifference.

'What about other employment?'

'You mean here? In England?'

'I suppose I do, yes.'

'Don't you read the papers?'

The interviewer smiled. 'I tend to lose sight of British problems – I spend so much time travelling. And of course our head office is in Germany.'

'I like the Germans,' said Howard. 'Really got it together, they have. Never understood how they lost the war.'

'Well then . . . .' The interviewer arose and put out his hand. Howard stood to his full five feet five inches and grasped the offered hand. The interviewer, looking down, felt as if he had hold of a lump of wood. 'You can pick up air tickets and expenses on the way out. They'll give you your instructions. Goodbye.'

'Yeah,' said Howard.

The interviewer watched the short, straight figure leave, looked once more at his hand and gave a small shudder. He dropped his eyes to the folder and read: 'HOWARD. SIMON LAWRENCE. US ARMY. Long Range Patrol Unit 17. Body count: 52. Verification: Ears.'

'Ears,' he breathed. '*Ears!*'

Switzerland
Geneva

The Aeroflot Ilyushin airliner taxied to a halt on an outer perimeter runway at Geneva International Airport. The engines wailed downwards as two pairs of headlights sped toward it. The first vehicle was a black Mercedes saloon while behind it, struggling to keep up, was a mobile gangway truck. Reaching the aircraft, the Mercedes pumped exhaust smoke into the brisk night air impatiently as the gangway was driven into place. Two men emerged finally from the Mercedes; the first stood by the truck, ensuring the driver remained in his cab; the second dashed straight up the gangway, almost losing his hat in his haste.

Inside Vladimir Baranov, the KGB resident director in Geneva, began pulling his light overcoat from his shoulders, then, hearing a gruff order from a too familiar voice at the rear of the long fuselage, he tugged it back on and snatched off his hat.

'Comrade Secretary-General!' he blurted. 'I had no idea ... I was told ....'

'Nor should you have,' said the Soviet leader, coughing heavily. 'I am not here. What is Tavrin's position at this moment?'

Baranov blinked. Surely the most powerful man in Russia had not flown to Switzerland simply to ask how a Russian Grandmaster – even one who was the world chess champion – was faring in the championships? Baranov shifted his feet, warily. He pleaded silently – though he had no god or religion except Marx and his doctrines – not to be drawn into some Kremlin conspiracy. Involvement in such matters usually ended in the small man being hurt and he, under such considerations, believed himself to be a very small man indeed.

'Well?'

'Ah! He's winning – naturally – Comrade Secretary. It is only a matter of time before the challenger resigns.'

'Bring him here.'

'Now? In the middle of a game? Comrade ....'

'Pass him this message: Yuri cannot wait. Then he will win quickly.'

'But ....'

'Go!' The Soviet leader shut his eyes, removed his gold-framed spectacles and dropped his head to his chest. He had long before learned the knack of conserving his energy for the big issues.

Geneva

The two players sat facing each other over the board while behind them, on a larger chequered surface, an illuminated projection of the game was displayed for the hushed audience. Someone coughed and it was an explosion of immeasurable dimension.

The world champion shifted position and stretched his

long legs out, ignoring the petulant frown of his opponent. He placed one thin finger along the bridge of his great hooked nose in a characteristic gesture known by millions who followed the game.

His pale eyes were lightly closed, their lids almost translucent with tiny blue veins showing through – while another vein, thick and cordlike, travelled from above his nose through to lifeless light brown hair which began far back off his wide brow. His ears were prominent, due to his lifelong habit of cupping them forward when facing the board. Altogether it was a face of striking originality – as if the Creator had decided that no other man should share such looks.

Yet somehow He had forgotten – perhaps in His eagerness to perfect the genius of the brain – that the face of a man should display his humanity, for the face was devoid of compassion, a mere façade which mirrored the perfect brain and not the imperfect soul. His name was Mikhail Yaraslavovich Tavrin, Grandmaster of all the Soviets and, since his clinical annihilation of all international competition over the preceding four years, the chess champion of the world.

He was also the Rasputin of modern Russia. With certain differences. Tavrin was entirely sane and utterly invisible in his role and his power lay not in the supernatural but in the genius of his extraordinary mind.

Mikhail Tavrin had visited Europe and the United States on numerous occasions for tournaments, and his name and background in depth were stored in the computer banks of every Western intelligence organization. Each of the major powers had instructed their secret agencies to make a 'pass' at the Russian genius in the hope of pulling off a great propaganda coup, but all had been fobbed off with the same polite but firm answer. 'I am a Russian. I am not a Communist because I will not be controlled. The West could not control me just as the East cannot control me. Nevertheless, I am still a Russian.'

This repeated answer, though convincing and believed because of its apparent sincerity, was a complete lie. Mikhail Tavrin was a confirmed Marxist. He was also the secret advisor of the Soviet Union's leader and the master strategist of that man's strike for power upon the death of his aged predecessor. His every utterance was believed without exception by the man who controlled uncountable destinies and virtually unlimited power.

Tavrin had been born in Leningrad during the bitter siege of that city by Hitler's armies in 1941. Since his rise to fame, for propaganda reasons the Communist Party had built up the story that he was the son of a Russian patriot who had perished in the city's heroic defence after a marriage with an attractive peasant girl fleeing the Nazi advance.

In reality, he was a bastard. The illegitimate son of the same peasant girl after she had been gang-raped by five German infantrymen in a trench eight inches deep in muddy, freezing water. The rape had been stopped forcibly – and for two of the rapists, fatally – by a young, aristocratic Wehrmacht Oberleutnant who hesitated for barely five seconds before using the Luger automatic pistol he had drawn from his holster. One week later, the Oberleutnant had led her under cover of darkness to the edge of the starving city – a week full of personal danger to himself as he had tended to the girl's torn and humiliated body in a small cattle shed on a farm used by the German Army as a forward artillery position. Later, in Leningrad, she was to tell her subsequent Russian lover that she had let the Oberleutnant make love to her to show her gratitude; love-making accompanied by the crashing of the big 88-millimetre guns which rained death on the city day and night. Afterwards, she said, she had watched him through a crack in the planking as he sat playing a game with total concentration, the back of his opponent toward her, so that she could see the cold rigidity of the Oberleutnant's face under his blond hair. Chess! she had exclaimed with surprise. A Russian game. Her father had played it constantly, even up to the night before their family home had been over-run by the advancing German tanks.

Tavrin was born amid starvation and death and survived only because of the sacrifices made for him, and infants like him, by the collective courage of the citizens of Leningrad. And though he realized quickly through his gift of pure logic that all loyalties are subject to the demands of reality, he had never forgotten his debt.

The young German Oberleutnant froze to death the following winter after being wounded by a Red Army tommy-gunner, and the peasant girl lived to see the siege lifted and the Nazis forced out of Russia.

She died in the early 1950s when the young Mikhail (named after her Russian lover who had indeed died a patriot during the siege) was barely thirteen and already showing signs of genius at the chessboard. By the age of eighteen he was already famous within the Soviet Union and the outside world was also beginning to hear of his immense ability.

At some point in his crucial, maturing years he was spotted by a rising Party member who saw more than just the movement of carved figurines on a chequered surface as a vehicle for that complex mind. An ambitious and ruthless man who realized that if the board were bigger, the rewards gained from the use of that icy logic could be incalculable.

The silence of the auditorium was again disturbed as a dark-suited figure tiptoed across the platform and placed a small slip of paper between the fingers of Tavrin's folded hands. The struggling challenger hissed his displeasure at the interruption and glanced scathingly at the offending messenger.

Mikhail Tavrin did not move. Then his eyelids lifted slightly and he gazed at the note. He pocketed it and turned back to the board, his pale, expressionless eyes fixed on his challenger's face. 'You lose,' he said quietly, and made his killing move, then uncurled his long body from his chair and strode away from the board, ignoring the applause.

Outside, Tavrin stepped into the waiting Mercedes and leaned back into the cushions, waving away Baranov's congratulations as the car sped through the busy traffic towards the airport.

'How is he?' Tavrin asked, his face still turned away to the window.

'A cough troubles him, Comrade Grandmaster. Otherwise he seems well enough.' Baranov's voice was a mere whisper; he rubbed his hand across his permanently blue jaw, producing an ugly rasping sound.

Tavrin glanced at him contemptuously. He detested nervous men; they made mistakes. 'Go faster,' he ordered and shut his eyes. The driver depressed his foot even more firmly on the accelerator.

At the airport Baranov used his diplomatic pass once more to gain admittance to the guarded strips of tarmac which led out into the night.

'Wait in the car,' Tavrin ordered as the Mercedes drew up at the foot of the gangway leading up to the Soviet airliner. The driver leaped out and heaved the door open, stealing a quick glance at the legendary face as the strangely birdlike head ducked out from the interior of the car. Then, with long strides, the Grandmaster was up the gangway and inside the airliner. What a story to tell his mates, the driver thought, but knowing that he was going to be told to keep his mouth shut. He'd got used to things with that certain smell. Why louse up a plum posting like Geneva for the sake of a moment's second-hand glory?

The Soviet leader was already awake, though he feigned sleep. He sensed the extraordinary presence of the tall figure above him. 'Mikhail Yaraslavovich,' he said and opened his eyes, slipping his gold-framed spectacles back on immediately.

'Yuri Vladimirovich,' Tavrin responded and sat in the seat across the aisle. 'I am told you have a cough. You must stop smoking.'

'Impossible.'

The Grandmaster stared down the long body of the airliner, then turned and looked directly at the fleshy, bespectacled face which might easily have belonged to a successful Western banker. '*Nothing* is impossible,' he said.

The full lips smiled. 'Allow me one human failing, Mikhail.'

'In your position you can afford none. The wolves are at

your door within and without Russia. Ill health is like any other weakness, comrade – your enemies can use it against you.'

The Soviet leader pinched the cardboard filter on the cigarette between his fingers but left it unlit. Tavrin noticed the beads of sweat at his hairline. The words when they came at last were taut: 'I am on the brink, my friend. The edge of the precipice. Perhaps, in my past, I have made too many enemies. The cabals are growing – the conspiracies fester around me like sores. The Americans back my opponents in secret but I can prove nothing! They *embarrass* me with their sanctions, they *reduce* me in the eyes of others, they are *forcing* me into concessions I feel unable to give. The NE-04 programme is a total failure and without the new missile I shall have to accept cutbacks on our SS-20s without the certain knowledge of a replacement programme. If I do this the hyenas will have my throat when I return to the Kremlin.'

'Yes,' the Grandmaster agreed.

'There are some who suspect your position with me. They will not allow your reputation – your popularity – to stand in their way. Memories are short in this world, even for such as you.'

The Grandmaster looked out of the porthole at the sudden roar. A row of illuminated holes flashed past, then lifted at a sharp angle and sped like tracers to the stars. 'That is so,' he said.

The Secretary-General grunted and removed his spectacles, polishing the lenses slowly with a silk handkerchief. 'My courier has been keeping you up to date on the matter we discussed in Moscow?'

Tavrin nodded. 'This information the KGB has purchased from the former employee of this corporation – how firm is it?'

The Soviet leader raised his eyebrows and slipped his glasses back on. 'When information is bought one must always distrust it – and that would have been the case here if our agents in Washington had not informed us of this rumour of top security meetings the American President has been holding with some of his scientific advisors. There is a document – a file, or report – which is causing concern at these meetings. That is the story which is being passed around. What it contains is not known, not even the subject matter.'

'You cannot penetrate their administration any further?' Tavrin asked.

'Impossible. Even now we are risking deep-penetration agents every time we ask them to delve deeper.'

Tavrin sat silently, quite still, for a while, then spoke, choosing every word with care. 'If the information you have bought *is* genuine – and the reports of these rumoured secret meetings seem to give it some basis in fact – then you have no choice but to act. Your position will be eroded most severely if you do not.' The Grandmaster hesitated, as if measuring the man before him. 'But if you act there are considerable risks.'

'Each step I take is a risk.'

Tavrin leaned across and flicked the wheel of a gold lighter. The Soviet leader dipped his cigarette to the flame, coughing immediately the smoke hit his lungs. 'Advise me,' he said, his face reddened.

The Grandmaster gave a bleak smile that never touched his eyes. 'Logic, Yuri Vladimirovich. Pure, indisputable logic. If you cannot go to the Americans in a position of strength then you must not go at all.'

The jowls of the fleshy face wobbled impatiently. 'You *know* that is out of the question. Their sanctions are harming us more than I would dare admit – even to you. If I do not go to the Americans they will certainly starve us to death. Their new regime was voted in on a platform of strength – they cannot be seen to be weak.'

Tavrin swept the words away with his hand. 'I am laying out your options. Our death by starvation is not an issue. Death itself is an issue – one of the options. The other is life. There are no others. If you accept what I shall say to you then at some point you might have to face the worse of the two options.' Tavrin's gaze was steady. 'When I say you, Yuri, I mean all of Russia.'

The Soviet leader's fleshy lips parted drily; he blinked and his mouth remained open.

Tavrin continued: 'You told me you were at the edge of the precipice. It is possible you may have to look over it.'

'But I *cannot* take such a decision! In such a situation I would have to consult with . . . .'

Tavrin stopped him dead. 'Oh, you can, Comrade Secretary-General. You can! Up to a certain level it is entirely within your power. *If* you are prepared to risk your position.'

Even through the thick flesh of the neck Tavrin could see the Secretary-General's Adam's apple move. 'What must be done?'

Taking long fingers of one hand, the Grandmaster began counting off points and the fleshy, mottled face opposite him grew paler as if stricken by a sudden, unexpected illness. The cigarette burned right down to the cardboard filter, then the stained fingers, but the face did not flinch.

The Grandmaster talked on.

The Mercedes sped away as the engines of the Ilyushin restarted, whining up the scale to an unsuppressed roar. Inside the car, Tavrin turned to the KGB officer. 'It is essential that I contact our naval base at Severomorsk, Murmansk. The call must be immediate and entirely secure. Do you have such a facility here in Geneva?'

Baranov's nervousness had grown, but he made an attempt to cover it. 'Of course, comrade.'

'Take me there.'

Baranov leaned forward, gave instructions, then said: 'Ten minutes.'

Tavrin shut his eyes, letting his head fall back against the headrest, his brain sifting smoothly through the facts at his command.

'We are here,' Baranov murmured, thinking that the Grandmaster was asleep.

The house was large and surrounded by trees with dense foliage, but even in the darkness Tavrin could see the massed antennae against the skyline. The half-circle driveway was gravelled and the feet of the two men crunched into it as they made their way to the heavy, reinforced door.

Baranov worked the triple locks with practised ease while Tavrin watched the peeping eye of the concealed camera in the frame of the porchway. Inside, Baranov led the way into a comfortable-looking study, furnished in dark wood and depressing, murky-coloured materials.

'A particular number?' the KGB resident inquired, his hand resting on the telephone he had unlocked from a wall safe.

Tavrin looked coldly at him.

'Ah!' Baranov uttered, apologetically. 'You may dial direct, Comrade Grandmaster. Use the instrument as if you were back in Moscow.'

Tavrin took the phone from him. 'Alone,' he said. 'Wait in the car.'

Baranov scuttled to the door, eager to be out of such high-powered games.

Tavrin placed the instrument on a large leather-topped desk, then moved to the thick drapes. He watched the KGB officer re-enter the car, then waited a full minute to check that he remained inside. Satisfied, he walked back and dialled the number.

The connection took longer than he had anticipated but finally a deep resonant voice, echoing, and touched with an odd vibrato caused by the electronic scramblers along the route, boomed down the line. 'Ulyanov,' it said gruffly, as if woken from sleep.

'Tavrin.' The Grandmaster answered. 'The moment has come. Act now, do not delay. Make your preparations tonight but be entirely sure of the men you choose. Do not consider any you doubt – even in the slightest. Sergei, *tonight*!'

The deep voice rose with concern. 'And you?'

Tavrin hesitated, then moved again to the window and checked the figures in the darkened Mercedes. 'I will bring Chebrikov,' he said, closing the tiny gap.

'What must I do when I have the men?' the voice asked, and Tavrin could hear the tension and the desperation to end the call.

'Listen to me and follow everything I say without deviation. *Do not act on your own* no matter what might happen.

I have control of everything. Make no decisions – just follow my instructions as if you are a man whose life has been planned in advance. If you do not you are lost. Believe me.'

'I believe you.'

The Grandmaster spoke quickly and concisely, his free hand moving through the air as if each instruction was a chesspiece placed into position in a game in which he alone could see the opponent and the outcome. Finally he replaced the receiver in the small wall safe, then walked outside to the car.

Baranov rolled his window down. 'Is everything satisfactory?' he asked, eager to please now that the conspiracy seemed to be over.

Tavrin indicated the driver with his odd pale eyes. 'Send him away,' he said.

Baranov spoke rapidly while moving over for Tavrin to enter the car. They watched in silence as the driver walked along the gravel driveway, taking cigarettes from a pocket and lighting one as he strolled.

'Ask no questions,' Tavrin ordered. 'Do what I tell you in every respect and I will ensure that your career will improve. Do *not* – or consult with *anyone*, even your superiors – and I will destroy every dream you have for yourself. You understand me, comrade?'

Baranov's head jerked readily. 'I am at your orders, Comrade Grandmaster. I know who was on the aircraft.'

'No one was on that aircraft. It was empty.'

Baranov nodded dumbly. 'The plane was empty, you are right of course.'

'I am. Here is what you will do for me. Tonight, at Severomorsk, the crew of one of our submarines will mutiny. They will sail underwater to Norway – to the Sogne Fjord. Do you know where that is?'

Baranov's face was a death mask in the darkness. 'I can find out,' he stammered. 'I do not understand . . . .'

'Don't attempt to understand,' Tavrin advised. 'Just accept. Between now and tomorrow evening you will make secure arrangements to get me and two other persons to that fjord and the submarine.'

33

Baranov nodded unhappily. 'The other persons . . . they are in Switzerland?'

'In Geneva.'

'Then there is no problem, comrade.'

Tavrin raised one eyebrow sharply. 'You accept too easily, my friend. The other persons are Josef Chebrikov and his grand-daughter.'

The KGB resident started and flicked his eyes uneasily into the darkness beyond the steamed-up windows. '*Impossible!*' he whispered. 'The defector is guarded day and night by the Swiss.'

Tavrin snorted. 'Chebrikov defected more than a decade ago! He is an old man now. Any secrets he held have been passed over by time and technology. When was the last time you had a look at him?'

'I . . . .'

Tavrin ignored him. 'It does not matter. I shall do most of your work for you. Chebrikov was not just a scientist, he was also a Grandmaster – he taught me much of the game. He must know that I am in Geneva, so I shall call on him as an old friend. I guarantee that he will come willingly – wherever I ask him to go. *After* I have spoken with him alone.'

Baranov faced the pale eyes. 'I am in your hands,' he said, resigned now to his position.

The Grandmaster nodded. 'Yes, comrade, you are.'

The house was very Swiss but small and simple, not palatial, nor in extensive patrolled grounds as other defectors from the Soviet Union had demanded as part of their price for treason. It was no more than Tavrin had expected.

A single police patrol passed as the Grandmaster got out from behind the wheel of the car he had borrowed, but they seemed as interested in all the other properties as they were in the Chebrikov residence. Nevertheless, one of the officers swung his head around as the patrol car passed and Tavrin guessed he had been recognized – a fact which did not disturb him at all.

He pressed the bell and waited.

'Who is there?' a girl's voice asked, speaking German.

'Mikhail Tavrin.'

The door opened but only as far as the chain allowed.

The girl gasped and put her face to the gap, pulling the chain taut. Her eyes looked not at him but past him. He stepped aside to show her the empty car.

'You!' she said, changing to Russian which by her accent was not her first language.

'*You*,' Tavrin countered with mock gravity, 'were a crawling child when I last saw you. It is Tanya?'

'Yes,' she whispered. The chain rattled in its fitting with her trembling.

'Girl, I am not the secret police! Open the door so that I can speak with your grandfather. Is he well?'

'He is well,' she answered, but still the chain remained in place.

'Tanya?' a voice called, crisp but fragile. 'Who calls here?' Russian, but the Jewishness came clear through, unashamedly.

The girl opened her mouth to answer, but her throat was dry and Tavrin had to speak for her.

'A boy who could always beat you at the board, old man!'

Tavrin heard china being pushed aside and the squeal of a chair on a wooden floor, then Josef Chebrikov was there in the hall.

'I would speak with you, old man,' said Tavrin. 'If your guardian here will let me inside.'

An old claw of a hand was cupped and the fingers moved all at once – because they could no longer be used separately – in a drawing-in motion. 'Come! Come! Tanya – Mikhail Yaraslavovich is our friend! He does not bring enemies to our door.'

Reluctantly the girl slipped the chain and stood aside for Tavrin to step into the narrow hallway.

Chebrikov was small and stooped, with a cane for support in his right hand. His clothes were immaculate and clean with none of the careless signs of old age, but, like their owner, they had seen their best days. He thrust out his hand, clutching at Tavrin's as if to assure himself that he was not an apparition from an unhappy past. 'Yes, it is you. How is the Master of the World? Is your brain still cold steel and your heart frozen ice?'

'Were they ever, old man?'

'Always – probably from the day you were born. You should have been born a Jew – then you would have been a complete man. We Jews are the only race who can live with a great intellect and a soul in the same body.'

'Russia is my soul,' Tavrin answered, feeling the weight of the frail body on his hand.

Chebrikov smiled, wistfully. 'Ah! And mine also. But a very different Russia from the one you live in, my clever friend.'

'Both our Russias are dying, old man. That is why I come to see you now. I would speak with you, alone.'

Chebrikov formed a small frown, but it passed as quickly as it had appeared. 'Tanya is all I have, Mikhail. If you cannot speak in front of her then do not speak at all.'

They had moved into a long room, combining both dining-room and drawing-room. The floor was wooden, deeply polished and warm; the overall smell of wax that pervaded the house came from it. There was burnished brass everywhere, dominated by a samovar on the sideboard and the fine, ritual Hebrew candlesticks on the table.

Chebrikov sat in a well-used, high-backed, winged leather armchair, watching the Grandmaster with quick, intelligent eyes. 'Sit, sit!' he urged, and smiled at his grand-daughter, clucking quietly at the concern on her young, almost pretty, face. He said: 'Tanya trusts no one – not even tradesmen. No one delivers any more, she has to go and shop herself. She has a car. You know what kind? Volkswagen. Hitler's People's Car. Imagine such a thing! After *everything*, our grandchildren drive themselves for shopping in that monster's car?'

'It is just a car,' Tanya said.

Chebrikov waved the girl down with his stick. 'So tell me why Russia is dying?'

Tavrin sat crouched forward, but even then he was looking down on the older man. 'Because she is ruled by a tyrant. The satellite states are beginning to crumble from within . . . .' He pointed at a television set: 'You have seen it all – and without them we could never feed ourselves. His iron fist is squeezing too hard. There are some who are ready to take the Kremlin from him. Freer thinkers, intellectuals like ourselves, who are sick of the repression and the failure of the system.'

Chebrikov shook his head wearily but his eyes held a glint of fire – like a forgotten ideal suddenly and unexpectedly smouldering once more. 'Russia has been ruled by tyrants for most of its history, Mikhail. You know that as well as I do. And there has always been unrest in the satellite states. They are all unpredictable – what occupied nation is not? Only God knows how the Warsaw Pact manages to function! And repression? Failure of the system? For these reasons I defected – not for gain. Not because I wanted to betray my country. But we Jews are so used to repression now . . . ' his shoulders drooped '. . . we accept. We *accept*.'

'*You* did not accept, old man. You spoke out. People listened.'

Chebrikov laughed sharply. 'Especially the KGB. They tried to make gruel of my brain in the Kaschenko – but they failed.'

'Yes! They failed. And there are those who remember that. You are needed, Josef Chebrikov – you are needed badly, *now*! Come with me to Murmansk. The sailors are ready to act again – as they have done before . . . .'

'Like 1975!' the girl snapped. 'In the Baltic? They were *shot*! Do not listen, Grandpapa!'

Tavrin turned on her, his grey eyes almost opaque now. 'Men have died and men will die – do not reduce their memories nor their ideals with your bourgeois suspicions. Children of your age live in fear of their lives in Moscow because under their beds they hide printed words which express their feelings. They sit, with blood in their mouths, refusing to answer the questions which will snap the fragile chain which gives them hope. *You* sit in your German car and pour scorn on *this*? Who are you? Bah! You are a child.' He dismissed her with an arrogant twist of his head and turned back to Chebrikov. 'They need men like Josef Chebrikov to show them the way – to give their cause

37

strength and meaning. Come to Murmansk, old man, come back to Russia. Here, you are a Jew only – come back with me and be a Jew *and* a Russian once more.'

Chebrikov laid his white head back against the leather wing of the chair, his eyes pink-rimmed with unshed tears. 'Aaah! there is no one more useless than an old revolutionary. No fire left, no strength.'

Tavrin stood up, his eyes icy. 'Then at least die a revolutionary. Die on the same soil with those who admire you still – and believe in what you once said.'

'Leave him alone!' Tanya cried, quite suddenly. 'He's done enough. What can he do? He's an old man! Can't you see that?'

The tears were now on Chebrikov's face. 'So tell her, Grandmaster. What can this old revolutionary do?'

'Do? You don't have to do anything. You are Chebrikov! Your name – your presence – is enough. Be there! That is all you need to do.'

'Murmansk?' Chebrikov asked, very quietly.

'Murmansk.'

'Stop!' Tanya shouted. 'It is a trick! They want you back so that they can beat you and lock you away. Don't go back to *that*!'

Tavrin said: 'Would you believe me if I took you to the sailors – would their words convince you?'

'In Russia I believe no one!' she spat.

'Not in Russia. They are prepared to take over a submarine and come for you – on the Norwegian coast.'

'They would steal a Soviet submarine?' she asked in wonder.

Tavrin glanced at his watch. 'The submarine has already been stolen. They believed I would be successful – they cannot turn back now. They are committed to this course whether Chebrikov is with them or not.'

Chebrikov prised himself up with his stick. 'Old I may be – but a Judas I have never been – I will not fail them. Pack clothes, girl.'

'Warm clothes,' Tavrin added. 'It will be cold. Very cold.'

PART TWO

Gambit

I

From the air the island was a deformed claw clenched tight, its talons the black cliffs, tucked under so that from their tops you could not see where they sank into the sea. Its surface was lashed mercilessly by freezing spray which was part foam, like floating white handkerchiefs landing softly on the rocks, and part ice splinters, like razor-edged diamonds.

The pilot of the helicopter swivelled his head backward. 'We go down in that – ' he snapped gloved fingers uselessly, ' – three minutes, maybe four . . . dead. OK?'

Simon Howard craned his neck forward for another look at the Arctic Ocean, impressed. Anything that could kill a man that quickly got his unreserved respect.

'Not much ice?' he yelled over the rotor's clatter directly into the pilot's headphoned ear.

'Too early! Give it a couple more months, then we set down here and walk to the Pole.'

'No thanks, I like sunshine.'

The pilot shook his head gravely. 'Not too much here – only sunlamp. No women, only . . . .' He made an obscene pumping gesture with his fist.

Howard frowned – though not because he cared that much for women, for he had gone without sex for months at a time in the jungle – but more because he hated being misinformed. He protested: 'In London they said there was a woman.'

The pilot waggled a finger. 'One. Taken. Bossman's woman. You don't fool around none. Big man. Break your neck, OK?'

Howard said nothing, then pointed downwards quickly. 'What's that place?'

The pilot leaned over in his seat, looking down at a cluster of jagged rocks crowned by a solid-looking square concrete hut. 'For shipwreck. Has food, medicine. Maybe some survivors come in lifeboat – use radio inside, ask help.'

'Anyone ever make it there?'

The pilot turned and gazed at Howard pityingly. 'I told you. These waters no one survives.'

Howard patted the blond Norwegian on the shoulder and stepped back down into the passenger cabin.

'I've spotted Beacon Island,' he told the three seated figures, as if he personally was responsible for the navigation of their journey.

The fur-hatted West German with the strange fine white scars which stood out like stretch marks on his sunlamp-browned face grunted, then closed his blue eyes once more. Herr Reinhardt Weissleder, a director of INTERSAT, was not pleased by the interruption of his dozing. He was cold and he detested the helicopter trips to the island, but also he did not like the little Englishman who had been appointed as bodyguard for travelling INTERSAT directors. If he needed a bodyguard – which he did not – he would have driven to Hamburg and picked any one of a hundred bruisers who did front-of-house duty for St Pauli night clubs.

Howard made a face and leaned over the man beside Weissleder. 'Sir Henry,' he said, 'we're almost there.'

The Englishman smiled gently, looking up from his journal. His skin had that smoothness that only the really wealthy seem to be able to achieve. He sported a grey moustache which matched the widow's peak under the large fur ear muffs he affected. Ledden reminded Howard of certain missionaries he had met in the jungle: calm in the face of God's seeming indifference to suffering, but zealous – even fanatical – in their conviction that He, and only He, could see the true pattern of things. Howard believed in the Devil more than he did in God – the Devil, he figured, was more in touch with real things.

'Very good,' said Ledden. 'Thank you, Howard.' He began packing his papers into his briefcase.

Sir Henry Ledden was tall, elegant and immensely wealthy. He was also a first-rank scientist with numerous patents bearing his name. His inventions – and his brilliant exploitation of them – had made him a sterling millionaire by the time he was thirty and secured him a knighthood five years later. By the age of forty, when most men begin to look backward at their failures, Ledden surged forward to even greater success by committing his entire fortune to the science of miniaturization. Whenever he saw the possibility of reducing size with the aid of microchip technology he simply went ahead and did it, ignoring his many critics. There were some who counted Ledden a hypocrite for, although he was actively – and profitably – involved in the military-industrial establishment, in private he preached a strong anti-war gospel. He had a vision of world peace achieved through technological advancement rather than pure pacifism. He believed that man had it within his power to do anything he set out to do, no matter how difficult the task. Now, only weeks away from his sixtieth birthday, he was chairman of the most powerful multi-national communications corporation in the world: a corporation with enough financial and technological muscle to have developed and produced their own launch vehicles for space communication satellites. INTERSAT was a powerful – and independently minded – giant that even major governments had to reckon with.

'Seat belts, please,' the pilot said through the intercom as he circled the unwelcoming black rock below.

Ledden indicated that Howard should sit down, then turned to a lanky, sleeping figure in the seat behind him.

'Mr Stracey,' he called. 'Wake up – we're above WHITEFIRE ONE.'

So this is it? Ed Stracey thought, opening one cold eye and peering down through the porthole at the approaching rock. Shit! If it were much smaller we'd drop off the damn place. Drowsily he surveyed the island, taking in the huts which seemed to buttress the phallic light tower at the highest point of elevation. Goddam! It's unfriendly. How can these people have lived here, in isolation, for almost two years? Looking lower he noted the cracked concrete jetty, its rusted railings still intact, then the dizzy path leading down to it. Those Krauts sure knew how to build things – still do! All right, let's see exactly what they've got here that's got the Institute so all fired up? He buckled his seat belt and took a long, careful look at the men who had brought him almost to the roof of the world.

Ledden, apart from a certain self-righteousness which he found slightly jarring, he could take – even admire – but the German was like a splinter in his flesh: too much aggravation without enough cause. He had only to look at Weissleder's heavy, overfed face to feel the burn of irritation.

Strangely, Ledden deferred to Weissleder whenever the three of them discussed the project and this annoyed Stracey intensely, for it was plain that the German was no scientist and had only his powerful position on the board of INTERSAT as his credentials for even *being* in the conversation. All right, he was the negotiator in the deal and if this exploratory trip for the benefit of the United States Institute of Strategic Studies, America's war-game think tank and Stracey's employers, worked out, then Weissleder would be up front, justifying his position. But right now he was supercargo and a pain in the ass.

Stracey found himself looking at the malicious, grinning face of Howard. And *you,* he thought, need watching like a rattler! Where the hell did they find you, you little bastard? Under some rock? Howard reminded him, painfully, of a Khmer Rouge leader in Cambodia who, after Stracey had been captured on a hearts-and-minds mission, had given him a three-hour, completely reasonable lecture on *how* American aid should be dispensed. Then, without reason or warning, he had grabbed Stracey's left wrist and lopped off the end joints of his fingers with a machete. Stracey had gone back to the States minus his fingertips and his belief that America could win any war with one hand toting a gun and the other holding out aid. War wasn't for nice guys and heroes, he decided; it was for profiteers and the psychopaths who enjoyed killing. Anyone else involved was just pulled along by the swell and had just about as much chance of surviving as a non-swimmer caught in a rip tide.

The chopper hovered, swayed, bounced once on the white-painted landing circle, then settled, its jet exhaust screaming and the rotor blades whipping murderously at the air.

Stracey was out first – he hated helicopters like death since Vietnam – and rolled expertly, using his soft travel bag as a buffer when a vicious blast of wind caught him in mid-jump. He stood up to face the biggest man he had seen for a long time.

'Matt Jordan!' the figure bellowed, fighting the racket made by the chopper. 'You OK?'

'Sure, just a tumble! Ed Stracey – ISS. You're head man here, right?'

Jordan smiled broadly. 'Something like that! Hey, excuse me?' Jordan stepped past and stretched up for Ledden. 'Easy there, Sir Henry, it's really blowing up today. Thought you people might have had to turn around.' He swung Ledden down, then offered a hand to Weissleder who growled and jumped down unaided, landing heavily on the rocky surface. Howard leaped out lithely, landing with a springy bounce at Jordan's feet. For a moment the two men stood looking at each other, the disparity in height between them ludicrous.

'Wasn't expecting anyone else!' Jordan shouted with surprise.

'That's what Hitler said when you Yanks decided it was time you joined in the war!' Howard shouted back, heaving a battered rucksack out from the aircraft.

Jordan reached for it. 'I'll get it!' he yelled. The bag was unreasonably heavy for its size, taking him completely by surprise. It thumped onto the rock.

Howard lifted it one-handed, then casually slipped the straps over his shoulders, grinning throughout like a demented child. He gave an amazingly loud click of his tongue, then strutted off as though he knew the entire layout of the island. He did. Howard always checked things first.

The pilot gave a thumbs-up sign as Jordan slammed the door closed, then heaved the helicopter up into the dangerous crosswinds.

'Down?' Jordan bawled into Ledden's ear muffs. Ledden nodded firmly, let the American take his bag, then followed the others to the lighthouse. Inside they let Jordan lead the way down a narrow railed stairwell to a circular basement filled with packing cases, some half open with their fibre packing falling out. He approached a large floor-to-ceiling powerboard and said: 'Open her up, Ray.' The board slid noiselessly behind a large, immovable packing case.

'Dummy?' Stracey asked.

Jordan nodded. 'All power controls are below. It was the best way. The Nazis built the original underground installation but this entrance had collapsed and some of the underground chambers were risky. Didn't dare enter them. Sealed them up – permanently. Which meant we had to do a lot of new work.' He rapped the metal of a gleaming door. 'Titanium armour. Nothing will get through it.'

The door slid aside to reveal an elevator. Stracey whistled in admiration.

Jordan ducked his head toward Weissleder. 'Congratulate Herr Weissleder – he was in charge of the construction. He went into the dangerous areas alone – took one look and said seal them up and start over. All this is his work, his achievement.'

'I do,' said Stracey. 'I certainly do. Very impressive. I'm sure glad you people are on our side.'

Ledden said sombrely, 'I rather feel we're not on anyone's *side*, Mr Stracey. It really is more a question of expediencies.'

Jordan tugged at his ear lobe, then grinned cheerfully: 'Let's just say that the States are the first to see it.'

Stracey grimaced. 'If the data you've let us see is anything to go by, I hope to God no one else has!'

The elevator slid downward in silence.

'Some hole in the ground,' Ed Stracey remarked as Jordan showed him around the underground installation.

'Who called it that?' Jordan asked, turning as they walked the length of the corridor, lined on both sides with the cabin-style rooms which were the station's living quarters.

'Your boss – I asked him about this place in the car just after I flew into the USAF base at Frankfurt. He dismissed it. Called it "just a hole in the ground".'

'He'd never discuss Beacon Island except in the most secure circumstances. Security has always been our greatest problem on the project. But take my word, this installation is the most important thing in Sir Henry's life.'

'More than INTERSAT'S satellite launching zone in Africa?'

'Right.'

Stracey gave Jordan a thoughtful look and followed on. 'So when do I get the full tour, Dr Jordan? The business end of the place, I mean. Your facilities are terrific – a real Arctic Hilton – but they're not what I flew up here to see.'

Jordan said: 'I'd better leave that side to Sir Henry. I don't know what kind of deal he's making with Washington, so it's best he shows you what he wants you to see.'

'But you're the project head, right?'

'Right, but it's still his project. I'm just hired help.'

'Hardly that! I understand you've been working with him on this for almost four years and you've been stuck on this rock for two of those.'

'You know a lot.'

'Once the news of the project was broken – to the right people – in Washington, we really started digging.'

'Well, I hope to God your digging hasn't knocked down any fences?'

Stracey held up a hand, fingers splayed. 'Less than that got to see the file with INTERSAT's proposals. One was the President and I'm last in line. Even *I* don't know everyone on the distribution list.'

Jordan stopped. 'Here's your bunk. You're on your own.'

But Stracey was not listening. His full attention was on a woman walking towards them wearing white overalls, zipped from neck to crotch like a fashionable jumpsuit, and big round tortoiseshell reading glasses jammed into her short auburn hair. She was not classically beautiful, but she did have that indefinable sexual quality that can turn heads instantly. And, moreover, she knew it.

'You being checked into this fur-lined Alcatraz?' she called, then stuck out her hand. 'Jemma Elliot. I don't suppose I'm allowed to tell you what I do here.' She swivelled her large eyes up to Jordan and gave a dry smile which could have become a sneer with a fraction more movement of her lips.

'Ed Stracey,' Jordan said. 'ISS.'

She raised her eyebrows, lowered the glasses onto her nose, then peered over them mockingly. 'Say! We must have hit the big time. Our little project going national, Matt?'

'You were with NASA, right?' Stracey said, suddenly remembering. 'Guidance expert? Didn't you go to work for the Brits on the revised Trident package?'

'Who's a clever ISS man, then? I thought you people studied methods – not personnel. People don't count in war-game scenarios, surely?'

'You had a pretty good reputation, Dr Elliot. So *this* is where you've been hiding.'

'Jemma, please. I leave the titles for those who've got something to prove.'

Jordan had opened the cabin door and Stracey heaved his bag up onto the higher of two bunks. 'Neat,' he said, taking a quick look at the compact but complete living unit.

'If you don't mind being a battery hen, sure it's neat,' said Jemma Elliot behind him. 'OK, see you men later. Oh! Ladies' hour in the sauna and sun room is between five and six every day. The doors have no locks – like all the best men's clubs – so don't forget, will you, Ed?'

They watched her walk away. Stracey said: 'Great-looking broad but that tongue's better than a whip! I'd hate to share a space this size with her.'

'I do.' Jordan smiled.

Stracey looked up at the big man. 'I retract. Don't hit me, for Christ's sake – I gotta live to make my report to Washington.'

'I won't. You're right.'

Stracey gave an exaggerated sigh of relief. 'Thanks. Listen, you're in good shape – how d'you keep it up down here? Don't get me wrong now, I'm talking strictly about solo exercises.'

'We've got a good recreational area – weights, cycling machines, rowing – all that stuff. And we've got movies on video – we're well set up. Have to be, some of us have been here for more than a year at one stretch.'

'So you've got a bar?'

'We've got a bar.'

'Well, screw your project, let's have a drink.'

A shrill electronic scream blasted down the corridor, then dipped in tone while Jordan's name was called over a PA system; then the screech rose again, then died. 'Alert Stage One,' a male voice said, metallically. Stracey guessed it was a computer audio system.

'What's up?' he asked.

'Our satellite link pre-warns us when the Soviets are about to launch a test missile.'

'You people got an "Eye" on Tyuratam?' Stracey exclaimed.

'Sure. We can patch into any of INTERSAT's satellites, but recently the corporation launched a high-definition TV satellite with an orbit that cuts straight over Vladivostok, part of China, Mongolia, then straight out over Sevastopol. Nearly as good as your *Big-Bird*.'

Stracey's weathered face broke into a wry grin. 'And it just *happens* that that orbit takes in the Red Chinese Shuang Ch'eng rocket test centre, their nuclear test area at Lop Nor and the Soviet missile test centre at Tyuratam? Nice orbit, Doc!'

The alarm screeched again and announced Jordan's name once more. 'Got to go. Make yourself at home – we'll see about that drink later.' Then he was gone.

Stracey began unpacking his bag, his lean, lined face disturbed. Christ, he thought, Washington is going to love this – they're playing nuclear ball without a book of rules!

Edmund Stracey was what the Institute of Strategic Studies might, in lay terms, have called an 'evaluator'. His job, and he was arguably the best in his field, was to report on any new development in the field of strategic weaponry and play the results – when a project seemed feasible – into the regular studies conducted by the Institute.

Stracey was a mathematician and physicist by training but a USAF fighter pilot by choice. At the end of the Korean War he came out with enough kills to be considered a minor ace and had no difficulty landing a civilian job with the Rand Corporation where he developed into something of an expert in national security planning. Soon, however, he had found the routine of a desk job crushing and applied for a post with a new and quite secret government department which sent 'advisers' into what, in those days, were termed 'second-theatre war zones with threat capability'. What they really meant was that some small country was kicking the US in the ass and needed to be given a lesson in manners – or so Stracey realized very quickly.

He got the job – even against the objections of the National Security Agency who considered he would be too big a catch as a prisoner of the Communists – but had to agree to the tired old routine of the hollow tooth and its measured dose of lethality. 'If you're under too much pressure,' the tame dentist had said, cheerfully, 'just bite it. You won't feel a thing.'

'How the hell would you know?' Stracey had growled and subsequently chewed all his food on the opposite side.

His cover was that of a Peace Corps officer, which enabled him to penetrate 'non-friendly areas' with relative impunity. He travelled across Laos, Cambodia and Vietnam assessing the success – or more usually the failure – of American methods of conducting such 'policing actions', and came out of this experience a changed man who believed that any real nuclear threat would evolve, not from a clash of heads at superpower level, but, instead, from the disruptive policies of Third World nations – nations with too much power and too little responsibility.

Like the friendly lunatics on this Arctic rock, he thought.

Ten days before he had been called into the Director's office at the ISS to find himself in the presence of the

President, the Secretary of State and the Director of Strategic Technology. They were all sitting around the ISS Director's desk staring at a slim file as if it were an unexploded bomb – and Stracey had the uneasy feeling as he entered that he was the man they had chosen to defuse it.

The contents of the file made his skin crawl all the way up to the roots of his spiky crew-cut. His orders were sharp and simple: find out if what they have been working on is genuine, and if it is let us know immediately, by satellite link, and we'll make arrangements to get the damn thing away from that location. What they are doing is too damn dangerous and too damn close to Russia.

They were right.

He would have given what remained of the fingers on his left hand to know what price INTERSAT was asking for the technology they had developed – in fact he'd have given his entire arm and not flinched – because, if the initial reports of success were accurate, a whole bunch of thinking and decisions were going to be upended overnight!

Stracey lay down on the bunk, lit a small brown cigar and linked his arms behind his head, puffing thoughtfully. 'Whitefire?' he murmured aloud through a stream of blue smoke.

Jemma Elliot had turned the handle on the door of her own scarcely used cabin after leaving Stracey and Jordan and stopped dead. 'Who the hell are you?' she exploded.

Simon Howard gave his evil grin and humped his rucksack onto the bunk. He made a show of looking around the room. 'They told me there was an empty cabin bottom right, and this one looks empty to me. Where're all your things?'

'Mind your own goddam business – get out of my room before I get Dr Jordan to throw you out!'

'Ah, you're the bossman's bird, then. The chopper pilot told me to watch out for you.'

'Are you going to get out of here?' she snapped, infuriated by the little dark man, though at the same time getting a fleeting warning inside that he needed to be handled with care. 'Who are you?' she snapped again, but forcing her notoriously quick temper down. 'The house snooper?'

Howard held out his hand, very formally. 'Actually it's Howard. Simon Lawrence Howard.'

She took the offered hand puzzled by the abrupt change in Howard's accent and also the familiarity of his new voice. Ledden! she realized suddenly. He's mimicking his upper-class English drawl.

'I look after your chairman, you know,' Howard drawled.

Jemma Elliot laughed. 'Now I've heard everything! Don't tell me that Ledden needs a valet down here? Jesus!'

'Bodyguard,' Howard said, and his eyes were suddenly black and dangerous. He stood perfectly still, his thin fingers curled, the blunt cutting edges of his hands outwards.

If he hits me with those hands, she told herself, I'll crack like an egg.

'You need to watch your lip,' Howard warned. 'I'm nobody's servant.'

'I'm sorry, I was wrong. I apologize, OK?'

'That's all right, then.'

'It's the next room that's free,' she said.

Howard was not listening; he had dropped his eyes to her body. 'I like white,' he said. 'Reminds me of nurses. Nurses are good luck for me – always patched me up right when I caught a packet.' He reached out and touched the material over the swell of her breast but she didn't move. 'Nice. Crisp. Feels good.' He placed his fingers at the top of the starched, stuck-together pocket and pushed downwards, separating the material with a small tearing sound. She felt hypnotized. 'Nice,' he repeated, and though she fought against it she felt her nipple hardening against the back of his slim fingers.

She felt the flush on her cheeks and knew he could see it too. 'I'll help you settle in if you want,' she offered.

Howard removed his fingers. 'No thanks – like to do things on my own. No offence?'

She shook her head.

Howard hefted the rucksack onto his shoulder and eased

her aside. 'See you, then. What time do they serve grub in this place?'

'Any time really – if you want to cook for yourself.'

'I usually do. You're Jemma Elliot, right?'

'Yes. How did you know that?'

Howard grinned. 'Lady, this time tomorrow I'll know the colour of your underwear – 'cept you don't wear no bra, do you?'

She closed the door quickly behind him and leaned against it.

And who spawned you? she thought. Do you eat big girls for supper, little Simon Lawrence Howard, with your bright white teeth and your hard waiting hands? She recalled her immediate impression as she entered the cabin, realizing that even then with her anger flaring that his effect on her had been instantaneous. Dark and quick; with the eyes of a thief and an urchin's grin. His body was slim, almost vulnerable in appearance, though she very much doubted the latter. The sheer suppressed violence that simmered beneath that cruel grin both terrified and attracted her. No man had ever had that effect on her and she doubted if her liberated hard-headedness, which was her single defence in that isolated male-dominated community, would have any effect against Howard. Instinctively she detested him, because he was a perfect example of everything she hated in men. Over-confident, self-opinionated, and he used the superior strength of his gender like a blunt weapon. Yet that same physical presence which should have repelled her had attracted her, and for Jemma Elliot that was a disaster.

The sudden shriek of the alarm warning of an imminent Soviet missile test pushed the incident from her mind. The cool scientist in her taking over from the woman.

2

The Soviet Strategic Missile Test Centre at Tyuratam is north-east of the Aral Sea in Kazakhstan on the banks of the Syr Darya. It is a sprawling complex comprising, nearest the river, a support staging area; the main support complex; leading off that, by either road or rail, a fuel storage area; an earlier space/military booster complex; a new research and development complex; and the launch site proper.

Below ground, at the launch site, a technician watched the giant NE-04 missile boring its way through the illuminated tunnel, a massive black finger pointing menacingly at him as though intent on his destruction. He felt the rush of its passing, its oppressive bulk causing him to press back against the curved wall.

The wheels of the flat-car which transported the missile to the launch pad screeched appallingly as the braking system cut in; the entire unit swinging through an arc of 180 degrees before coming to a dead stop. Next came the movement which the official Soviet Rocket Forces operations manual describes as 'the higher point of readiness', but which the personnel of the secret base have crudely renamed, in Russian slang, 'the hard on'. The missile slowly rose so that the top of the huge nose pointed at the circle of sky at the top of the silo.

At the launch monitoring centre the blast-off was followed as the missile climbed higher. The worried technicians hovered nervously over their screens, breath held, as the NE-04 re-entered the atmosphere over the Kara Sea.

Sir Henry Ledden stood behind Matthew Jordan, leaning forward, knuckles whitened, as he gripped the back of the American's chair. His eyes, like all others, were fixed on the great video-screen at the farthest end of the large equipment-filled room.

Jemma Elliot, below Jordan and Ledden on the master console, blinked as Jordan's deep voice murmured in her ears. Instinctively, she raised her hands to the headset.

'When it happens,' Jordan's voice told her, 'you'll only have seconds. If you manage to lock onto it give me ten seconds of steady control – after that lock off it and let the bird fall. Ten seconds only – any longer and they'll begin to doubt their instrument read-outs – if that happens the entire project will be in jeopardy.'

She pushed her glasses up her nose, her eyes flicking impatiently up at him. 'If I lock on "guidance" I hold for maximum ten seconds. That is *ten seconds*,' she affirmed into the slim curved microphone before her mouth, then began punching in co-ordinates on her computer keyboard. All around her rows of other scientists and technicians performed their various functions with ice-cool efficiency, the only sound being the persistent clicking as fingers pressed buttons. The secret heart of the island, the control centre, was fully manned.

'Test for rotation,' Jordan's voice said in the headsets.

A brief delay, then another voice said: 'Affirmative'.

Jordan began his checklist, noting with his eyes the direction of the anonymous replies as they reached his ears.

'Outlets?'

'Check.'

'Electromagnets?'

'Check.'

'Injectors?'

'Check.'

'Resonators?'

'Check.'

'Wave reflection?'

'Negative.'

'Very good,' Jordan said. 'Linear accelerator: wave velocity?'

'Good.'

'Phase velocity?'

'Good.'

Jordan leaned back in his chair and Ledden pushed himself upright. 'We have "Go",' said Jordan. 'Do you confirm "Proceed"?'

Ledden nodded tightly and Jordan noted, as he looked upward, the finger pressed hard against the high cheekbone and, above it, a sheen of perspiration across the wide forehead. The whole weight of awesome responsibility was stamped on his face.

'Sir Henry, I need "Proceed",' he urged, gently but firmly.

'Proceed,' said Ledden, letting his hand fall to his side as if he had expended all his strength. Beside him, on his left, was the heavy-set German, Weissleder, hunched forward in the observer's chair, his fists tight balls, his hard eyes angry at the Englishman's hesitation. He turned away toward the image of the missile on the giant screen, jaw set and eyes glittering now with power.

'Whitefire,' Jordan said.

On the surface, above the huge reflectors of the lantern, within the white dome of the lighthouse tower, a mass of complex electronics formed a glowing pyramid. At the apex of the pyramid, a device which might easily have been mistaken for a piece of futuristic sculpture in steel and fused glass moved hesitantly around its own axis – the movements erratic, as though the device was searching for something beyond the confines of the white dome. Momentarily it seemed perplexed, then stopped and fixed its twin cylindrical protrusions on one part of the curved enclosure. Briefly it crackled, a sound felt rather than heard. Like fork lightning.

At Tyuratam, red flashes warning of systems failure in the test missile began in turn on each of the monitoring consoles, the Soviet technicians becoming increasingly frantic as each electronic function within the sophisticated weapon began to die. Then, like all its predecessors on the NE-04 test programme, the giant missile plunged downward, out of control.

In a mad rage the programme director slammed his fist onto the master control console. 'No!' he bawled, his total frustration overwhelming him. 'It cannot be! There is nothing wrong! *Nothing!*'

In a glass booth overlooking the centre a Red Army (Rocket Forces) general lifted a telephone linked directly to the Kremlin and reported the latest failure, visualizing, as he spoke, his own bleak future.

In Moscow, the Soviet leader replaced his telephone, then his hand hovered momentarily over another instrument. He was appalled to see that his hand was trembling. He withdrew it, lit a cigarette and coughed rackingly. But the nicotine calmed him. He lifted the telephone. First he dialled the office of the Chairman of the KGB, then the Admiral commanding the major submarine base at Severomorsk near Murmansk.

When he had finished both calls he pushed his cigarette away from him and sat very still. All he could do now was wait.

Deep in the heart of the Cheyenne Mountain complex in the Colorado Rockies, behind thirty-ton steel doors the personnel of the Combat Operations Centre, North American Air Defence Command live in a small city of eleven buildings two and three storeys high which rest on mammoth steel springs weighing a ton each. These springs co-operate with shock absorbers to dampen bounces from explosions or earth tremors. With the massive doors closed the base can remain sealed off for one month, tied to the outside world only by communications. In this underground city the personnel work, eat, sleep, shop at an exchange, receive medical and dental care and are completely independent of the outside world.

Inside the brain of the NORAD centre a United States Air Force officer – a specialist in computer programming – worked on the tape for an imminent practice alert simulating a nuclear attack. His face was grey and his heart banged against his ribs as though it might burst through the bones, for what he was about to do would certainly finish his career and with it his usefulness as a long-term penetration agent for his true masters – the Soviet Union.

As he worked, he considered briefly that if the consequences of his act were as terrible as he foresaw then he was, quite literally, sealing his own tomb. Yet not at any time since receiving the order from his KGB controller earlier had he questioned the command. Whatever the reason, if his act served to further the Communist cause it would be worth it – whether the cost was his freedom or the lives of the entire population of the United States.

When he had completed his treacherous task he thought, in a moment of vanity, that he might be one of the few men who were privileged to change the course of history.

Nobody questioned his actions as he placed the altered tape on the machine; he was, after all, apparently just performing his normal duty.

The vast camouflage net was like some colossal spider's web spun flat over a pit and imprisoning the thick black slug below. Even at that distance the new Soviet nuclear submarine looked enormous.

Admiral Ivan Pavlovich Myshko gazed down in awe – not for the first time – at the *Leonid Brezhnev*, the largest submarine ever constructed and the pride of the Soviet Navy.

Displacing 30,000 tons of water, 600 feet long – nearly three times as long as a jumbo jet – and twice the width of America's latest and biggest submarine, the Trident-class *Mariner*, the *Brezhnev* was a world-beater.

Admiral Myshko glanced at his watch. He had been awake all night because of the disappearance of one of his submarines along with a crew of mutineers. And now, from the Kremlin, had come this extraordinary order: seek out and destroy the mutineers with the *Brezhnev*.

But why the *Brezhnev*? Why? What was the man up to?

All right, hunt the mutineers down and destroy them. Avoid a trial by all means – he did not want his dirty linen laundered in public – but *why* the *Brezhnev*? Just to prove his power? Why squash a bug with a steamroller when a foot was adequate?

Myshko looked down at the oily water, flat and heavy like blackened mercury, as it gurgled between the sloping titanium hull of the vast submarine and the concrete sides of the pen.

He turned to the officer beside him. 'Flood the pen,' he ordered.

Matthew Jordan put his head into the communications

room on Whitefire One. 'Morning! You still on duty, Ray? You're over-running your shift.'

Simpson yawned and sipped coffee from a mug. 'There was some Russian traffic that Bill couldn't handle so I took over.'

Jordan's face registered alarm. 'Nothing serious, I hope?'

'Not for us. They lost one of their submarines out of Severomorsk. Mutiny by the sound of it. Stole the boat – Foxtrot class, non-nuclear – and put to sea before anyone twigged it. Then I got a BBC World Service flash that a Russian sub had surfaced off Norway earlier this morning. Eye witnesses reckoned they picked up three people.'

'Same boat?'

'Could be, if they were going flat out. Funny thing is that the BBC say that the people they picked up might have been Mikhail Tavrin and that old dissident . . . what's his name . . . that scientist who defected years ago, lives in Switzerland?'

'Chebrikov,' said Jordan. 'Josef Chebrikov. But why them?'

'They both disappeared from Geneva yesterday.'

'That's not possible. You told me that Tavrin was defending his world title.'

'Was. He's gone. Won a game and left with someone.'

'No warning?'

'Got passed a note, thought about it for a minute, then wiped out his opponent and pissed off. Didn't go back.'

'Strange. I suppose he's blown the title now.'

'Not yet, his advisers are pleading for time and screaming foul play by you Yanks.'

'Normal. But what's the Norwegian connection? The mutineers in the sub?'

'Search me. The BBC didn't mention anything about that – just said *a* Russian sub was spotted. The Kremlin is hardly going to announce something like that, are they?'

'You definitely heard "mutiny" on the Russian air?'

'I got this job because of my Russian, remember? It was all on their military frequency – short-range, but long enough for this equipment. They were frantic – most of it was in clear language.'

'And someone saw Tavrin and Chebrikov go aboard the sub?'

'*People* were seen. Three of them. Two men and a young-looking girl. But the descriptions fit. One man very tall and thin, another small and seemingly old. The BBC definitely made the link.'

'Weird?' Jordan said, pouring coffee. 'You'd better keep an ear on the Soviet naval frequency – they might just start a search for that sub up this way. If they do we want plenty of warning.'

'OK, I'll stick with it for a while – who needs sleep anyway?'

'Thanks. Right now we don't need any surprises – not with the US government aboard!'

At nine o'clock that morning, Murmansk time, the *Leonid Brezhnev* put to sea, and by ten o'clock the massive vessel had entered the Gulf of Dvina, making its way on the surface toward the White Sea.

Two hundred miles up above the surface of the White Sea the television lenses of the United States spy satellite *Big-Bird* zoomed in on the *Brezhnev* and the controllers in the Satellite Command Control Centre at the Pentagon in Washington whooped loudly, hardly believing their luck.

It seemed impossible that the Russians would be so incompetent as to sail the vessel out, on the surface, when *Big-Bird* was just beginning its great looping arc over their territory, yet, there she was, on the big screens, smashing her way through the seas. The pictures were so clear they might have been looking down on the *Brezhnev* through a crystal window a few feet above.

An officer was already on the telephone to Naval Intelligence. He cupped his hand over the mouthpiece and called out: 'They say it's the first visual on her anywhere!'

'Look at that picture,' someone whooped. 'Fantastic!'

A computer read-out gave the *Brezhnev*'s surface speed at 35 knots. 'Just idling,' the officer holding the phone said. 'NavyInt believes that the reason for the size of that thing is a much bigger power plant. They estimate 20 knots on top, maybe more.'

As if in confirmation the *Brezhnev* surged forward immediately, creating a huge bow wave. The computer visual display unit flashed up: '45 knots est.'

The room fell silent.

'And holding,' a subdued voice said.

'Maybe it's not extra power?' said the controller who had spotted the submarine first. 'Maybe back-up missiles?'

The controller talking with Naval Intelligence repeated the suggestion into the telephone, then shook his head. 'They say unlikely. With a secondary stock of missiles they would *have* to surface to reload their tubes. With radar, sonar and spy satellites working against them, that's like waiting to get your head blown off. If the extra size is for missiles it's got to be a surface-to-surface system for sea battles, not ICBMs.'

'Damn! She's flooding her tanks.'

'Too bad.'

'No problem, we've still got the sonar boys to keep us informed of her progress.'

Someone called out: 'They'd better! Whatever their reason for pushing that boat out, it must be a damn good one.'

In a raised glassed-off observation area the commander of the Satellite Control Centre, an Air Force general, stood up, leaned over a panel of complex electronics, and put his lips to a desk microphone. His deep voice boomed out into the room below: 'That place down there looks like a McDonald's on a Saturday night. Get it policed, I'm calling the President.' He tugged his sleeve back and checked his watch, then dialled the number of one of the President's aides.

A mumbled 'Hello' came down the line, followed by the distinct clunk of a thick coffee cup hitting its saucer.

'Bad for you, coffee after midnight,' the Satellite Commander advised, and heard a chuckle in reply. He turned and watched the big screens. 'That area the President wanted monitored? Thought I'd better pass this on in case he decides it's important. The Russians have just let their biggest piece of underwater hardware loose. That's right

– the *Brezhnev* – and it's heading clean through that bit of sea at around 45 knots.'

'I'll wake him,' the presidential aide said quickly. 'He'll want to come down there.'

'It's past two in the morning – you sure he'll want to do that?'

'Very sure,' the aide replied, and hung up.

Above the earth *Big-Bird* continued to beam down television pictures of a cold sea which, as if in protest at this intrusion of privacy, was beginning to whip up its surface.

Before he had given the command 'Open main vents' Admiral Ivan Myshko had ordered that the *Brezhnev* was checked for 'tightness', ensuring that all hatches were shut and clipped.

He sat on a high stool fixed to the massive, gleaming steel column which housed the submarine's two periscopes. In front of him, to his left, a radar operator checked his scanner. To his right, a senior officer oversaw every movement made by the two planesmen who operated the vessel's aircraft-style control columns while strapped into high-backed seats, bolted to the deck. Of these, a petty officer controlled the more important after-hydroplanes, assisted by a leading seaman who handled the rudder and forward-hydroplanes.

As the ballast tanks flooded the hydroplanes were angled for diving and the *Brezhnev* moved forward and down in one smooth movement, the huge single bronze screw forcing her down to the depths where the Barents and White Seas merged.

Admiral Myshko fixed his attention on a television screen, set amid the mass of instruments between the planesmen, which displayed a computer image of a 'highway' beneath the sea and the vessel's attitude in relation to it.

On illuminated digital depth and pressure gauges the changing status of their progress was recorded by flickering figures which only a practised eye could decipher.

Abruptly, Myshko gave the order for the *Brezhnev* to be levelled off and slowed to a speed of 20 knots.

A signals officer approached Myshko, his face stunned. Myshko took the message slip from him. The man said quietly, avoiding the curious glances from the faces around him: 'From Central Nuclear Command, Comrade Admiral.'

Myshko read. 'United States ICBMs readied . . . no exercise code received. Motors fired . . . missiles static . . . US and Canadian interceptor jets airborne . . . no exercise code received . . . Strategic Air Command nuclear strike patrols reported turning back toward Soviet borders . . . no exercise code received. Prepare for immediate retaliation on codeword KARINA.'

Myshko straightened, his face impassive, and sounded the alarm for imminent nuclear attack. His mind was spinning but in control: if the Americans had made a mistake – or were prepared to climb down – they had better do it soon. There were only minutes remaining.

'Submarine on the screens!' said an officer urgently.

Not now! Myshko cursed. Not now!

The President of the United States stood in the Satellite Control Centre, his eyes fixed to the huge screens beyond the plate glass of the observation room.

Since his arrival the flat grey lead of the Barents Sea had become a rolling swell dashed with white feathers of spray.

He turned to the Centre Commander beside him. 'I doubt if you'll have clear vision much longer if this weather deteriorates any further,' he observed.

The general nodded gloomily. 'Three days of clear weather and it turns to shit now!'

'Even we can't control the weather – yet!' the President replied.

'Damn it, sir! This is the one time we could really see the boat in action. NavyInt are screaming for anything on the *Brezhnev*. I'm beginning to wonder if God is on the side of the Russians. Someone makes the crass error of sailing her out right under *Big-Bird*'s opening sweep – and what happens? We lose the goddam weather!'

The President smiled drily. 'God doesn't take sides any more, general. He's just sitting up there waiting for us to

63

blow each other to bits, then he'll drop a big hand down, gather up the pieces and rewrite the scenario.'

The two men glanced sideways at each other, both wearing the same tight smile which displayed the cynicism born of familiarity with total power.

The shrill ring of a telephone distracted them. The presidential aide picked it up, listened, then said: 'Mr President, you'd better take this, sir.'

'Problem?' the President asked quickly, but seeing his aide's face did not wait for an answer. The aide flipped a cigarette from a packet, lit it and inhaled deeply, but his eyes did not leave the President's face for an instant.

'Of course I know about the exercise,' the President was saying. '*Of course* it's an exercise – do you think I'd be standing here calmly talking to you if it wasn't? What? Are you sure? Jesus, what do I have to say to con . . . ? Check the code, dammit . . . the Russians recognize an exercise code as well as we do. WHAT!'

The aide's eyes met with the President's and he nodded. 'THEN STAND IT DOWN!' the President roared. 'Stand the damn thing down – NOW!' He jerked his head around, hearing the sudden uproar from the main room, and saw the dreadful mushroom-shaped cloud growing on the big screen.

'She's gone!' the general gasped. 'Just gone!'

The President's face had aged in seconds. He snatched the phone back up to his mouth. 'Full alert!' he said, with a calmness he did not feel.

The voice in his ear pleaded: 'Sir, we daren't do that! Moscow will think you've gone crazy. I've just given the order to stand down . . . .'

'I know that!' the President snapped. 'That's a chance we'll have to take.'

3

Commander Sergei Ulyanov of the Soviet Navy was a big man for a submariner. He stood a full inch above six feet and filled his blue uniform well with a solid, if rather hirsute, physique. He sported a grey-flecked black beard which appeared to be a continuation of the thick mat of coarse hair which hid the skin of his deep chest, and had a gold cap on a front tooth, which in the Soviet Union, where steel is more usual, was very distinctive.

Sometimes, in the late evenings when Ulyanov drank vodka in one of the waterfront bars he frequented, he could look positively piratical, and sometimes cruel – even fearsome. But if he actually had any of these traits it was only that of the pirate, for Ulyanov was a fiercely independent man prepared to back his own judgement to the hilt and always ready to follow the tug of his heart. Especially if that tug was toward his beloved Russia.

He was not cruel – though he could be utterly ruthless when occasion demanded – and the old salts who frequented the same bars, the barmaids who served him and the small children who tagged behind him delightedly on the streets, would all bear immediate witness that he was certainly not fearsome.

Sergei kept his own counsel on most things but slowly, over the years – he was now thirty-nine – he had realized that the only way to do anything about his discontent with the way things were going in Russia was to talk with like-minded people.

He met with small, dangerous groups who mostly just talked of change with little positive action – but sometimes they gained the courage to put their words into print on underground presses, though their efforts were rarely read by any more than the small handful of dissidents who were already converted.

He had a passion for the game of chess and counted as one of the greatest moments in his life his meeting with Mikhail Tavrin, Grandmaster of all the Soviets, at an exclusive chess club in Moscow one chill autumn evening some three years before.

His other great moments were – and depending on his mood they varied in importance: gaining his first command; marrying the girl he loved; and the birth of his only child, a bonny, dark and surprisingly blue-eyed girl. His disappointments were many, but he never counted those for he had no time for petty regrets; however he nursed two tragedies like wounds which could never heal, and whose pain could only be numbed by the consumption of copious quantities of neat vodka whenever a maudlin mood took him over.

The first came early in his manhood when he returned to his native Georgia in the middle of the famine following the failure of yet another Five-Year Plan, to find his young wife hopelessly ill after religiously starving herself so that her child could eat. She had died, his beautiful Katya, one month after he had returned and Sergei had buried her, dry-eyed but with a weeping heart, in the useless soil. Then he had packed his sack, lifted his daughter with one thick black-haired arm and, after spitting on the earth to give release to his contempt for the system which had failed him, had travelled back to Murmansk. There he had searched for and found an elderly couple who could be trusted, for a modest payment, to care for his child while he voyaged beneath the seas.

His second tragedy had, he reckoned, always been with him – he could not remember a day when he had not felt a deep sense of loss because Russia, his country, his people, could never be free. *Truly free.* He granted the system its achievements – was sometimes proud of them – yet he knew that not he, not anyone, was *free*. Whatever he did would always be restricted in some way. No freedom of thought or expression; no freedom to travel without someone's permission and yet another slip of paper with a stamp on it. Sometimes he wondered why the bureaucrats bothered with all the paper – why didn't they just stamp straight onto his body, then he'd be just one great walking example of bureaucracy gone mad!

Only Mikhail Tavrin – who hinted, never stated nor confirmed, at great undercurrents of free thought bubbling just below the surface in the Soviet Union – only Tavrin could ease that sense of loss and give him hope for a different future. For Tavrin could not be better placed. He was revered at all levels in Soviet society, from the awesome heights of Kremlin power to the lowest collective. He trav-

66

elled without restriction and he could see – could feel – that things were changing. He had pointed at Poland as being a fine example. Yes, certainly their revolution had been crushed, but they had proved that a certain level of freedom *could* be achieved as long as people acted in a concerted manner and under the strong guiding hand of a respected leader. The world watched *everything* nowadays, he had said. The eyes of television cameras were *everywhere!* Everything was noted and reported on – and that was where the real strength of revolution lay. Its strength *and* its weapons. Spilling blood was unnecessary if you could only get the world to watch what you were doing – for even the Kremlin was loath to show itself as being the suppressor of human rights.

The phone call from the Grandmaster had made Sergei's heart bang with both fear and hope, and his voice ached to shout out the importance of his mission but – as always – he kept his own counsel and tenderly kissed his daughter as she slept. Then he walked the streets of Murmansk calling at the homes of the men he knew he could count on, even to the extent of their lives.

All of this made Sergei Ulyanov the man he was, and gave reason for his presence – when lesser men would have crept safely away – in the command seat of the out-dated patrol submarine named the *Stoiki*. He had little idea what the Grandmaster intended to do, nor how he would over-come the wrath of the Kremlin, which was bound to be terrible, but he was certain – *he knew* – that Tavrin would have some carefully considered plan. Such was the power and confidence the man exuded. And the small crew of mutineers, too, gazed at the Grandmaster in awe – and though they felt the twist of fear in their bowels they obey-ed, like blind sheep, the firm but gentle prodding staff of their chosen shepherd.

'Sir!' the sonar operator said, urgently. 'Submarine. *Very big!* Only three miles from our position.'

Ulyanov stepped off his stool and listened to the echo. 'The *Brezhnev*? Never. They wouldn't send her out to deal with this heap of scrap.'

'They might,' Tavrin said, softly. 'Intimidation is sometimes the most effective weapon of all. Would *you* attack her? Would you *dare* attack the pride of the Soviet Navy?'

Ulyanov grunted. 'More to the point, Mikhail, will she attack *us?*'

'Of course. If it *is* her, then she has been sent to blow us into so many small pieces that nothing will ever be found. What we have done – are doing – is a greater threat to the Kremlin than a thousand American missiles. They cannot afford to lose. They cannot afford to be *seen* as having let this happen.'

'So what must we do?'

'Will you have any warning of attack from her?'

'Of course, we are linked with the same Central Command. Every word passed to the *Brezhnev*, if that's who she is, we can monitor.'

The Grandmaster frowned and glanced at his watch.

'Mikhail?' Ulyanov said.

The signals officer broke the brief silence. 'It *is* the *Brezhnev*. I've got them on the Central Nuclear Command emergency frequency. They've just been advised of an American nuclear alert.'

'Exercise alert,' Ulyanov corrected.

'No sir, no exercise code given.'

Ulyanov twisted his head around, a dead look in his deep brown eyes. 'Repeat!' he ordered.

'No exercise code given, sir. I'm holding the frequency.'

'Battle stations,' Ulyanov ordered calmly over the PA system, an automatic reaction from years of training. He turned to a young, pale-faced sailor. 'Vladi, see that Comrade Chebrikov and his grand-daughter are not alarmed. Tell them it is just a precaution. Go!'

'You'd be informed – normally – if an exercise went out of control?' Tavrin asked, cool as ice.

Ulyanov nodded. 'Immediately. In such situations, time is what counts. There is a stand-off period before the missiles are released. Even if their propulsion motors are ignited they remain static – but not for very long, my friend, not long at all.'

'I will suggest something to you, Sergei – but this you must decide yourself. I cannot force you.'

'I understand.'

'If the *Brezhnev* is going to strike at you, her commander will do it now. His options are too limited; he cannot watch two situations at the same time and function without the possibility of error. And a nuclear alert is more crucial at this time.'

Ulyanov nodded again. 'In his place that is how I would see it. He will release a missile at us within the next two minutes.'

'You can avoid it?'

'No.' The negative was flat, emotionless. 'The *Stoiki* is too old, it does not have the sophisticated equipment to blind the missile. We could dive deep, then cut our engines . . . but it will still find us. What is your suggestion?'

'Kill the *Brezhnev* – then run for safety.'

Ulyanov dropped his eyes momentarily, avoiding the powerful will before him. But he knew that that was impossible.

The signals officer said: '*Brezhnev* has moved to battle stations, sir. Alert still running – no code given, yet.' His voice was taut; fear battened down.

Ulyanov straightened his broad back. All around him frightened eyes were fixed on his pirate's face, not a body moving. Time is frozen, he thought, detachedly. Only I really exist at this split second.

'They will hunt us down – we cannot outrun them,' he said to Tavrin, his voice low. 'I know this! I am . . . was . . . them.'

'Neutral ground?' Tavrin suggested, perfectly calm.

'Too far.'

'No. The satellite weather station on Beacon Island has international status. Effectively it is neutral ground. If they allow us to land we could plead for asylum. Could we reach it?'

Ulyanov had beads of sweat along his brow – he wiped them off with nicotine-stained fingers. 'I know the place. Bring her around,' he ordered the helmsman. 'Ready bow torpedo tubes, one and two.'

'*Brezhnev* surfaced, sir!'

'Periscope depth!' Ulyanov pulled down the handles, crouching low. 'Periscope up!' His face was jammed to the eyepiece. 'There she is, magnificent!' He took his eyes away. 'We can't wait to make sure,' he told Tavrin. 'We must crash-dive immediately we fire.'

Tavrin's face was immovable. 'Your decision.'

'Fire both!' Ulyanov snapped. 'Down periscope. Crash-dive!' He smacked his palm hard on the klaxon horn and the grating bellow began as the deck tilted crazily beneath their feet.

'God save us!' he whispered as he clung on tightly – for he still believed in the Almighty. The thunder was in his ears, threatening to squeeze his brain from its cavity. He closed his eyes, picturing only the sweet, sleeping face of his child as he had bent to kiss her.

The *Stoiki* heaved over sideways while still plunging downwards, then, with every rivet screaming for release from the impossible task they were being forced to perform, began to roll.

Admiral Myshko gave the order 'Arm missile' as the *Brezhnev* broke the surface of the freezing sea while watching, without breathing, for the stand-down from the alert. He heard the warning 'Two torpedoes running!' but somehow it did not quite register. He could not believe that one of his own submarines – mutineers or no – would actually *fire* at the *Brezhnev*. That fractional delay on his part was fatal.

Both torpedoes struck the *Brezhnev* at her bow, though one would have been sufficient. The mighty submarine was ripped apart as, first, the torpedoes exploded, and then her reactor blew. She vapourized, displacing tons of water in a gigantic spout and leaving a monstrous mushroom cloud as her tombstone. So total was her destruction that she might never have existed.

The shock wave of the explosion was almost exhausted by the time it reached the jagged cliffs of Beacon Island.

Simon Howard felt it first, while he was lifting the last rock which had covered an old, moss-covered rusted steel door he had discovered near the cliff edge. He had reckoned to have explored every inch of the island by midday that morning, but his sudden discovery of the old door had put an end to that.

He talked to himself constantly – that was his way and he saw nothing strange in it – and usually he complained about other people's failings. On first sight of the odd clump of rocks and the secret they covered, he muttered: 'Stupid bastards! Bloody Ivans could creep in through here whilst those fuckin' geniuses are taking sauna baths and getting brown and cut our throats! Well you don't say a dickey-bird to *no one*, mate!' Then he'd started heaving the rocks aside.

Howard was knocked flat by the shock wave.

'Fuck!' he exclaimed, picked himself up and inspected the brand-new fur-lined anorak he'd purchased in Germany from the allowance issued to him at the INTERSAT head office. He was inordinately proud of it and had actually worn it out of the shop into the afternoon sunshine, scowling at the stares he received. Then he saw the growing cloud on the horizon and sprinted for the tower as if Lucifer was behind him – who, for some obscure reason, he believed in quite seriously.

The crew of the 'cover' surface weather station were grouped shakily around the entrance of one of the huts. Howard dashed past them at a dead run muttering 'Stupid bastards' through deep controlled breaths. He sprinted down the stairwell to the basement of the lighthouse and pulled up in front of the dummy power panel. 'Open up, Ray!' he called, his accent suddenly North American, a parody of Jordan's own. He waited for ten seconds, then lashed out with his high, lace-up paratrooper's boot. 'Open up, cunt!' This time his odd London – South African accent was back in use.

Behind him the weather station crew had filed in.

'Easy, lad,' one said in a warm Scottish burr. 'In an emergency they seal themselves in – with a thump like that the master computer does it automatically. We'll just have to wait.'

'Not on your life, mate!' Howard snapped and pushed

past up the stairs and out onto the surface again, avoiding looking at the growing monster on the horizon. In one of the huts he found two rubber-covered torches and a pair of binoculars, then dashed back to the cliff edge. Here he surveyed the cloud through the glasses for a few brief seconds, then made for the rusted door in the black rock.

Matthew Jordan reached over Jemma Elliot in the narrow bunk and found the cleft between her buttocks, then the tight ring and the softness beyond. She stirred.

'I've got to do a run-down with Stracey,' he murmured, nuzzling her ear with his mouth. She found his erection and gave a fierce squeeze. 'Well, you'd better get rid of *that* first!'

He rolled onto her, forcing her face into the pillow and penetrated her quickly, knowing she needed no prolonged foreplay. She thrust her bottom up at him, letting him force himself deep into her. Forcing his own orgasm down, he lifted her higher, bringing one hand around to her while lifting her with the other. She began thrashing under him, snatching at the pillow to stifle her own cries. The walls shuddered and the instant shriek of the alarm was like an explosion.

Immediately, Jordan leaped off her and began pulling on his clothes.

'Shit!' she screamed over the nerve-shattering noise and threw the pillow across the cabin. It flopped into the wet well of the shower cubicle. 'Shit! Shit! Shit!'

'Shut up!' Jordan snapped. 'Didn't you feel that?'

'*What* for Chrissake?'

'The tremor. Get dressed.'

The alarm continued, unabated.

'Get dressed, dammit! That's a full emergency.' Then he was gone, leaving the door open.

With quick anger, she lifted one naked leg and struck at the door but the expected crash never came as the pressure hinges caught it at the last instant and eased it into place.

'Sonofabitch!' she swore, then sat up, pulled on her jumpsuit and ran down the corridor fighting with the zip.

The men emerging from their rooms barely gave her a

glance – the sudden exposure of her full breasts had no place in their immediate scale of importance.

Jordan burst through the clamour outside the communications room to find Stracey, Ledden and Weissleder already inside. The monitoring speakers were emitting a hailstorm of static and both radar screens were whited out.

'Christ! What happened?' Jordan gasped.

No one had an answer.

Ray Simpson pushed his way into the room and gave the duty officer a quick nod. The man stood up and let Simpson take his place at the console. Simpson began a series of checks, to no avail. He looked back. 'Can't understand it. Nothing – nothing at all!' He worked his way through emergency frequencies, then world stations. 'Absolutely nothing. This is crazy!'

'What's all that static?' Jordan asked.

Simpson shook his head. 'Search me. There's nothing wrong with the equipment, or the computer would be bawling at me to get off my arse and fix it.'

Both Ledden and Weissleder were dishevelled from disturbed sleep after the late night they had had going over the results of the latest test of their device. Ed Stracey, however, was groomed and collected – but his face was grave.

Jordan noticed it. 'Ed? You ever see anything like this?'

Stracey held Jordan's eyes, very still. 'Never outside the game room. We can simulate it there – but this . . . .'

'What is this you say?' Weissleder demanded. 'Someone is making games here?'

Stracey shifted from the desk he was leaning on. 'I am saying, Herr Weissleder, that what you have right here is exactly what we project conditions would be like – communications-wise – if a pre-emptive strike took out our distant early warning line followed by a multi-warhead attack on major targets. In other words, a full-scale nuclear war.'

'That's crazy!' Jordan protested.

'Not the way you people have been fooling around, it isn't,' Stracey answered. '*Sure*, Washington wants your

73

technology – but they also wanted this project out of your hands before a dangerous situation blew up.'

'No!' Ledden objected. 'We set out to produce a device that would end the threat of nuclear war. And we've proved that we can do that!'

Stracey smiled bleakly. 'All you may have proved, Sir Henry, is that you can start one.'

The giant mushroom cloud seemed to hang over Simon Howard's shoulders as he worked frantically at the pulpy growth around the rusted steel door with a heavy, bone-handled, folding knife. He yanked at the old lever, pulling with all his might, but the door remained obstinately shut. He yelled at it in fury, cursing it, the island and INTER-SAT for bringing him to the wretched place. But only after he had used up his large vocabulary of expletives did he notice the wedges jammed into the frame. It took him five more cursing minutes to extract them. With a resounding *clung* and an expulsion of foul air the door gave in. He paused, peering down the low, sloping, uninviting shaft into the rock. Then, with a last backward glance before he entered the tunnel, he saw in the far distance a black smudge break the surface of the ocean. He ducked into the tunnel and dragged the door inward, leaving a gap for the binoculars. He saw the black hull – and as if it were springing at him through the lenses – the red Communist star on the conning tower.

'Bleedin' Russians!' he breathed and pulled the door shut, squatting on the cold gritty concrete to think. Inside, it was as black as Hell.

Sergei Ulyanov had regained consciousness to find himself draped over the now horizontal shaft of the periscope housing. His eyes were stinging and misted with red. He eased himself down onto what had been one of the side walls of the craft and wiped at his eyes. The white sleeve of his thick sweater came away smeared with blood.

A sailor picked his way cautiously over smashed equipment to Ulyanov's side with a first aid kit. 'Comrade Commander, you have a bad cut!'

'Stop the bleeding,' Ulyanov ordered. 'We must right the boat .... Mikhail!' he said suddenly, his voice rising with concern. 'Where is the Grandmaster?'

'Here,' answered Tavrin, hanging by one long arm from a row of pipes, his feet splayed for support. 'I am all right, but you must get us out of here.'

Ulyanov looked over at him and laughed. 'Out? Out! he says, comrades. Mikhail, before we can get out, we have to go *up*.'

'Are we on the bottom?'

'I don't think so – we hadn't gained enough depth. I think we have struck a shelf. We are lucky – very lucky – by rights we should all be dead.'

'But we are not,' said Tavrin. 'So up – then out.'

Ulyanov shook his bearded head. 'We will have to see.'

He began giving orders and making checks of the submarine's systems with a controlled urgency, for he knew that in such a situation panic could easily begin, so it was essential to estimate any damage as fast as possible. Finally, and then only when he was satisfied enough to take the risk, he began the delicate manoeuvres designed to right the *Stoiki*. Suddenly he smacked his forehead with his palm. 'Chebrikov and the girl!' he exclaimed.

Tavrin said. 'They are well. Your young sailor strapped them into their bunks. Some of the men freed them while you were unconscious.'

'Where are they now?'

'The boy is looking after them. They are not the immediate problem. Do what you have to do first.'

Ulyanov nodded and rapped out sharp orders. Slowly, and with a long, protesting moan, the *Stoiki* came over onto her belly. He called the crew together.

'This is the moment,' he said, studying the grim, scared faces. 'If we are going to go up at all, it must be now. If we reach the surface we will have to abandon ship very fast. There is too much damage done. The rudder is jammed and we are shipping water from many small leaks. It will be impossible to steer her and too risky to stay aboard her. We have lost many comrades,' he said sadly, noticing how small his original crew had become, 'but we have one chance to survive. We must use it now before more systems fail.' He looked directly at the frail, supported body of Josef Chebrikov – all but unconscious in a sailor's arms. 'If we reach the surface safely, Comrade Chebrikov and the girl must go first. Next Comrade Tavrin, and then the rest of us. Good luck to all of you – and my thanks . . . .' his words trailed off. 'Blow all tanks!' he snapped in an altogether sharper voice.

With a hideous tearing sound the *Stoiki* ripped herself free and rose, bows first and excruciatingly slowly, towards the surface.

The *Stoiki*'s bows smashed through the waves and kept on going as if rearing up to the sky itself. Then, her momentum gone, she crashed back sickeningly to the icy water.

Ulyanov had the hatches opened within seconds and two grey inflatable dinghies on the deck slats, blowing themselves into shape, almost before the foam had run off the slippery hull of the submarine. He barked orders rapidly, making sure that the three civilians were safely in one of the inflatables with some of the men before he allowed the launch of the second.

At the last moment he flung himself, arms stretched, toward Tavrin's boat and landed on the rim, his legs in the freezing water. Willing hands dragged him in and he shouted: 'Row! Get away from her!' He turned to the other small boat and waved his arm frantically towards the distant mound of Beacon Island.

Behind them the *Stoiki* gave out a deep moan and turned turtle, then went down as if every rivet in her had given way at the same instant.

The second inflatable had lagged behind and Ulyanov screamed at them but, although the sailors drove their paddles into the sea like men demented, the undertow at the edge of the great swirling whirlpool caused by the descent of the *Stoiki* caught them, and they disappeared into the black depths of the vortex, their screams of terror cutting through the cold air like blades. The screams seemed to continue long after a huge bubble of air and black oil burst on the surface.

Sergei Ulyanov laid his head onto his thick forearms in grief, impervious to the cold which would soon render his soaked legs useless. Tanya Chebrikova slipped to her knees, rolled up the drenched heavy serge trouser legs and began massaging the flesh furiously.

Ulyanov looked up at her. 'God bless you,' he said, his deep voice choked with emotion.

'God?' she queried. 'There is no God. But I am a nurse. I cannot stand aside and watch suffering. Your men are dead – I cannot help them – but I can help you. If there is a God he would have helped them. How much power does it need to pull a few men in a boat to safety? There is no God.' She turned to the black, mushroom-shaped cloud. 'There is the power that has replaced your "God"!'

'Commander!' the young sailor shouted. 'Look, the island!'

4

'What's happened up there?' Matt Jordan exclaimed, looking up at the worried faces which filled the closed-circuit TV monitor.

'Haven't you seen it?' one of the surface crew answered quickly.

'Seen what?'

One of the men eased forward so that his face filled the screen. 'Macpherson, sir. You'd better turn on the south-facing camera.' The Scotsman's voice was quiet. Too quiet.

Ray Simpson flicked a switch and another screen in the row lit up. 'Jee . . . sus!' he breathed.

Ed Stracey jerked upright.

'It doesn't *have* to be war,' Jordan muttered, his eyes locking with Stracey's.

'No,' Stracey agreed. 'Could be a nuclear sub blown away – that's happened before – but it wouldn't account for the loss of all communications, would it?'

'You tell me.'

'I just did. You can't turn off the world by blowing up one sub.'

'But *we* are here, Herr Stracey,' Weissleder cut in roughly. 'How can we be standing here talking if there is an atomic war outside?'

'Like everyone else, Weissleder, you believe that a nuclear war is total destruction in seconds flat. It isn't. Many places won't be harmed at all . . . until the fallout drops on them. We certainly felt the shockwave from one bomb – or something – but the nearest target to us would be the Soviet naval bases near Murmansk and Archangel and they're a little too far away. My bet is a sub has blown, but it doesn't *have* to be an accident. The loss of communication tends to support that. If a series of targets were hit – missile installations first, then major cities, the radioactivity would turn the airwaves into spaghetti. Right now – if that *is* what has happened – we're out of it.'

Ledden said: 'So my decision to keep the station sealed up is not an over-reaction.'

Stracey gave a twisted grin. 'Sir Henry, if you hadn't I'd have knocked you on the head and done it myself.'

'You sound convinced that we *are* facing a nuclear situation, even war,' Ledden said.

Stracey shrugged. 'I've seen it on computers – their projections seem identical – but thank God I've never seen the real thing.'

Jemma Elliot had pushed her way in and was standing, very subdued, in the doorway. 'Till now,' she said.

'Mac,' Jordan spoke into the desk microphone. 'We'll open the lift doors for you – get straight down here, just leave everything as it is up there.'

'Doctor,' the Scot said with a frown, 'that chappie who came in with Sir Henry is still out there. Wouldn't wait for you to open up.'

'Howard,' Ledden said.

'He'll be back,' Jordan told Macpherson. 'You get yourselves down here right away.' Jordan stabbed the lift release mechanism.

Jemma Elliot faced Stracey. 'So if you're right – who's

left out there? Us and who else – the goddam politicians, I suppose!'

Stracey could see the stark fear in her eyes. 'There'll be plenty of underground bases which might escape – or survive – a hit. Many countries will be entirely untouched – but like I said, that's before the dust starts to blow. That's when the men get separated from the boys.'

'*Men from the boys*! Jesus, you're all heart, Stracey. What are you – some kind of analytical machine?'

'I'm a realist, ma'am.'

'Well, all right, Mr Realist! What are we – the men or the boys?'

'Ask your boss, he knows how this place is set up.'

'No immediate problems, thank God,' Jordan answered. 'We've got a massive air filtration plant and scrubbers and plenty of food. INTERSAT's policy has always been to keep Whitefire One supplied on a one-year reserve basis. I'm talking about basics and dehydrated products, naturally.'

'Water could be a problem,' Ledden interrupted. 'When the winter starts we might be able to rely on snow, but it could be contaminated by radiation like everything else.'

Jordan frowned. 'The desalination plant should cope as long as we're careful – *I don't believe we're talking like this!* This is *unreal*.'

'That cloud looks pretty damn real to me!' Jemma snapped.

A voice called out from the crowd of technicians at the door. 'Sir, maybe the Russians have finally caught on to us and the nuke is a warning?'

Jordan shook his head. 'Even if they'd worked out that we were responsible for their failures, they'd hardly go to that extreme. They'd just hit the island with a task force – but not before we destroyed Whitefire. We've always accepted that risk and we're fully prepared for it. I don't buy that theory . . . even though I'd rather not face the other.'

Ledden said: 'I think we have to discuss this in depth. We'd better get the entire staff together in the recreation area. If your theory is correct, Mr Stracey, we are going to have to review our present values. Take away all this high technology and we will be reduced to living like primitive man – or animals – in a very dark hole in the ground.'

Stracey grimaced. 'And that's another thing our computers projected, Sir Henry. But I don't believe that, right now, any of you want to know the results.'

Behind Stracey, Reinhardt Weissleder's face had become a mask of terror. It was as if his worst nightmare had suddenly become a reality.

Simon Howard had encountered and perpetrated enough horror in his twenty-eight years as a mercenary killer to have given most men nightmares for the rest of their lives.

But Howard suffered neither pangs of conscience nor regret; he rationalized his killing of fellow human beings by calling it his 'profession'. He took great pride in the undoubted expertise he employed in his work, and kept a grisly account of every method he had used and others he might at some future time get to use. Also, in the same black notebook, he kept a meticulous record of every victim he had summarily dispatched. For this record, when names were not readily available he could be satisfied by a careful physical description of the victim ranging from the colour of hair and eyes, and estimation of height and weight, down to the smallest deformities such as moles or scars. Dates and times of death he noted in a separate column, and he pondered over these at great length, working out hideous averages in his sharp, cunning and entirely brutalized mind.

He began keeping this dreadful record when – after completing his voluntary period with the Australian Forces in Vietnam – he immediately volunteered his skills to the US Army Long Range Patrol Unit, the silent search-and-destroy patrols known as LURPS. Since in every guerrilla war the only realistic method of keeping an account of defeat or victory against a hit-and-run enemy is by a physical body count of every single member of the enemy shot or otherwise killed, the Americans – who dearly love statistics – had adopted this method.

Howard soon had the highest body count per mission of any other LURP in his region and – after some disbelieving looks at debriefing sessions – he gave physical confirmation of his prowess by supplying pairs of ears as proof. The problem with this method was that it was difficult to know exactly how to pack such items in quantity. He tried, at first, stringing them like a necklace, then different methods of pressing them like some dreadful species of flower, but in the end he gave up and simply kept a written record. By this time his debriefing officers were willing – even eager – to believe whatever claims the 'crazy little Limey' made, so actual physical proof became redundant. 'And anyway,' Howard had told a fellow patrol member, 'a notebook doesn't stink.'

He considered these facts to be no different from a salesman's record in the field. After all, he liked to joke, his victims were hardly likely to give him a reference!

But none of this had prepared him for what he found at the end of the cold, dank tunnel.

His progress had been slow, because he lived by caution, so it had taken him a while to reach the main chamber and *there*, in the stabbing beam of the torch, he was faced with a nightmare scene. He shut his eyes, feeling his hair actually *rising* on his head, then, gathering himself together, opened them again. His thin face was a ghastly white in the reflected light above the torch. He moved the beam and encountered even more dreadful sights in another part of the chamber. There was only one thought in his mind – and that was to get out fast.

He darted back along the tunnel, barking his shins on the narrow gas lock, then threw himself at the steel door, breathing in the fresh air with deep gulps.

'Holy shit!' he exclaimed between gasps, and squatted on his haunches to recover. If he had not already spotted the dinghy he would have made his way over to the light-house and demanded admittance, but now he could not do that. His instincts told him to stay right where he was. He brought the binoculars up quickly, just to keep the nearing boat in his sights. He watched, and he waited.

He thought of everything that had happened, arms

clutched around his knees, and finally came to a conclusion. There was no way he was going back to the station and possibly get trapped underground and starved to death . . . like . . . but he shut the recurring image from his mind. *No way!* He was above ground and free to move – and if he *had* to go back down the tunnel for safety, well, next time he'd be better prepared. He would wait. He would find out *exactly* what was going on, then he could do something about it.

The dinghy was still some way off, but closing. He decided that he must stock up with a little food and drink – just in case – so darted over the rocks toward the concrete huts and raided the weathermen's stores. There was very little food. They eat below, he thought furiously. He grabbed a few tins and dashed back to his door.

Through the glasses again, he saw the dinghy change direction and head toward the jetty far below his position. When they landed they would have no choice but to pass him, and for a moment he worried about them seeing the door, but then realized that with the lessening light and the poor visibility, because of the constant spray, they would head straight for the swinging beam of the lighthouse and the warmth of the huts. He studied the cloud again, which had now become anvil-shaped from the stratospheric winds. Good! The wind was blowing it the other way. Straight back to bleedin' Russia.

He waited. He was cold. He was angry.

Come on, you Commie bastards, let's have you!

Ulyanov blinked through the haze of icy spray and his heart plummeted. There was no earthly way that the old man could even begin to climb the sheer overhanging cliffs to the angled plateau at their summit. Looking around him, he doubted if the rest of the beaten-looking party of survivors could get halfway to the top – even if they had climbing gear. He turned, staring at the great cloud behind them, wondering what the people on the island would make of it. They would be frightened, bewildered and probably very edgy, even hostile. He decided that he had no choice but to take a gamble: if his party could not make it to the top unaided, then he would have to enlist the help of the people on the island. He hefted the emergency radio he had snatched at the last moment from the doomed submarine, pulled out the long, whip-like antennae and switched on the set. Every frequency he tried was blocked by an unbroken field of static. He gave it one hard slap, in desperation, but the grating sound continued.

'Useless!' he shouted over the roar of the waves pounding against the cliffs ahead, and in anger tossed the set into the sea.

Tavrin shouted back: 'What was wrong with it?'

Ulyanov shrugged and yelled. 'We can't climb those cliffs!'

Tavrin pointed. 'There's a small landing stage on the south-east face! We can make it to the top from there.'

Ulyanov looked at the Grandmaster sharply. 'How do you know?'

'What does it matter – get us there!'

'There!' Tanya cried with relief. 'Look! Over there!'

'Take her in!' Ulyanov ordered, and gave Tavrin another careful look. Then, judging the timing and force of the waves expertly, he brought the inflatable alongside the jetty. Blue with cold, the party hauled themselves onto the slimy concrete, but Ulyanov urged his men to their feet and had the boat dragged to a place of safety on the rocks, then secured it to one of the rusted steel hand rails which the sea had bent but could not dislodge. Looking up, his hands cupped around his reddened eyes, he surveyed the zigzag railinged path cut into the jagged black rock and leading to the plateau above.

Ulyanov counted heads before they began the ascent. His losses were appalling: of the twenty-two men he had persuaded to join him, only six remained. So with himself and the three civilians, all there was to show for the entire disastrous enterprise were ten, cold, defeated people. Never try to put ideals into practice, he told himself wretchedly. His burning idealism had sent sixteen good men to the bottom of the ocean.

Grimly, he gave the order to begin the ascent.

5

Sir Henry Ledden assembled the staff of the secret base in the recreation area, the largest single space on Level One in which they could all be addressed. He watched them filing into the open-plan area in stunned silence, for, though not all had actually heard Stracey's view of the situation, word had spread very quickly and in the process had become accepted as fact.

Leddon knew he would have a hard job bringing the situation back to a semblance of normality. He waited while they sat at the tables in the dining section or perched themselves on the few pieces of gymnastic equipment or on the bar stools around the small bar. They were completely still and Ledden himself felt a reluctance to break their silence. Then someone did it for him.

'Sir Henry!' A voice came from the bar. 'We want to know the truth – we're entitled to it.'

Ledden acknowledged the man. 'Indeed you are – we all are – and if I knew the truth I should tell you immediately. But at present we have total communications failure.'

'Some of us heard what was said in the communications room,' the man said. 'If Mr Stracey is with the ISS he must know what he's talking about. We're not looking for soft options here. All we want to know is – if he's right – what are our chances?'

Jordan took over. 'I've already reprogrammed the computer in its life-support functions. We're entirely self-sufficient and protected. The air you are breathing right now is being filtered and scrubbed. Simpson is keeping all emergency frequencies open and we shall continue to maintain a round-the-clock monitoring rota. Beyond these initial procedures we can do no more. Food is no problem – nor is water . . .' Jordan smiled, ' . . . and if we run out of that we've got a year's supply of alchohol left.'

No one laughed.

Jordan scanned the faces. 'Nothing's been proven – if we

get confirmation of a nuclear conflict *then* we can look at the wider issues. Right now let's keep everything battened down tight and wait.'

'Isn't that cloud enough proof for you?' Jemma Elliot snapped, angrily.

Jordan watched her closely, and suddenly she was very much one woman alone with close on fifty men. Trapped men. He recognized that her anger was actually fear. Before the station had been made operational he had made a point of studying every report he could get hold of concerning men under stress so that he would be prepared for the difficulties of keeping his staff under control – and underground – for almost a year without a break. Now the conclusions of those studies came back to him hard. Psychological collapse was inevitable. Deterioration would set in at an alarming rate once the stabilizing factor of a world outside their closed environment was cast into doubt. Tempers would shorten, then not be kept in check at all; normal values would lose significance; behaviour patterns would be subject to aberration. Inevitably, the system would collapse. No wonder she's scared, Jordan thought. If I were in her place I would be terrified.

Another voice called out: 'She's right!'

'No, she's *not!*' Jordan retorted, coming down hard on the man. 'You're supposed to be scientists and technicians – yet you're acting like laymen who have no conception of the sort of accidents that can happen with nuclear energy. You're letting your emotions take over your brains! I *know* you've got families out there, I *know* how you feel, but goddammit, we all share those fears. We're just going to have to sit this out and not lose our grip on the situation.'

'So what if it *is* true?' said the same voice. 'What if we can't leave this island? We rely on the chopper. All we've got up top is a couple of rubber boats!'

Ledden answered the question, his voice displaying the bitter defeat he felt inside. 'If there has been a major nuclear conflict then, no matter what facilities we had to get off the island, we would still be wiser to remain. Because this underground installation is the only place we could hope to survive in. God alone knows what might lie out there!'

'What do *you* believe has happened, Sir Henry?' Jemma Elliot asked.

Ledden shook his head. 'I don't know what I believe any more. With the arms race going out of control as it is – or was,' he added grimly, 'I would say that it was inevitable that at some point one side or the other would use their nuclear weapons.'

The emergency alarm shrieked and instantly everyone was moving.

'Calm down!' Jordan bawled, managing – just – to keep hold of some sort of order. He forced his way through the crowd blocking the passage leading to the communications room and ordered them to go back, then opened the door. Simpson turned to him and cut the alarm.

'Visitors,' he said, 'up top. Sailors. Russian sailors.' He lifted his chin toward the bank of video screens.

Jordan could see, in the haze, two white hats and bulky bodies beneath them. 'Can you improve the picture?' he asked.

'No. But they'll make for the main hut, for sure. I can use the cameras inside.'

'We've got sound in there, right?'

'Condensor mikes. No problem.'

Ledden ushered Stracey and Weissleder through then, and reluctantly allowed Jemma Elliot to pass. Jordan could hear the rumble of noise in the passage from the rest. 'Russian Navy,' he said.

'How many?' Stracey queried.

'Can't tell. Wait till they get into the main weather hut – we can pick up their conversations in there.'

'They've got someone hurt by the look of it . . . .' Jordan said, peering at the grey blur of the screen. 'They're supporting someone.'

'They sure don't look like any task force,' Stracey murmured. 'More like they've been shipwrecked.'

'Maybe you were right about that sub, Stracey,' said Jordan.

'Maybe,' Stracey breathed, casting a sideways glance at Jordan. 'But don't go pinning your hopes on that.'

'I'm not. But if it *was* a sub then they could be survivors of the crew. They can tell us a lot.'

'You don't get survivors from a nuclear blast. These guys must be from some other vessel. Hey, that's no goddam sailor! They've got a woman with them.'

At the rim of the cliff, Mikhail Tavrin had pulled Ulyanov aside, speaking urgently, fighting the wind and spray.

'Sergei, listen to me! You must not mention to these people that you destroyed the *Brezhnev*. Tell them that and they may not want the responsibility of us.'

Ulyanov laughed harshly, the wind snatching away the sound. '*Responsibility!* Mikhail, I heard no cancellation of the nuclear alert – and there were only seconds to go before both ours and the American missiles were to be released.' He stuck out a solid arm. 'Maybe there is *nothing* out there!'

Tavrin made a gesture of impatience. 'These exercises have gone wrong before, but they have always been corrected in time. Come, let us get out of this weather before we die of exposure!'

But Ulyanov had grabbed Tavrin's arm, restraining him. 'Mikhail! I have *never* known an exercise run so close to launch. The time factor was at a critical stage. Perhaps it was too late to stop it?'

Tavrin turned away, making the bearded sailor release him. 'If anyone can answer your question, the people on this island can.' He pointed at a large dish antenna. 'That is for satellite communications. They will know everything that is going on in the world – even at this second. Remember, my friend – not one word about the *Brezhnev*.'

Ulyanov followed him, puzzled. 'How do you know about this place? The jetty, the steps, their satellite link? How, Mikhail?'

Tavrin turned his back on the rising storm, his face close to Ulyanov's, his pale eyes impenetrable. 'Because I *know*. Because I have access to sources which you could never have. Because I am Mikhail Tavrin!' He swung away into the wind.

In front of them, the sailors had reached the huts, aiding the barely conscious Chebrikov and Tanya over the treacherous rocks on the way. Tavrin and Ulyanov ran, heads down against the freezing, blinding spray, to catch up.

Ulyanov reached the door first and almost fell inside. He flicked on a light switch and surveyed the deserted hut. 'They've gone,' he said, helping the others inside.

'Why leave the doors open?' Tanya asked.

Chebrikov smiled at her weakly as he was placed on a chair. 'My child,' he said, 'who would come all this way to steal?'

'Tavrin!' Ray Simpson blurted. 'Mikhail Tavrin!'

'Are you certain?' Jordan questioned, moving closer to the extraordinary face on the screen. 'You're right,' he said.

'The Russian Grandmaster?' Ledden said.

'World chess champion, sir,' Simpson corrected, his eyes still on the screen.

'What world?' Jemma Elliot muttered.

'Shut up!' snapped Jordan.

'What's he doing here – with Soviet sailors?' said Ledden.

'He disappeared from the championships . . . in mid-tournament . . . .' Jordan began, but Ledden was no longer interested in chess players.

Stracey said: 'You recognize him too, Sir Henry?'

Ledden nodded. 'Chebrikov. The last person we'd want here . . . if he were still working for the Russians.'

Weissleder, who until that moment had remained icy calm, suddenly exploded, jabbing a finger at the row of screens. 'And what are those, if you please, Sir Henry? American GIs? This is a conspiracy – we must stop it!'

Jordan turned. 'Keep calm, please. There is an explanation. Simpson picked up a news bulletin – BBC World Service – before we lost the radio. It said that Tavrin, Chebrikov and a woman were picked up by a Soviet submarine in a Norwegian fjord.'

Simpson nodded. 'An eye witness saw the three go aboard.'

Jordan continued: 'And Simpson also picked up some

Russian radio traffic hours before, which indicated that they'd got some kind of naval mutiny on their hands – a sub had gone missing and they were trying to track it down.'

Simpson added: 'The mutineers had taken over the sub and had made a run for it – that was the story.'

'Surely that's not feasible?' Ledden said.

'It's been tried before,' Stracey countered. 'Not a sub, admittedly, but a guided missile destroyer called the *Storozhevoy*. She slipped her berth in Riga, Latvia and attempted to sail west – 9 November 1976, if I remember rightly. She was manned by a skeleton crew – dissident sailors who'd had enough – but a Soviet task force outran them and brought them back. They executed the ringleaders on the spot and the rest got the usual trip to the labour camps without the option. If they'd chosen a nuclear sub they might have made it.'

'All right,' Ledden conceded, 'but *these* people were already as far as Norway – why come back?'

'Pick up the phone and ask them!' Jemma snapped acidly. 'We're standing here jabbering when we should be asking them what the hell has happened out there.'

'Jemma's right,' Jordan said. 'In a Soviet Navy submarine they'd have had access to every military order as it was given. If they were being hunted they'd have been certain to be listening. We've got to speak with them.'

'No!' Weissleder growled. 'No speaking. We stay here. They have come to make us open the doors. Do not trust them.'

'Dr Jordan is right, Herr Weissleder,' Ledden said. 'They are certain to know what has happened – however there is one factor here which is most disturbing. The old man on the screen is Josef Chebrikov. Both Mr Stracey and myself have recognized him, so there is no mistake. I think you'd better tell them yourself, Stracey.'

Stracey nodded. 'Chebrikov defected from the Soviet Union some twelve years ago. He was a great scientist, way ahead of his time in almost everything he worked on. The poor bastard had it rough all his life – the Nazis lifted him out of Russia and put him to work for them, then

Stalin grabbed him back and stuck him in a labour camp for a few years before putting him back to work again – re-education in Marxist principles, I suppose. He did a lot of underground rebel-rousing for a while, then they put him in the slammer for more re-education. In the end he managed to get out of Russia just when they thought they'd got him thinking their way. He was one of the pioneers of the Soviet "chain-lighting" high-energy lasers and charged particle beam programme at Semipalatinsk, Kazakhstan. Do I need to say any more?'

Weissleder spun Ledden round to face him, his blue eyes blazing. 'You see! They are making a conspiracy. They *must not* be allowed to see what is here!'

'Where is everybody?' Tanya Chebrikova said, bewildered by the deserted huts. 'They cannot just disappear. Look. All their possessions are here . . . ' she snatched a coat from a peg '. . . they were working . . . look!' She held up papers.

Ulyanov raised his bushy eyebrows hopelessly. 'The men have checked all the huts. There is no one.'

'If I saw such an explosion on the horizon, I too would disappear,' Tavrin observed. 'But where? Your men must have missed something, Sergei. Make them search some more.'

'No,' Ulyanov objected. 'They are exhausted. And the weather is too bad – we might lose a man off the cliffs. These people must return . . . where can they go? Into the sea?'

'Perhaps there is some underground shelter for the winter months? They would be afraid of radiation fallout, would they not, Sergei?'

'Of course! *I* am afraid of fallout! If this storm turns toward the Pole we will be in grave danger. You think I wish to remain on the surface?' Ulyanov moved over to the radio transmitter and switched it on, working his way through various frequencies. Like Simpson beneath him, all he got was a haze of static.

Tavrin stood over him silently.

The heavy bearded face turned upwards, the ruddy complexion had turned grey. 'It is as I said,' Ulyanov whispered.

Tavrin frowned. 'Impossible!'

Ulyanov flicked angrily through all the wavelengths without result, then fell back into the chair as if stunned.

'What is wrong?' Tanya demanded, looking up from Chebrikov, who seemed to have lost consciousness entirely.

Ulyanov switched off the set and stood up. He spoke to her slowly as if she were a small child. 'Before we encountered the *Brezhnev* we picked up a message from our own Nuclear Command Centre that the Americans were preparing a nuclear strike. Naturally all Soviet missiles were readied also.'

'Yes?' she said, not quite understanding.

'We heard no order for the countdown to be halted. At first I thought it was an exercise, but there was no code put out by the Americans to show that it was. This is a safety factor agreed by both sides. There was no exercise code . . . and we did not hear the countdown stop.'

Tanya's hand was pressed to her mouth, the flesh white from the pressure she exerted. 'And the radio?' she asked, deathly pale.

'Blocked. All wavelengths are blocked. This will happen when the radiation level rises to . . . .' Ulyanov moved just fast enough to catch her before she hit the floor.

Simon Howard had let the party of Russians pass his position, then followed like a shadow, stopping as the tallest man drew a big bearded officer aside and spoke in a low conspiratorial manner. Their conversation seemed urgent and without doubt was about something they were planning. Or so it seemed to Howard, who had not a word of Russian to his name.

All right, you bastards, Howard thought, let's see what your game is.

He tracked them to the main hut, then spread flat as the sailors came out and searched the area before trudging back exhaustedly into the hut. Carefully he approached the window, gazing covetously at their AKS-74 assault rifles and the automatic holstered at the bearded officer's belt.

Howard had seen many people pass out in his lifetime, and could see the girl was going to seconds before she actually did. Nevertheless he was impressed by the speed at which the big officer moved to catch her. Then the sound of an amplified voice came clearly through the glass.

Simpson translated Ulyanov's words as they watched him sit Tanya in a chair and push her head down between her legs.

'That settles it,' said Ledden. 'We have our answer. We can't leave those people up there any longer – the radiation hazard is increasing all the time.'

'No!' Weissleder shouted. 'They must not come down here. If they see what is here – we are finished. Finished! You are throwing billions of dollars away. Billions!'

Ledden looked at the German sadly. 'Can't you understand that it's over anyway?'

The German's face had darkened with anger but now it cleared, and he seemed to withdraw inside as if he had lost interest. He moved away and stood very still by the wall, watching.

'Speak to them,' Ledden ordered Simpson. 'Tell them we are underground. Get them to identify themselves – just confirmation – then we'll get them down.'

Simpson spoke into his microphone in Russian: 'Please do not be alarmed. I am speaking from an underground facility of this station. I can see and hear you through television cameras.' He watched the faces of the Russians turn immediately to a speaker, then swivel around searching uselessly for the concealed cameras.

Tavrin moved forward to the speaker. 'We would like to speak with whoever is in charge here – it is very important. Quickly, please.'

Jordan said: 'Get him to confirm who he is.'

Simpson continued, still speaking Russian: 'You are Grandmaster Mikhail Tavrin?'

'Correct,' Tavrin agreed, mildly surprised.

'Please identify the rest of your party.'

'Who is speaking here? Are you in charge of this place?'

'Please identify the other people,' Simpson repeated.

'Survivors from the Soviet submarine *Stoiki*,' Tavrin stated impatiently. 'Here also is Josef Chebrikov, a Swiss citizen, and his grand-daughter. I speak English also and German if that is better?'

Ledden took over. 'Very well,' he said in English. 'Can you tell us what has happened up there?'

Tavrin glanced at Ulyanov, then said: 'We wished you to answer this question. You don't know?'

'We have only seen evidence of a nuclear explosion. We thought perhaps it was a submarine. Yours?'

Ulyanov answered in heavily accented but passable English. 'I am Sergei Ulyanov. I commanded the *Stoiki*. Our submarine was wrecked by the blast from another boat – the *Brezhnev*.'

Underground Ed Stracey sucked in breath sharply. 'The *Brezhnev*! That's their latest boat . . . the biggest sub in the world . . . nearly 30,000 tons!'

'How was the *Brezhnev* destroyed?' Ledden said into the microphone.

Ulyanov shrugged, then looked warily at the radio. 'Perhaps a missile? We were monitoring an American nuclear exercise which seemed to go wrong. The *Brezhnev* exploded as the countdown was nearing its crucial phase.'

Ledden said: 'We picked up Soviet radio traffic last night. Are you the mutineers they were hunting?'

Ulyanov's face clouded. 'We do not call ourselves mutineers,' he said heavily.

Tavrin broke in. 'Who is speaking, please?'

'My name is Henry Ledden. The island you are on is owned – leased – from your country by my company.'

'This is good, we seek political asylum.' Tavrin stated. There was a long pause and Tavrin repeated his statement. 'We seek your protection. Did you hear me? Political asylum.'

But Ulyanov was tapping the radio urgently and spoke before Ledden could answer. 'What is wrong with this radio? Is it unserviceable?'

'No,' Ledden answered carefully. 'There is a possibility that the exercise you heard might have been a pre-emptive nuclear strike by the United States. We have other equipment which is also picking up the heavy static. We fear it may be a radioactive haze which is blocking all radio traffic.'

Tavrin cut in. 'Then you *must* take us in! If there is radioactivity then we are in danger. Our submarine has sunk – we have no other place to go. If you are underground you have protection . . . there are not many of us. We are not your enemies. I ask you, please, *help us*.'

The speaker fell silent and around the room, heads bowed with exhaustion, the sailors seemed oblivious to the sudden lull in the conversation and totally unaware of the revelations made by the disembodied voice speaking a language they did not understand.

'Very well,' Ledden said at last. 'But all your weapons must remain where you are. I will have no firearms down here. Go to the lighthouse and we will let you into the underground area.'

Ulyanov gave an order, then took charge of the assault rifles, placing them on a table along with his automatic.

Outside the hut, his ear jammed against the window, Simon Howard spat out an obscenity, then moved swiftly across the sloping plateau toward the steel door cut into the black rock.

The Russians were greeted with a wariness that bordered on hostility, but slowly the eagerness for information broke down the initial barriers and the atmosphere warmed enough for questions to be asked. Between them, Ulyanov and Tavrin recalled the incidents of the stealing of the submarine, the approach made to Chebrikov and the meeting in Norway, then, avoiding their involvement in the destruction of the *Brezhnev*, the nerve-straining last moments of the countdown to nuclear catastrophe. As many of the secret base's personnel were avid chess players the presence of the world champion was akin to having a god suddenly transported into their midst – for some it even lifted the memory of the dreadful cloud which had scarred the horizon.

Chebrikov had lapsed into unconsciousness almost as soon as he had entered the warm air of the underground level, and Tanya had not left his bedside in the small sick bay from the moment of their arrival. She was amazed, and thankful, that the medical facilities were as good as they were.

Finally, and with some reluctance, Tavrin and the rest of the Russians were allowed to escape from the endless barrage of questions and were shown, utterly exhausted, to cabins vacated for them.

As soon as they had left Ledden insisted that Jordan should go with him to Level Two; once there he wasted no time in expressing his fears. 'You realize that we will have to close down this level entirely? We can't risk the Russians coming in here – not until we can be absolutely certain of what has happened.'

'You don't trust them?'

'Oh, I believe what they say – but it's a question of the extent of . . . well, the damage that's been done. Are we talking about total nuclear war or an incident between the two superpowers that may have been stopped before it was too late?'

Jordan shook his head slowly. 'If it wasn't for the loss of all our communications I'd go along with you – but to lose radio, radar – and our satellite link – all at once, paints a rather black picture, Sir Henry.' He surveyed the rows of consoles and the banks of complicated equipment. 'All this advanced technology turned into very expensive junk in minutes – it's unbelievable.'

'It's *tragic* – not unbelievable. Given a few weeks more and we might have been able to avert this terrible . . . *atrocity!* I've always believed that the human race can achieve anything it really wanted and, Matthew, we were so close – so very close – to achieving what has always been thought impossible: the nullification of war. Or at the very least the constant fear of nuclear war. But I suppose, going by man's past record, that it was inevitable he would destroy himself before he could save himself.'

'From himself,' Jordan added, folding his brown arms behind his head. 'I gave up philosophizing about the human race right after I left college. Somehow the "real world" destroys any ideals one might have. But I suppose that's called growing up?'

Ledden sat down and sighed. 'My dream was that all the money that would have been saved once Whitefire was operational could have been used to *improve* this world we don't deserve . . . not destroy it. I have recurring nightmares about how much the superpowers – and the rest – spend on "sabre-rattling". And most of the time that is all it is – only a complete lunatic contemplates total destruction.'

Jordan looked pointedly at the massed equipment and said: 'Adolf Hitler contemplated it.'

Ledden nodded sombrely. 'That really is the supreme irony, isn't it? The man who almost destroyed civilization could have been the catalyst which started the process of saving it in its darkest hour. Do you know that I was almost at the stage of believing that all the suffering he inflicted might after all have been justified if – in the end – we could produce Whitefire?'

'That's not a judgement I would care to make,' Jordan said, grimly.

Ledden tugged a pipe from his jacket and lit it. 'The other thing I wanted to discuss is the women. If we are stuck down here for . . . let's say a long time . . . I foresee problems.' He lifted his eyebrows in inquiry. 'You do realize that the men are going to have a lot of time on their hands – something they're not used to down here. We can't continue with work on the project – for obvious reasons.'

Jordan nodded agreement. 'I've thought about it already. So has Jemma – you can see it in her eyes – but God knows how she will react to any loss of her independence. She won't take easily to any suggestions that she might have to . . . .'

'Be circumspect in her behaviour?' Ledden suggested.

'That's one way of putting it.' Jordan grinned, but there was little humour in his eyes. He knew that she was going to be very difficult to handle.

Ledden tapped ash from his pipe and stood up. 'Well, that matter I must leave with you, I'm afraid. I know she's acknowledged to be one of the finest guidance experts in the field, but as a woman I have no knowledge of her at all.'

'I'll talk with her,' Jordan said, standing.

They walked to the lift. Ledden turned, then said: 'It really is quite extraordinary that here we are standing under the most advanced defence system ever developed in human history, and probably all we'll ever have to use it against is barbaric scavengers armed with clubs!'

Jordan put his finger on the sensor and the doors opened. Ledden stood quite still, surveying his lost dream, his warm eyes filled with regret. 'But perhaps that is how all civilizations end?' he said.

'I'll seal it up,' Jordan said, gently.

Mikhail Tavrin was not sleeping. Exhausted though he was, his mind was working smoothly. He switched on the small light over the bunk and checked his watch, then lay back, his eyes lightly closed.

Below him, on the lower bunk, Sergei Ulyanov was snoring grandly with deep bass undertones. A soft double knock on the door and the sound of his name stopped his snoring instantly. He pulled himself up and shook his head to clear the effects of sleep. 'Yes?' he answered, recalling that the voice had spoken in English.

A woman's voice said: 'Will you come straight away to the communications room . . . we've picked up a distress call through the static. There's another Russian ship in trouble. Please be quick!'

'One moment,' Ulyanov replied, and dressed quickly in the clothes he'd been loaned while his uniform was dried out. He opened the door, casting a glance at Tavrin who seemed to have slept through the interruption.

Jemma Elliot stood outside waiting, her white overalls replaced by a light polo-neck and denims. Ulyanov hardly recognized her as the same attractive but rather severe-looking young woman who had sat with the big blond American while he had eaten and answered questions with Tavrin. Then she had hardly spoken, but had watched him intently as if judging him for what he had done. Now the coolness had gone, and he wondered if this was her way of accepting men – the judgement first, and if they passed her test, a little warmth? Also gone was that hint of mannishness – perhaps it was only the change of clothes or the removal of the heavy glasses – but now she was entirely female and unusually beautiful.

He let her lead, admiring the sway of her hips and the hugging tightness of her denims. He noticed the movement of her breasts and knew she wore nothing beneath the sweater. If you were my woman, he thought, I would not allow you to do this. If you were mine no other man could see the softness of your body.

He said: 'Please, I forget your name?'

'Jemma Elliot,' she said, not turning, and he sensed her fear. 'You look better – did you sleep at all?'

'Thank you, yes. I had . . . bath?' He made a cupped-hand movement over his head.

'Shower.'

'I had the shower – then I took some sleep.' He glanced at his watch. 'Not too much.'

'I'm sorry,' she said, and this time she turned. 'Simpson told me to wake you.'

'Do not worry. In Navy all commanders sleep little.'

'Here we are.' She opened the door for him. Only Jordan and Simpson were inside. Simpson spoke quickly in Russian.

'We still have the static but I picked up a distress call through it, very faint but definitely there.'

'She told me,' Ulyanov said, breaking into English. 'How long?'

'Just now – only minutes.'

'You're sure it is a Russian ship?'

'Certain. *Admiral Grechko*.' Simpson gave a call sign.

'Not ship, submarine. Old boat – maybe twelve, thirteen years but nuclear-powered. Named Charlie class by NATO. Message says what is wrong?'

Simpson paused. Jordan answered: 'They reported a hit by a missile. An American missile.'

Ulyanov looked straight into Jordan's eyes. 'You are American, yes?'

Jordan nodded.

Ulyanov tugged his beard. 'Then this position is difficult for you. Do you wish to answer this call? Our countries are fighting in war which can take no prisoners. Leaves only ashes. What is your feeling . . . Dr Jordan?'

Jordan's eyes were troubled. 'I honestly don't know. You people are an exception – you came here for asylum. My country would have let you in under those circumstances . . . but I don't know what to do in the case of a Soviet warship.'

'You can't let them drown!' Jemma exclaimed.

'I have to think of our survival,' Jordan said.

'You have no more space?' Ulyanov questioned.

Jordan shrugged his wide shoulders. 'Depends on how many make it here. We can squeeze in quite a few, I suppose – if we clear the recreation area. The rest would have to take their chances in the surface huts . . . but you realize that the radiation level could become lethal if there is a change in wind direction.'

'Then you'll just have to open up Level Two!' Jemma snapped. 'It's not much use for anything else any more.'

'There is more space underground?' Ulyanov inquired. 'Under here?' He pointed at his feet.

'Machinery,' Jordan said, vaguely. 'Life-support systems . . . computers, that sort of thing.'

Ulyanov frowned, and a fleeting look of suspicion touched his eyes. 'Arctic weather station usually has huts and sometimes maybe one tunnel. But always small . . . not with equipment like in here. This place is like military base.'

'It used to be,' Jordan answered, locking eyes with the bearded Russian. 'The Germans built it during the last war. We developed it further – added more underground space.'

Simpson waved a hand, then pressed his headphones hard against his ears, his pencil darting over the message pad. 'They're abandoning ship,' he said, turning fast. 're-questing assistance from anyone in the area.'

'How far away are they?' Jordan asked, his voice taut.

'Ten miles? Maybe more. I'll work it out.'

Jordan's forehead creased, then he made his decision.

'All right, give them our position and tell them to try and make it here – but if they can get picked up by another vessel tell them to take it. Got that?'

'Right,' said Simpson.

Ulyanov put out his hand. 'Thank you. Sea is the only enemy once ship is sunk. I speak with the men who make it here. Don't worry for your safety.'

Jordan shook the proffered hand and nodded briefly. 'They'll be hours getting here in this weather – if they make it at all. Ray, wake me if anything else happens. Coming, Jemma?'

'How can you sleep with all this going on? I'm going to fix a drink . . . maybe I'll sleep after that . . . OK?'

Jordan gave her a steady look. 'As you like.' He nodded again at Ulyanov. 'See you later.'

'Coffee?' she asked the Russian after Jordan had left.

'For real coffee I would shave my beard!'

'Don't do that! You wouldn't look like a pirate any more.' She fixed three cups, handing one to Simpson. 'Commander, would you like something extra in that? Ray, we'll leave you to it.'

In the recreation area Jemma slid behind the small bar and held up a bottle of brandy. 'This do?' she said.

Ulyanov held out his cup while she poured. She slammed the bottle on the bar top, unexpectedly causing the coffee to spill.

'I'm sorry,' she murmured. 'I just can't seem to face what's happened.'

Ulyanov sat on a stool so that he could look into her face. 'You are hiding your fear too much. Sometimes it is better to let it show.'

'Can *you* believe there's been a nuclear war?'

'Of course. For many years I have stood with my finger over a button which could send destruction to the other side of the world in minutes. It is a little like being God in this moment, believe me. But I am not God – and man is not God – he makes mistakes or he is so proud that he allows himself to make decisions which force his own destruction. Yes, I believe there is a war.'

She poured neat brandy into a glass and swallowed it. Ulyanov placed his broad, thickly-haired hand over hers.

He said: 'We are all frightened – you are not alone. We are like small children made into orphans very quickly. Our security has gone, our lives changed so much that we may never be the same people again. But orphans grow up and they accept the new way of things. It is life. Here we stand, drinking, while others have died – perhaps thousands, perhaps millions. Perhaps we live now only on time lent to us? I do not know. I said before, I am not God. But I think we will survive – we will all change – but we will survive.' He leaned towards her over the bar, feeling the sadness in her, and their faces almost touched.

Her eyes filled with tears but they did not spill over. 'Have you lost someone? A wife? Children?'

'My child. Murmansk was a first-strike target. No one would have survived such a firestorm.' Ulyanov's dark eyes seemed to mist over. 'Perhaps she is better dead. I pray she died quickly with no pain. That is the most I can hope for.'

Jemma poured two glasses of brandy and pushed one to him. 'Your wife?' she said. 'Was she in Murmansk?'

He said nothing and she clasped his hand hard, but he looked up at her and said, 'She died long before this,' then released his hand and swallowed the drink.

He stood up and touched her face. 'A woman needs a man to protect her – it is the way it has always been. Now, in this case, it is even more important. You are lucky, there are many men here who will give all they possess to be in such a position with you.'

'But I'm afraid of that too!' she cried. 'I don't want to be the cause of trouble – and that is sure to happen. I'd rather leave. I want the men *not* to see me as a woman. I don't want to be put into such a position.'

Ulyanov smiled. 'If you were my woman I would not leave you to be afraid. Go tell your man what you have told me. Let him see inside you and perhaps he will see what I have seen.' He finished his drink. 'Now I must sleep a little more before I become too drunk and then too sad.'

He left her standing at the bar, her hand still clutched around her glass.

'What took you so long?' Jordan asked, still awake in the darkness as Jemma entered the cabin.

'Sorry if I woke you,' she answered, pulling her sweater over her head. Jordan pressed the light switch and watched her as she tugged her jeans down her long legs.

'Did you have to put the light on?' she said in irritation. 'Can't I get undressed without you ogling me as if I were some bar-stripper?'

'What's the matter?' he asked.

'What's the matter! Jesus! We're sealed up under a mountain of rock with the rest of the world blown away and you ask what's the matter? What's the matter with *you*!'

'Come on Jemma . . . until we hear something definite there's no point in . . . .'

'You know what you sound like?' she blazed, cutting right across him. 'A damn computer that doesn't like the program it's been fed. So what do you want – a personally autographed copy of the declaration of war? Why don't you face up to it? You've already been knocked out of bed on your ass by one nuke . . . and oh, a couple of minor things like Soviet submarines being blown out of the water by US missiles, and radio stations that don't exist any more . . . ! When are you going to believe what's happened? When *we* get hit? Is that it? Will that be proof enough?'

'You've been talking with that Russian, Ulyanov – that's what's started this . . . right?'

'Sure it has! Why not? He's lost his child . . . what have you lost? This project? So Whitefire goes down the tube and you and Ledden can't play God any more . . . is that the sum total of your life? I must have been crazy to get involved with you and this whole lunatic organization.'

Jordan's face darkened. 'You, I, all of us have lost people – loss isn't just on one side, dammit! Why should Ulyanov corner the market on loss – what makes him so special?' Jordan recognized the dangerous edge of jealousy in his voice, but found it impossible to control.

'Well, maybe he *cares* more! Maybe he actually *feels* his loss and doesn't just shove it under the rug and pretend nothing has happened. Christ, you've got about as much *feeling* – as much *compassion* inside you as . . . this wretched island! You don't *react* – you *compute* and spew out careful measured statements in case anyone gets scared shitless and tears their hair out. Well, maybe what we've lost was so important that the only way to react *is* by tearing your hair out! Does that make any sense to you *at all?*'

'It makes sense, but it doesn't ease the situation. We need to keep calm and consider our position – not start losing our heads. That's the surest way to anarchy down here. You're a woman, I don't need to remind you what can happen if things get panicked.'

'*Oh no!* Don't think you're going to tie me up like that. You're not the only man who'd be prepared to watch over my welfare . . . and maybe for other reasons than getting me into bed.' She pulled her robe from the wall closet and threw it on angrily. 'It's a fallacy that a woman needs a cool, calculated man in a crisis. She needs someone who'll show her he cares and understands . . . not correct her if she starts to crumble a little.'

Jordan sighed. 'I understand, Jemma. I just don't think it does any good if *any* of us start to crumble.'

'That's why you're so damn good at your job. Scientific problems have logical and predictable solutions – they don't weep on your shoulder or slap you in the face for no apparent reason. You got me into your bed down here right at the beginning for one reason only – I was available. If I hadn't been here you'd have done without . . . and it wouldn't have made any difference.'

She gathered a few things off the washbasin and moved to the door.

Jordan said: 'This is not the time to be apart – you know that, don't you?'

She opened the door. 'Maybe – but it's not the time to be together either. Not like this. Sleep well . . . not that I really believe you won't.'

Jordan let her go, wanting to stop her – hold her – but

at the same time knowing that he could not do that. It wasn't his way.

He switched off the light, closed his eyes, and wondered if perhaps she might be right, and he completely wrong. If that were true he simply did not know how he could face the circumstances which had, so incredibly swiftly, destroyed the entire pattern and purpose of his life.

Before he finally fell asleep, in the twilight of semi-consciousness, he imagined himself a child again in his parents' lavish – but unhappy – Virginia home. He half heard again the rows which were conducted in soft, civilized, but desperately cruel tones – but which still, for all that, reached his ears like the scuttling of sharp-clawed rats in the floor beneath his bed. And he remembered that his only defence was the silent, and hopeless, threat to bring the house crashing down.

And so much, he thought, in the last moments of wakefulness, for *controlled* man.

6

As the party of Russians entered the lighthouse Simon Howard had made straight back for the huts. First he stole Ulyanov's automatic pistol, knowing that it would be a superior close-quarters weapon to the assault rifles, then he raided the weathermen's storeroom. He took down a row of emergency lamps and a spare box of nife-cell batteries. There was one thing he was quite certain of: if he had to re-enter the chamber at the end of the tunnel he would do it with as much light as he could muster.

The lamps were large – more than a foot high – and illuminated by twin fluorescent tubes. He strung a length of thin nylon rope through their handles, then, hanging them around his neck, ran across the darkened plateau, the beam of the lighthouse whipping over his head like double blades.

At the steel door he switched on every lamp and started down the tunnel, able to stand almost upright because of his diminutive size, the lamps dangling from him like some grotesque luminous necklace. At one point he stumbled and his hand grazed the wall. The surface of the concrete was soft, like a gritty paste.

At the end of the sloping shaft he pulled open the circular gas lock and stepped down into a corridor. The swaying blue-white lights lit up the walls around him and he breathed more easily – though he knew exactly what he was going to find further on. He pushed an old, rusted Schmeisser machine pistol aside with his foot and the metallic scrape echoed ahead of him along the curving corridor. He stopped dead, willing himself to move on but for a moment quite unable to continue.

'Silly sod!' he cursed himself aloud, and forced his unwilling body around the curve.

In the stark glow of the lamps he could see the wall facing him across the chamber stacked high with dried-out corpses, half-skin half-skeleton, arranged head to toe. On the floor around this grim pile lay the spent distorted bullets which had killed them. They had fallen out, Howard decided, as the bodies rotted. He wondered – a little crazy at that moment – if all the bodies had reached the same stage of decomposition together so that the bullets fell at once, like some leaden hailstorm, to the cold concrete. The corpses wore rags, like long coats which somehow made them even more fearsome, and their shoes had fallen from their feet as the flesh had gone and were deposited in two untidy piles at each end of the stack.

Howard felt as if he were invading the sacred tomb of some lost, ancient civilization, and the large photograph of Adolf Hitler hanging on the wall did nothing to dispel that feeling. There was a star-shaped crack in the glass covering the photograph and below, on the ground, the heavy bone which had caused it. Howard could not see who had thrown it in the large chamber but he knew he would find him somewhere – anyone who had waited long enough for the bodies to rot so that he could throw the bone was either insane, or trapped – or, more likely, both.

Shuffling forward in his necklace of lights he found small alcoves like doorless cells, each with iron double bunks which made the narrow corridor seem like part of some derelict prison – which, for all Howard knew, it might have been.

In these cells he found more corpses; some still covered by blankets holed by both age and other, quicker, forms of death, and some kneeling up in supplication, their knee bones poking right through the rotted hair mattresses and the collapsed springs beneath. One was on a single bedstead and could have been the model for some ghastly martyr, so pious was the death pose. Howard could not resist touching the slumped, finely balanced skull, which immediately snapped from the neck and fell at his feet. He yelped and kicked it away, just moving fast enough to avoid the rest of the carcass collapsing over him. It clattered at his feet and he jumped back with a shudder of disgust.

Somewhere, he knew he would find what remained of the killer – or killers – and he was beginning to be very afraid that what he might find would not be a pleasant sight. He remembered the collapsed rocks over the entrance – and the wedges around the door. No one dies easily, buried alive, he thought.

At the end of the corridor he found a narrow staircase which led upward to another level. Or it should have done. The dried, rough mass of concrete which sealed the way up ran like a petrified stream down the stairs to his feet. He bent over and touched it. Compared to the condition of the rest of the place this concrete was new and dry, with none of the soft grittiness he had so far encountered.

'Uh-ha,' Howard uttered aloud and moved on.

There were three more rooms leading off the main chamber: one, an office which Howard avoided because of its proximity to the pile of corpses, another a kitchen which appeared to have a new wall built across its breadth, and finally a dining-room. At this last, Howard stopped. The severed, gnawed, oversized bones told their own story. He felt his stomach churn but controlled the reaction.

There were more bodies on the floor, flung backwards off their chairs and sprawled in grotesque poses. They were caught napping, Howard thought, examining their uniforms. Didn't know it was coming. One minute they were tucking into their horrible nosh, the next they get blown away. And they got it from the table. Not from the door, not the ceiling, from the table – while they all sat together.

There was one man at the table, the top of his head blown away. The Schmeisser in his mouth was wedged under the edge of the table to hold down the kick. His own legs were strapped to the sturdy legs of the table holding him firmly in place. He strapped himself down, Howard surmised, so that the blast didn't deflect the bullets, leaving him a vegetable – or blinded – or whatever else he imagined could be worse than being what he had become. Suicide ain't easy, mate, Howard said silently. You just proved it. Carefully he lifted the sheaf of yellowed paper from in front of the black-uniformed body and looked at the irregular writing. But he could not read German. He folded the papers carefully and stored them in the back pocket of his trousers – he would find out what they said later.

He had already decided that there was no way into the INTERSAT base from where he was, when he heard the voice, and literally jumped with fright. Between that instant and his recognition of the speaker he was rooted to the spot, white with fear. He heard – as though at the end of a tunnel, but clear nevertheless – Sir Henry Ledden say: 'You realize that we will have to close down this level entirely . . . .'

Howard looked up and saw the thick square iron tube. He leaped onto the table, uncaring now about the terrible human bones at his feet, and stood on tiptoe to press his ear to the ice-cold metal. Jordan's voice answered, hollow but recognizable. Howard jumped down and followed the tube as it disappeared into the wall, then emerged on the other side. There it branched out into the large chamber and left towards the cut-in-half kitchen. He headed for the kitchen and, as he had guessed, the tube ran straight into the new wall. He grinned with self-satisfaction, jumped onto the old cooking range and listened again.

Then he took out his knife and began working on the screws at a joint in the tubing. The joint parted easily and the voices came through clearly, as if a door had been opened.

'Right, gotcha!' Howard exclaimed aloud. He unslung his lamps, peeled off his anorak – after tucking the automatic into his belt at his back – then grabbed one of the rubber torches and heaved himself up.

He knew he had passed into the new part of the installation when the temperature began to rise and the hollow booming in the ventilation shaft deadened. The shaft was just large enough for him to crawl on his hands and knees and he had stuck the torch into his midriff so that the beam illuminated the way ahead from under his hard stomach.

Howard knew all about narrow tunnels.

Once, in Vietnam, he had followed three Viet Cong down one of their earthen escape tunnels after being pinned down by their ambush. He admitted later that it was a crazy thing to have done, but he had been so furious that he had been determined to make them pay for their audacity – and the loss of two of his LURP unit.

The Cong had not expected such a thing and were crawling ahead of him at an easy pace. He shot all three dead – from the rear – each being hit in turn by the burst of fire as the man behind him fell. They stood no chance whatsoever in the confined space.

After that incident, Howard had developed the tactic with the aid of the other members of his patrol. They would wait for 'Charlie' to hop into his system of jungle burrows, then Howard would go in like a terrier to flush them out onto the waiting guns of his partners on the surface. It worked – as he often recounted – like a dream. The Cong could be caught in the same way every time for, as far as they were concerned, Americans were far to big to go in after them. Unfortunately for 'Charlie', Simon Howard could stand eyeball-to-eyeball with the smallest Vietnamese.

His hand caught on a strip of raised metal; he stopped promptly and picked out the square inspection panel with the torch. Using the heavy blade of his knife he prised it open. Below was a square of yellow plastic – soft and yielding to the prodding of his calloused fingertips. Thick insulation tiles, he guessed – the walls and ceiling of the base were covered with insulation materials to keep the temperature constant in all weathers.

He was no longer listening to the voices, for inside him was the growing realization that whoever had built the INTERSAT base must have known about the other chamber – and what was in it. The concrete seal which overflowed down the steps, the new wall across the kitchen – someone must know about those. And the ventilation shaft. A shaft has to lead somewhere. It doesn't just drive straight into solid rock! There was no air being pumped through the shaft, so he supposed it had just been encased in the suspended ceiling rather than go to the trouble of removing it. So why hadn't that someone cleared out the chamber of horrors? Why hadn't they cleared the place up and used the extra space? Why – if they didn't need more space – hadn't they just dropped the corpses into the ocean? Howard had strict views on the burial of soldiers – *real* soldiers, for he did not count terrorists as soldiers at all – and those views did not encompass the practice of burial alive, nor the neglect of a body discovered by accident.

Not that for one moment did he consider that what he had discovered was in any way an *accident*!

He laid the blame at the door of INTERSAT. They were a German-based corporation and the chamber was a Nazi base – that was plain. So, bad publicity, hold-up of work, slimy pressmen crawling all over the rock . . . all that would be bad for business and would mean the death of any secret project under the nose of the bloody Russians. So INTERSAT must have bribed the construction engineers very well to keep them quiet.

Not nice, he thought, more than a little angry. Someone needed to be taught a lesson in manners.

Below him the voices of Ledden and Jordan droned on; he pressed his ear onto the insulation and listened intently without moving, for he was a born watcher and listener. He heard them go, at last, then punched hard at the tile which flopped down onto the control consoles below. He had never before seen this part of the installation – it was a restricted area for anyone except the crew of scientists who manned it. He swung down onto the carpeted space between the consoles and stalked over to the polished steel door of the elevator, snorting derisively at what he had heard of the conversation between the two scientists.

War! What fucking war? One bomb don't make no war, mate! Lesson one – learned the hard way – don't trust no sodding Russians. They talk peace like it was their religion, then hand out brand-new Kalashnikovs to the Dinks like fruit gums. OK, say there is a war! Who're we fighting, then? The fucking Russians, that's who . . . and who's crawling all over this place? *Well?* Well *he* was not going to jack it in that easily – *no way.*

The lift door was sealed tight and pressing the funny button did no good whatsoever, so he gave it a furious kick and sat down heavily at one of the desks. He did not like being thwarted; he did not like people making decisions that affected his life without asking his permission; and he did not like being trapped.

Again – and quite unreasonably because he knew that someone had to come down to the second level sometime – the frightful fate of the dead soldier slid into his mind. He forced the dreadful image away. They probably think I fell off the bleedin' cliff, he mused. OK, let 'em think it, effing fairies, ready to chuck it in after just one whiff of smoke. Jesus, eight of them, a geriatric and a bird and they're opening the doors like a Saigon cat house! Well *sorry,* but he wasn't ready to do a Lazarus yet . . . not until he knew exactly what had happened outside. This was how he liked it – working on his own – almost invisible to the enemy. Except of course this wasn't the jungle and he'd be hard put to keep under cover. What he really needed was to be able to see and hear what was going on and still be invisible. And he'd need some help sometime – a bolthole if he screwed up. He kicked at the tile and his evil grin spread over his dark elfin face, ear to ear. He climbed onto the console, the tile clamped between his ankles, and reached upwards.

Jemma Elliot was dreaming and her dream was, at once, both erotic and terrifying. She dreamed principally of Sergei Ulyanov who stood before her quite naked, his solid thick-trunked body forcing her against a bed which was, strangely, upright. She felt that if he let go of her she would plummet into the nothingness below.

Her state of arousal was so extreme that she might have reached orgasm except that there were other men, waiting, all around her, but though she searched for Jordan's face it was not among them. Her eyes alighted on a dark flitting figure which seemed to appear wherever she looked, and yet when she focused intently on it was not there at all. She began to scream because Ulyanov – who had suddenly become Jordan – had withdrawn from her and was letting her slide downwards. He clamped a hand over her mouth and that was all that could save her from the pit that would seal her up forever. She awoke, her eyes wide with fright.

Simon Howard pressed harder with his hand, then said: 'Scream and I'll break your nose.' She stared at the poised cutting edge of the hand above her face. He said: 'I'm taking my hand away, right? Not a sound.' She nodded, then as his hand was removed raked at his face with her nails. She gasped in pain as his fingers circled her wrist, unable to believe that anyone could react that fast. He slapped her hard, once, and she lay still.

'Stupid!' Howard hissed, and shook her face. 'Come on, you crazy bitch!'

Jemma blinked, stunned by the blow, and warily pulled the sheet over her exposed breasts.

'For chrissake!' he fumed. 'I'm not interested, get it!'

'Then what do you want?' she whispered furiously. 'You sneak in here when I'm half naked! What do you expect?'

'What's going on down here?' he asked, releasing her and dusting off his clothes.

'What happened to you?' she demanded. 'Where have you been?'

'You wouldn't believe me,' he smirked. 'Come on, what's going on?'

She told him everything, still afraid of his deadly hands.

'So there's more bloody Ivans coming down here? You people are nutters!'

'They're in trouble.'

'No, *you're* in trouble – the whole bunch of you.'

She watched him, trying to calm herself down. 'You just won't accept it, will you – you're as bad as Matt. *I* didn't at first but Sergei . . . .'

'Who's he?'

'The submarine commander . . . .'

'The big geezer with the beard – the Russian? *Sergei* already, is it? Bloody women! You all think with your crotch instead of your brains.'

Jemma flared: 'You little bastard! He's lost his child because of what's happened . . . .'

'And I lost my granny in Basingstoke. Come off it, lady, you've been had. I've been out there – there's only one bomb gone off. You think the Reds can't afford one bomb?'

'You're mad! It wasn't a bomb. It was one of their submarines – Stracey said their biggest. You think they'd blow it up *themselves?*'

'Saw the bits, did you? Old Sergei came back with the nameplate? Here you are darlin', a piece of the old ship to prove I'm a hero? Commie bastard.'

'You *are* mad.'

Howard grinned. 'You're going to help me.'

'Like hell I am!'

'This is what you do. First you get me something to eat. Then you get out there and keep your ears switched on for anything – and I mean anything – that don't sound kosher. Understand?'

'Yes – but . . . .'

'Don't yap, do it. I'm going to kip right here in your bunk, got it? I'm not interested in your bloody body so you can forget squealing about *that!* And if you bring anyone back here while I'm kipping I shall very definitely break your neck.'

He began removing his clothes.

'What do you think you're doing?' she blurted.

'What's it look like? Go get the food if you're that embarrassed.'

Against her will, she watched the lean body below her, the taut muscles standing out in ridges all over Howard's torso. He seemed to be scarred everywhere.

'How did you get all those scars?' she asked, unable to stem her curiosity.

'Wars, lady, *real* wars. Not something the sodding Ivans dreamed up for your benefit. So what's on this lump of rock that they want so bad? Something to do with those poor sods cemented in next door?'

'I don't know what you're talking about.'

'Oh sure! You read German?'

'No – what's that got to do with anything?'

'INTERSAT's a Kraut company, isn't it? How come you don't know German?'

'It's not just German, it's multi-national. What do you mean, cemented in? You mean *buried?* In the old section?'

Howard smirked, enjoying his secret knowledge. 'You don't know what kind of people you work for, lady.'

'You definitely are crazy. What happened to you up there?'

Howard ignored her question. 'So what's hidden on this rock that's so important?'

'I can't answer that – you're not cleared. You wouldn't understand it anyway.'

'So I'm no bloody genius – but there is something, right? Something the Russians would want. *Right!*'

'I'm not saying a word.'

'You don't have to, lady. Come on, get your gear on and find me some food, I'm famished.'

Jemma clasped the sheet tighter. 'I'm naked – go in the shower while I get dressed.'

'Leave off!' Howard snorted and unzipped his trousers, then sat on the lower bed examining his feet.

She got down carefully, clutching the sheet to her front. 'Great ass!' Howard remarked appreciatively as she began dressing, unable to avoid displaying her naked rear as she pulled on her pants.

'I thought you said you weren't interested!' she snapped.

'Give me time – you might just pull me around.' He leered mockingly as she fought to pull her sweater down over her breasts.

Jemma turned away angrily.

Howard sighed and stretched under the sheets. 'You going or not?'

She nodded, reluctantly.

'You better come back alone,' he warned her.

She nodded again, surprised at her own readiness to obey him.

'Say it.'

She said: 'Alone.'

'That's better.'

She opened the door and made for the kitchen.

She woke him carefully, standing well away, her arm outstretched to his shoulder.

'They're here,' she said as his eyes snapped open. 'The Russians – on the surface.'

'Shit!' he cursed and swung his legs to the floor. All he wore was a pair of tiny black briefs. 'What time is it, then?'

'Just after eight.'

'*Eight?*'

'Eight in the morning – you slept right through.' She pointed at the untouched food. 'I didn't want to wake you – you were out cold. I'll get something fresh.'

'You've changed your tune?' Howard queried, studying her tense face curiously.

'I'm frightened. From what I've heard there are about twenty men up there waiting to be let in – and Ledden says they can. How do you think that makes me feel? That young Russian girl and I are the only females down here. If they're going to keep this place sealed up . . . .'

'I'd keep my legs tightly crossed if I were you,' Howard jibed.

'Being crude doesn't help. You're going to have to protect me.' She made the statement as if it were a foregone conclusion. Something she had worked out in the hours he had been sleeping.

'Go see your boyfriend, I'm not running a minding service for a couple of birds.'

'I can't. Not any more.'

'Fancy that? Nothing to do with you chatting up old Sergei, of course?'

'I can talk to whom I damn well like!'

'Sure,' Howard grinned. 'You know what happens to people who switch horses too often, lady? They fall off.'

'You're a bastard!' she snapped.

'Right! That's why you've latched onto me. So when are they coming in?'

'Sir Henry is discussing it with Tavrin,' she answered, controlling her quick temper.

'That chess player you told me about last night? What's he got to do with anything?'

'He's a defector, damn it! He's here with a crew of mutineers – what's left of them. I told you all this before.'

'Load of bollocks.'

Jemma raised her eyes in exasperation. 'Look, maybe Tavrin and the others don't think it's a good idea to have a bunch of loyal Russians down here.'

'Once a Commie, always a Commie.'

'God, you're bigoted.'

'Yeah.'

'Those sailors up there got hit by an American missile. One of *our* missiles. Maybe they won't feel very kindly towards Russians who've gone over to the enemy. Tavrin's trying to make sure there's no problem with them.'

'One of *your* missiles,' Howard pointed out. 'You're the Yank.'

'It doesn't matter *whose* missile it was . . . the point, if you can't see it, is that it proves there really is a war going on.'

'No it doesn't. It proves that *one* missile got fired and *maybe* hit something . . . that's not a war; that's a problem for the politicians and a slap on the wrist for the poor sod who pressed the button. Anyway, you've only got these Commies' word on it. When I see it on *News at Ten* I'll believe it.'

'I don't care what you believe. *I'm* still stuck here with too many goddam men.'

Howard reached out and squeezed her thigh. ''Course I'll take care of you. Cost you though.'

She looked down on him scathingly. 'I thought you said you weren't interested?'

He increased the pressure. 'Changed my mind, didn't I?'

'Christ! You're damn sure of yourself, you little creep.'

He squeezed very hard, his fingers digging harshly into a nerve. She gasped in pain. 'You have a very ugly mouth,' he told her, holding the grip still. 'You need to learn to keep it shut. Got it?'

She nodded, her eyes tightly closed. He released her. 'Right, now get out there and watch what's happening.'

'Why don't you go and show them you're alive!' she exploded. 'They've got volunteers offering to go and look for you. They could suffer from radiation poisoning up there. Haven't you got any conscience at all?'

'More fools them. You just do like I told you. And be sure to tell me if any of them come down here tooled up.'

'Tooled up?'

'Armed.'

'Don't be ridiculous – they wouldn't let anyone down here with a gun.'

Howard grinned and produced the Soviet-made automatic from under the pillow.

'Where did you get that!'

'Old Sergei left it up top – I nicked it.'

'If Sir Henry catches you with that he'll pitch it – and you – into the ocean. Believe me he will.'

'Well he won't – unless you decide to start squealing?' He laid the gun on her shoulder.

'Don't do that, it's not funny,' she said, very still.

Howard moved the gun and snapped the safety catch back on. 'I bet you,' he said quietly, 'that right now Sir Henry is wondering if it might not be a good idea to have a few firearms down here. In the right hands, of course. I mean, when your whole world gets tipped on its ass you tend to change your attitudes.'

Jemma gave him a look of scorn. 'I'll go check what's happening. Don't worry, I'll be back . . . I can't wait!'

Howard dipped the barrel of the gun at the tray of stale food. 'Don't forget breakfast.'

'What do you think I am – your personal goddam servant?'

'Lady, you want protection, you have to look after your protector. Otherwise, when they start ripping your gear off I might just be too weak to help.'

'You bastard.'

'You're getting boring,' he said and lowered himself to the floor, performing press-ups on the knuckles of his hands. He looked up. 'Nice legs,' he said and she closed the door viciously. He reached out, balanced on one fist, and caught it, then let it close gently. 'Crazy bitch,' he muttered, then continued punishing his hard body.

The survivors of the Soviet submarine the *Admiral Grechko* were hard, grim-faced men, all of whom suffered in varying degrees from both frostbite and severe – though superficial – radiation burns to the exposed areas of their bodies. Only a few of the men carried weapons and these – after some negotiation by Tavrin – were left on the surface. When they finally emerged from the lift, numbering twenty in total, they had the look of battle-hardened veterans returning from some massive defeat. But even allowing for their shaken, battered condition they seemed, to Ulyanov, to be far fitter than any crew he had ever commanded. Perhaps, he thought, the *Admiral Grechko* had been a much tougher boat to serve on than he might have imagined.

In groups of four they were taken to the small sick bay and tended to by the base's young medic with the volunteered assistance of Tanya Chebrikova. They were dealt with quickly and reappeared with their faces and hands smeared in salve for their burns, which looked for all the world as if they had been caused by severe exposure to the sun. Luckily, no major injuries were diagnosed and apart from three cases of frost-bitten feet they were all able to walk unaided.

Unhappily, the first encounter between the mutineers and the crew of the *Grechko* was a violent one, but Tavrin's presence restored order and both groups of Russians were reconciled to acceptance of their enforced – but mutually beneficial – predicament.

The *Grechko*'s crew told their tale in subdued voices, some of them not wishing to talk at all of the terrible things taking place in the outside world. Yes, they were certainly hit by a missile – very nearly a direct hit – and, yes, equally certainly that missile was American. They seemed oddly uninterested in the underground base, accepting Jordan's translated explanation of it without demur, though his obvious American accent caused a few hostile glances from the group.

To a man, they knew the story of the disappearance of the *Stoiki* and had themselves been placed on alert for some hours in case they should be required to crew the *Grechko* in a hunter's role. They were totally surprised by the inclusion of Mikhail Tavrin in the party of mutineers for, as they admitted, no announcement had been made by Moscow regarding the Grandmaster's defection. It was obvious to the listeners that Tavrin was held in such esteem that his entire involvement in the incident was completely – or perhaps hopefully – discounted by the survivors.

Later, when Ulyanov spoke with the senior man – a tough Slav-featured petty officer – he voiced the view that he and his men were more than a little lucky to be alive. The man told him roughly that luck had nothing to do with it: after the destruction of the submarine, when they were forced into open boats on that merciless sea, it had been a question of the survival of the fittest, and he reckoned that he had with him some of the hardiest sailors in the entire Soviet Navy – if not in any navy in the entire world. *What remains of it*, he had added with a voluble string of obscenities in the coarsest Russian for emphasis.

With this definite confirmation of the state of things beyond the immediate horizons of the bleak island, and the sudden overcrowding of the underground quarters, the morale of the base slumped visibly, creating an air of siege and, below that, a grumbling discontent which seemed to develop alarmingly as the long day dragged on.

All of this Jemma Elliot reported obediently to Howard – welcoming the chance to get away from the surreptitious, and she believed lustful, looks she received whenever she entered the jammed recreation area. She had made the serious mistake of taking her daily sauna regardless and had found to her horror, as she lay naked on the wooden slats, a face pressed to the small misted window. She had closed her splayed legs and thrown a towel at the door and the face had slipped away, but she could not forget the look in the eyes as they had fixed on her total exposure. Though she dearly loved her time in the tiny sauna cubicle she knew that she would never go in there again – not the way things were now. She told this to Howard too and, predictably, he laughed cruelly and accused her of doing it purposely, and because of that she decided it was time to make her peace with Jordan.

She found him in his cabin, writing up the day-to-day log for the base; something she had wholly expected of him even under the present – in her view, hopeless – circumstances.

'Is that necessary any more?' she jibed.

He laid down his pen. 'Maybe not. But it beats sitting at the bar with the rest getting smashed.'

'Any news of Howard?' she asked casually.

'None. Sir Henry refuses to let anyone go up to the surface any more. It's far too risky now that we know what's happened.'

'Don't tell me you *actually* believe it now!'

'I believe that it's happened – but I still doubt the *extent* of the conflict. I'm certain that they'd see sense after the first-strike hit. We should hear something on the radio in the next few days. It takes time for the radioactivity to clear.'

'Can't we get something on the satellite link? What about pictures? Cloud formations . . . all that?'

Jordan shook his head. 'We're blind, deaf and dumb. Although the radiation level here is not too dangerous, further away it's obviously bad enough to scramble the air waves. I'm sorry.'

'Why be sorry? It's not your fault.'

He shrugged. 'Is that what you came in for?'

'News of fresh disasters? No. I just wanted to say we can't go on this way. I know we fight. We always have done. I know I'm difficult! But this should have brought us together, not . . . .'

He looked at her steadily. 'Do you consider that it's over between us? Completely over? You know that I love you.'

She sat down. 'Do you? Oh God! I don't know, I'm confused right now.'

'Come on Jemma, you're a grown woman – but you're acting like a teenager with complexes coming out of her ears. What's the real problem? This situation? Don't tell me you can't handle it, because I find that incredibly hard to believe. You're a scientist – you know what could happen much more than the average person. Surely you've accepted that?'

'How can you – *anyone* – accept total destruction?'

'You live with it – just like you live with death.'

'That's too glib for me, I'm afraid. Anyway, I don't want to talk about it. I've had it with the whole subject. I just want to survive.'

'By saying that, you've taken the first step. Good.'

'Don't patronize me.'

Jordan returned to his writing. 'I'm not,' he said, then turned back to her. 'How did we get together anyway? I've never quite understood it.'

'It happened – just happened. Seemed the natural thing to do. *Then.*'

'And now?' he asked.

'Now? Now I don't know – so go ahead and call me a teenager again. This place isn't the same any more. Everything's changed. Our situation has changed.'

'Why? Because there are other men down here?'

'Don't put it that way . . . you make me sound . . . .'

'Is there another way of putting it that's as honest?'

'Matt, look, before . . . we would have finished this project and split. Gone our own separate ways. There was no long-term commitment. No licence, no kid, no dog, no indoor plants to water – no nothing. Just this cabin and us. That was it! OK, now there's a big bang and nothing's the same any more. So I don't know what I feel.'

'I'm prepared to wait for you to make up your mind.'

'Why are you so goddam *reasonable?* Why don't you just say – get the hell out! I would. I know I would.'

'I'm not you. You're too volatile – you'd decide too quickly and probably wrongly if I did that.'

'Well, I'm not now, am I? I've told you I need *time*.'

Jordan sighed. 'You need time to play the field. You're beginning to convince yourself that all the choice you'll ever have is down here. You're pushing yourself into a decision. You don't need to do that – not yet anyway.'

'Then when? So I shack up with you again, then in a year – maybe six months, maybe tomorrow – I say: sorry, Matt, but I think I'll try Joe down the hall. Is that how you see it?'

'Maybe that's the only sensible way . . . now.'

'And you'd accept that? You say you love me yet you'd let me walk away and get screwed by someone else a few doors down? Is that love?'

'At least it's not losing completely.'

'Not completely – just partially. That's a cop-out. You're pathetic, you don't even want to fight for me!'

Jordan laughed. 'Who am I supposed to fight? The entire male population on Beacon Island? Maybe the whole damn Arctic Circle if things get really bad?'

She wrenched the door open. 'Don't say I didn't give you the chance.'

Then she was gone, and Jordon returned to his work with a small shake of his head.

7

Mikhail Tavrin sat down beside Josef Chebrikov on the bed. 'How are you feeling, old man?' he asked, his pale grey eyes resting lightly on the drawn, clawed face.

'Is it true?' Chebrikov demanded. 'This story I keep hearing? Does nobody consider I am worthy of the truth?'

Tavrin dipped his large head. 'It is true.'

Chebrikov lifted one hand from the blankets, then let it drop in a gesture of futility. 'Madness! What kind of world have I survived into? All my life I have survived something, hoping each time that things would change -- maybe the world had learned its lesson. But no, alas no! Each time it is worse. First Hitler, then Stalin . . . and now this . . .' he lifted his hand again, feebly ' . . . this new prison.'

'No prison,' Tavrin answered. 'You will be treated well here. You are safe.'

'For what? To die underground like a rat because I daren't walk in the air above? Ach! I should have let myself be taken to the gas chambers long ago. In the end I shall finish up the same way. What is this place?'

'A weather satellite research station. It is owned by a German business corporation.'

Chebrikov peered at the Grandmaster over his spectacles.

Tavrin gave a dry chuckle. 'You accept nothing at its face value. Why must you always disbelieve? Not everything German – or Russian – is sinister.'

'Because every time I have believed I have been lied to. Always I have to do something because there is no other choice. Mikhail, you are here because you *want* to be here – not because fate brought you here. *Everything* you have done in your life you have planned – you could not exist otherwise. So what is this place – and why am I here?'

Tavrin rose. 'Don't be so suspicious, old friend. Even *I* cannot make a war!'

Chebrikov gazed at him steadily. 'Where are we?'

'I have told you.'

'*Where?* Where exactly?'

Tavrin raised his shoulders. 'Ask Ulyanov. Somewhere in the Arctic Circle.'

'Russian waters?'

'Our fleet controls them, yes.'

'North of Novaya Zemlya?'

Tavrin frowned. 'Yes.'

'This island, what else is on it?'

'A lighthouse, some huts you saw. Why do you ask this?'

Chebrikov would not answer, but just stared at his hands for long moments. Finally he said: 'When do I meet the people who run this "weather station"?'

'When you are well.'

'I am well enough to talk with you. I wish to meet them now.'

'Later,' Tavrin said. 'We will all eat together tonight – the directors of this place and us. There are plans to be made. There is little space on this level to accommodate everyone – we must try to persuade them to open the second level.'

Chebrikov looked up sharply. 'There is a second level? What is in it?'

'They say computers, machinery . . . these types of things . . . the machinery which keeps this place alive.'

'Why do you say "persuade them"?'

'They've sealed it up. I think they do not trust us yet. Perhaps they fear we will try to take over?'

'Would you trust so quickly, Mikhail Yaraslavovich?'

Tavrin smiled. 'Perhaps not. But we must learn to trust each other now . . . or we shall not survive the holocaust.'

Chebrikov grunted. 'Tell these people I shall meet with them tonight too. I should thank them for saving my miserable life.' He watched Tavrin leave, then lay back onto the pillow, staring at the ceiling. He sniffed at the air, lightly at first, then more deeply. The cleft of a frown formed between his white brows. Quietly, in German, he said: '*Der flüsternde Tod.*' The whispering death.

His grand-daughter was tending to one of the frostbitten men. Chebrikov watched her for a moment, then sat up. 'Tanya!' he called. 'Tanya!'

She moved to him. 'You sound better,' she said, happily.

Chebrikov clicked his tongue impatiently. 'The commander – Ulyanov? Find him for me. Tell him to bring maps showing exactly where we are.'

'Why?' she asked.

Chebrikov glanced carefully at the Russian sailor and continued in German. 'Child, just do as I say. Get the commander. I need maps!'

She shrugged and walked out into the corridor. There Tavrin stood hesitantly. 'Is he all right?' he asked. 'I heard him call out.'

'He wants Commander Ulyanov. Says he needs maps.' She shrugged again.

'Maps? Maps for where?'

'Here,' she answered, shaking her head.

'Is he thinking of leaving us?' Tavrin said, lightly.

'Where is left to go?' Tanya asked sadly. 'I'd better get the commander – you know how impatient grandfather can be.'

'Yes,' Tavrin agreed. 'He has always been too impatient.' He watched her young, stocky figure as she walked away, and for the first time since he had climbed down the steps of the airliner in Geneva a hint of doubt cracked his icy calm.

'Where's the meeting?' asked Howard, finishing the sandwiches Jemma Elliot had smuggled in to him.

'Why don't you give up this ridiculous game and stop people worrying about you?' she said.

'Where's the meeting?' he repeated, his mouth full.

'What difference does it make – they haven't asked me. I won't be able to tell you anything.'

'Where're they having it?' Howard insisted, munching.

'In Matt's office – what are you going to do, pretend you're a fly on the wall?'

'Sure. Who'll be there?'

'Sir Henry, Matt, Weissleder – and the Russians, of course.'

'All of them?'

'Don't be stupid. Tavrin and the old man – Chebrikov.'

'Not old Sergei?'

'I suppose so. Oh, and Stracey too.'

'The Yank who came in the chopper with me? What's he do?'

'He's Government. US. God knows why he should make any decisions though – it's people like him who started this whole thing.'

'Yeah, and the Reds finished it. You Yanks tear yourselves apart every time something goes wrong.'

Jemma brushed a hand through her hair wearily. 'I'd hardly describe this situation as just "something going wrong".'

But Howard was not interested. 'You did it after 'Nam, after Nixon got shit on . . . .'

'Oh shut up. If you want to gatecrash the meeting just go ahead . . . I'm tired. All I want to do is sleep. You'll never get near that room, you know. The whole rec. area is full, I don't think there'll be any booze left by morning the way they're all hitting it out there. Jordan's office is on the other side of all that.'

'I'll get there,' Howard said confidently.

'You're crazy . . . . I want to take a shower,' she added, pointedly.

'Who's stopping you?"

She looked at him, then in resignation stripped herself naked, not caring any more. She slid the glass door open and turned on the jets, closing the entrance to the cubicle behind her, and let her head fall back, luxuriating in the warmth of the spray. She felt the sudden coolness as the door was opened and the hard callouses of his hand as it fell onto her breast. She said 'No!' partially blinded by the streaming water and the steam, but it did no good at all. He turned her face to the cubicle wall and kicked gently but purposefully at her calves till her legs were splayed, bringing her to his level. His hand snaked around her neck and clamped over her mouth as if he were afraid she might scream aloud – though she would not have done that because she knew he could snap her neck in a second. Then, with a strange mixture of fear and arousal, she surrendered to him completely.

Reinhardt Weissleder was consumed by fury. All he had planned was being reduced to nothing, and he was impotent in the face of the threat to his plans. He glared at himself in the mirror, viewing with self-disgust the heavy frame which had once been slim, even elegant. Too much good living, he admonished himself, grasping in his thick fingers the jowls which covered the former handsome jaw-line of the younger, disciplined man he used to see. But his body, though heavier, was still powerful and he certainly would not have been afraid to take on younger men if he found himself in such a situation. His years of daily, punishing exercises had delayed the ugly processes of middle age. And you are lucky, he reminded himself; you have survived. You are rich. He glowered at his reflection on that thought. Rich! Yes, certainly he was rich – but he could have been more than rich; he could have been one of the wealthiest men in the world. He was standing above a fortune – or at least the means of making one – and an English fool was being deceived into giving it away. The Whitefire secret, the revolutionary technology and sheer power of the device, were pure gold – enough to burst the vaults of a hundred Swiss banks. He felt physically sick at the thought of such a loss.

Weissleder had dreamed of unlimited wealth for as long as he could remember – even as a child in the mean Hamburg dockland dwelling which was all his Communist father could afford after sacrificing his shipping clerk's pittance of a salary for the 'good of the Party'. 'Materialism is a sin perpetrated by the people against themselves; they must learn to eradicate this vice from their lives.' The boy would remember this utterance by his hated father all his life, for it usually followed a refusal even to consider the purchase of any plaything, however small. This harsh treatment of the growing boy was well known in the ugly street and he became an object of pity to the neighbours, but also the subject of their children's cruel scorn.

So later, when the Nazi Brownshirts came and dragged his hated father away to a brutal death, administered clinically with the steel toecaps of their boots, the same neighbours whispered that the son had betrayed the father. They were correct. Except that the son did not consider this a betrayal, but justice.

He remembered the entire incident in clear detail – as if it had happened just the day before. He'd watched the Brownshirts parade through the streets on many occasions – hidden in the crowd in case his father spotted him by chance – and the Nazis could not have had a more eager convert. The National Socialist Party hated the Jews; Karl Marx was a Jew. The Nazis hated and killed Communists; Reinhardt Weissleder hated Communism and Communists even more than they did. So it had taken no great soul-searching decision for him to direct a squad of Brownshirts to the door of his father's house.

He had watched the execution – for that was how he viewed it – from a doorway in the alley, waiting until the final boot crunched into the bloodied face, administering the brutal *coup de grâce*. Then, after the thugs had left, he had walked over to the body, checked it for life, then ground his father's already cracked steel-rimmed spectacles to glass powder in the gutter. That done, he walked home and, ignoring his weak mother's wailing, systematically destroyed any vestige of his father's presence and his creed.

In the mirror he smiled at the memory, but the smile was short-lived for once again he was being forced to live cheek-by-jowl with men spawned by a country whose political doctrine he hated. His ham-fist thumped down on the washbasin as his rage exploded, for there was nothing, *nothing*, he could do about it.

He turned from the mirror and dressed himself carefully. Tonight decisions were to be made, and if they went the wrong way he must be prepared to change them – and by force if that was the only way. The thought of the men he would have to meet only made his mood blacker still. Ledden, for all his scientific and business genius, was a weak idealist eager to avoid confrontation. Jordan he considered simply an administrator who would follow as he was directed – and Ledden was the man who would direct him. No, the only man he could hope to influence was the American, Stracey. He had to be told the full extent of the work carried out on Beacon Island – he *must* be made to understand just how much power was about to be handed over to the Russians. Stracey must be made to see that *somehow* – though Weissleder could not imagine how – the Russians had conceived an elaborate plot to get for themselves the Whitefire secret. He would talk with Stracey and ignore the others.

Sounds drifted down the corridor to his cabin. Singing. Drunken singing. Both English and Russian voices together. Sheep! he exclaimed inwardly. Nothing but sheep. So ready to give up. So prepared to accept whatever they were told – no matter how ominous the signs. Just like the

Jews! *Come on in, good people, they're only showers. How exhausted you must be after your journey in the cattle trucks. We are so sorry about the transportation, but proper carriages must be set aside for our brave soldiers. Of course you understand, we knew you would. Come on in, they're only showers.*

He tied the knot in his tie tight. *Nothing* really changes, he thought viciously – but with a secret delight. From his suitcase he extracted a beautifully tooled black leather case and opened it in front of the mirror. Embedded in rich black velvet was a nickel-silver Walther automatic, beautifully engraved. Above it, nestling in its own velvet bed, lay the fat matching silver silencer. Only one thing was missing from the box, and it had left the evidence of its removal on the black velvet of the inner lid: two tiny tears where the screws had been, and an oblong of flattened pile where the silver inscribed plate had pressed down on the cloth. He had no regrets about having removed the plate – he could hardly have retained it in any case – but he often wondered just how much the boxed pistol would be worth now, if the inscription still remained.

For safety, he had melted the fine silver down long ago, but he could still see those amazing words in perfect Gothic script: 'To Karl Muller, who has never failed me. Adolf Hitler.'

He lifted the gun from its velvet bed and screwed on the silencer, his pitiless blue eyes seeming to flash momentarily as the gleaming metal reflected on his face – or perhaps it was the ignition of old memories which caused the sudden fire.

He pocketed the gun and a spare magazine.

Ed Stracey too had been dressing after a welcome shower. A sharp rap on the door disturbed him. He opened it to find Weissleder filling the narrow doorway.

'Herr Stracey,' Weissleder said urgently. 'I wish to speak with you – alone.'

Stracey stood aside. 'What's on your mind?' he asked.

Weissleder stepped inside quickly. 'We must discuss this meeting.'

Once again Stracey felt the abrasive rub of the German's

personality, but forced his unreasonable irritation down. 'OK, so discuss it,' he agreed.

Weissleder sat unasked on the only chair. Stracey remained standing.

'Herr Stracey,' said Weissleder. 'We must not allow the Russians into the project area under any circumstances.'

'You're the INTERSAT director,' Stracey interrupted. 'It's up to you and Ledden.'

Weissleder frowned. 'I cannot believe that a man of your experience can believe this story. These people, they lie – always.'

Stracey curled the corner of his mouth, creating more lines on his weathered face. 'It's my experience which convinces me that they're telling the truth. I've seen this situation played out too many times, mister – if it was ever going to happen, this is the way it would go. They're not lying – the facts speak for themselves. Listen, let me tell you – if the Russians hadn't landed I'd have still made a bet on what's happened out there. But OK, let's play it your way. Let's say this whole thing has been cooked up by the Kremlin. Why? To get onto the island? Crazy! They've got crack troops who could do that – and the way you people have been messing they'd have every right!'

'No,' Weissleder objected firmly. 'If they had received intelligence about the work being carried out here then they must also know that Washington has been approached – has received, if you will, a sample of what we have to offer. No, they would not take the risk. They would make such a conspiracy so that they would be given the Whitefire technology freely.'

'They're not being given it. Ledden will give them some story about the equipment down there on Level Two.'

'Perhaps,' Weissleder said. 'But I think not. He has visions which make him weak, Herr Stracey. His dreams of this so-called "peace through technology", as he is pleased to call it, are very deep inside him. I am very afraid he will tell this man Chebrikov everything. He has much vanity, Herr Stracey, and a vain man does not like seeing his dreams – his achievements – made into nothing. He is a dangerous man, Herr Stracey, and we must stand together to stop him.'

'All right,' said Stracey. 'So we say our piece and he says: "What's the alternative?" And he'd have us by the balls. We need extra space – we can't all exist in this area. There'll be bad trouble if we do. Already things are edgy – so what happens in one week – a month – a year? What's the alternative, mister?'

'There is none. But we need time. If we can delay opening Level Two for a little more time perhaps Washington will begin to worry why there is silence from you. Was it not so that you must report to Washington via our satellite link? You said on the journey that this was the case.'

'That's right,' Stracey agreed. 'But your satellite link, like every other goddam thing, isn't working, right?'

'Exactly, Herr Stracey. So they will now be wondering why you have not called. Perhaps – if they have studied the Whitefire report properly – they will soon begin to worry?'

Stracey sat on the lower bunk. 'Mr Weissleder, I've seen the "sample" and that scared the pants off me. Now if you want to convince me to go along with you, you'd better tell me exactly what you people have got down there. If you can scare me some more then I'll back you all the way. Deal?'

'I will tell you everything.'

'Good, because if this is some kind of conspiracy – and it must be a mighty big one because they'd have had to doctor a NORAD computer program, explode a nuke and jam a heck of a lot of air space to do it – then they're playing nuclear roulette because Washington won't be kidded for too long.'

'Herr Stracey,' Weissleder said, very serious, 'to have what is on this island, the Soviets would risk *everything*!'

8

Matthew Jordan stripped his office wall of every vestige of the Whitefire project. He packed everything into a large steel cabinet, locked the door and pocketed the key. This done, he slumped into the chair behind his desk with a feeling of anger burning inside him – anger which consumed the defeat he had already faced. Futile! he thought. Completely futile. What is there to hide any more? Does it really matter now?

There was a knock on the door but he didn't hear it. Then, coming back to reality, he saw the tall, slightly stooped figure before him.

'Excuse me,' Tavrin said. 'You did not answer? Are you unwell?'

'Fine,' Jordan replied, rising. 'Just fine – thinking – got lost. Can't seem to get to grips with this whole crazy situation. Grab a chair.'

Tavrin sat. 'We are all thinking the same way, Doctor. Do not apologize for being human.'

Jordan lowered himself back to his seat. 'It's hard to come to terms with a catastrophe of these dimensions. I find it impossible to believe that my country – excuse me, our countries – are devastated, as they surely will be if what we have assumed is true.'

'There is still hope,' Tavrin said reassuringly. 'Until we hear some official pronouncement – there is still hope.'

Jordan leaned backwards in the chair. 'I'm not pinning my hopes very high, I'm afraid. Too much has happened.'

'We must hope. That is all we can do.'

'Tell me – and I hope you don't mind me asking this – why did you defect? Surely you had everything going for you in the Soviet Union?'

Tavrin smiled bleakly. 'Everything – and nothing. I had privileges that others did not, but in the greater issues I was as chained as they were. You think freedom is not a tangible thing, Doctor? Believe me, it is. Only when you do not have it do you realize how tangible it is. You Americans take it for granted – and for that reason you do not appreciate it.'

'I guess you're right. Drink?'

'Scotch whisky, if you please.'

'Not vodka?'

Tavrin smiled. 'One of the privileges of being Mikhail Tavrin is being allowed to develop "decadent" tastes which for others would be impossible. No vodka. Whisky please, Scotch whisky.'

Jordan poured a liberal measure into two glasses and pushed one across the desk. He raised his. 'To what might be the last case of Scotch in the world.'

'Let us hope not,' Tavrin said, then drank.

'Was there something you wanted to see me about?' Jordan asked.

Tavrin crossed his long legs. 'Doctor, I – and Ulyanov – have sensed a certain reluctance – even tension – among your people about opening the lower level. Are we imagining this?'

Jordan shifted uneasily. 'A great deal of our work is very advanced. Some of our equipment is so new that patents have yet to be applied for . . . .'

Tavrin raised a hand. 'I can understand this being a problem under normal circumstances – but surely none of this matters now?' He paused. 'Commander Ulyanov has told me that you have lost all contact with your satellites – so surely the lower level can no longer be operative?'

Jordan nodded carefully.

'So in effect the entire area could be converted into living space without any real loss whatsoever?'

'Well . . . yes. But we would hardly want to dismantle that equipment yet. Also it would take a great deal of time.'

'But time is one thing we have no shortage of, Doctor.'

'No, but I'd like to be absolutely certain that things *are* as bad as they seem before I start stripping Level Two.'

'But how do you intend to be "certain"? Surely you are not prepared to delay this decision until you receive news from outside? This might take weeks! I understand you have taken a radiation reading – does this not convince you?'

'The reading is not dangerously high yet. The storm should carry away the major fallout from the destruction of the *Brezhnev*.'

'And the *Admiral Grechko*?'

'Yes,' Jordan said, hesitantly. 'But we have no evidence of a nuclear explosion in her case.'

'No evidence? The survivors are here! On this island. Men burned by radiation. Are you saying that they are lying? They burned themselves? For what reason, Doctor?'

'No, I didn't say that. I mean that we did not physically see any explosion.'

'Were you looking, Doctor?'

'No,' Jordan admitted. 'Oh, of *course* I believe their story. I suppose I'm just splitting hairs because I don't want to believe it. But as far as tests on radiation levels are concerned we shall have to wait until the winter months and we start getting snowfalls before we can assess how far-ranging the extent of the conflict has been.'

'You wish to wait until the *winter* before opening the second level!'

'I didn't say that exactly . . . but in any case it is up to the two directors of INTERSAT to make the final decision. This is their installation, I merely run it.' Jordan thought silently for a moment before continuing. 'But I suppose that we will have to start thinking about some form of collective decision-making soon, otherwise we will have down here what has happened out there!'

'A war?' Tavrin laughed humourlessly. 'And how would we conduct such a war? What would be the point? Surely our collective survival is – or should be – our main concern?'

Sir Henry Ledden walked in. 'Exactly!' he said. 'Mutual interests make bedfellows of the oldest enemies. Matthew, pour me some of your excellent Scotch.' He turned to Tavrin. 'Where is the commander?'

'He will be here,' said the Grandmaster, accepting another measure of Scotch. 'Chebrikov is coming also,' he added.

Ledden raised his eyebrows. 'Is he really well enough yet? Though I must say it would give me great pleasure to include such a mind in our deliberations . . . .'

'He insists,' Tavrin said firmly. He is weak, but also stubborn. His brain might prove invaluable in this situation.'

'Oh, indeed!' Ledden agreed, casting an inquiring look at Jordan who nodded, but his eyes were cautious still.

Ledden said:'Matthew, all things come to an end. Our survival is the most important consideration now . . . as Mr Tavrin has so accurately pointed out. And maybe we will be able to build something worthwhile from the ashes. Ah! gentlemen, come in.' Ledden greeted Ulyanov and Chebrikov, the old man supported by the submariner's arm.

Jordan pushed a chair forward and Chebrikov, nodding gratefully, allowed himself to be lowered on to it. Ulyanov chose to remain standing.

Ledden glanced at his watch, impatient to begin. 'Where the devil are Weissleder and Stracey?' he demanded, then, as if unable to control his impatience any longer, turned to the three Russians. 'I have decided,' he began, 'in the interests of mutual trust in what are sure to be difficult times ahead, that it would be best to tell you of the *real* work that we have been carrying out on Beacon Island. For many years now I have been in possession of certain data from . . . .'

'Say *nothing!*' Weissleder barked from the door, his face dark with anger. '*Nothing!*'

'He's right,' Stracey said, standing with the German. 'Let's hold off a while longer.'

Chebrikov broke the silence. 'I know what is here,' he said very quietly. He studied the Englishman with a strange expression of sadness on his worn face. '*Der flüsternde Tod.* In English: the whispering death. I see you have heard that expression before, Sir Henry. So I am right.'

Ledden's face displayed his total astonishment, while Weissleder's face was a mask of hatred – but beyond the hard glint of his blue eyes there was fear.

Chebrikov raised a hand as if to stave off protestations

and began speaking, but though his words were for all in the room, his eyes constantly alighted on Reinhardt Weissleder's face.

'I am an old man now and becoming senile,' he began, resignedly, like a man taking the first steps on a long and unwelcome journey. 'Though I was not always this way. Once – another lifetime ago – I was dragged from my homeland and forced to work for that monster Adolf Hitler and his Nazis at their experimental rocket installation at Peenemünde – on what Dr Goebbels called the *Vergeltungswaffen* – the weapons of reprisal – or the V1 and V2. I am afraid that many people may have lost their lives because of my personal contribution to that madman Hitler's dream.'

'You were *forced* to work for the Nazis?' Jordan interrupted. 'Surely they could only force you into manual labour? You cannot be *forced* into using your mind against your will. No scientist could allow such a thing!'

Chebrikov chuckled like a wise man tolerating the naive, unrealistic idealism of a young pupil. 'It is Dr Jordan, yes? My Tanya told me of the giant American with the blond hair and the strong, handsome face. You think I describe you this way to make some lightness of this? No, I say this because, Dr Jordan, you – even just physically – are a privileged human being. You were reared by a society that expects privilege – perhaps even as its right. But how would you react, Doctor, if that fine body of yours was reduced to less than a child's weight? But forgive me, I do not talk of hunger here because hunger alone is not persuasion enough. There are greater pressures which can be brought to bear on any man – no matter how courageous he may be – no matter how sincere his dedication to the principle that science should only be used for the benefit of man.'

For a brief moment the old man seemed to reflect on his own thoughts, then he began again. 'I am a Russian Jew. I was taken to Auschwitz first, where I was forced to burn the remnants of my race, then moved to Belsen where my family had been gathered together, ready for the gas chambers. A large family,' he murmured in bitter recollection. 'Five sisters, two brothers and my parents. They looked as though they were dead already and I felt ashamed that I should face them with fat still on my bones. But you see, I was classed as a genius and that was why I was given an "easy" job feeding the furnaces with the fuel which used to be my people. Oh, yes! I was to be kept alive. Not with dignity, you understand; just kept alive until they were ready for me. But my family were not geniuses – just simple ordinary Russian people who happened, also, to be Jewish.

'The Nazis said to me – with remarkable honesty – that they were losing the war but that it was still possible in those dying months for them to win. *I* was able to help them, they informed me. Did I wish to do this? Did I wish for my family to survive?' Chebrikov leaned forwards as if seeing the Nazi inquisitor before him at that moment. '"What do you wish me to do?" I asked, thinking of survival, which was not easy at that time for I had long before given up hope of surviving through each day, never mind the war! "Help us with our new weapons," they said. "Rockets! Rockets so powerful they could be launched at Washington or Moscow with warheads which would destroy entire cities. Not parts of cities – *entire* cities." I knew immediately that they were talking of nuclear fusion.

'"No!" I said "Emphatically, no!" For I too was an idealist in those days and believed that human life should be advanced by science, not destroyed by its products. So, they shot my youngest brother, then my eldest sister, then began working through my family from both ends of the age spectrum until I changed my mind. Yes, Dr Jordan, in the end I agreed to do their work, and they left me with less than one quarter of my family. My collaboration may not now seem worth the price but then, under those circumstances, I can assure you it was.'

Jordan began to speak, abashed, but Chebrikov waved him down. 'No matter, it is not the first time I have been accused of collaboration. But let me continue.

'The Nazis believed that if they could make the long-range version of the V2 rocket fully operational it could be armed with a nuclear warhead, instead of ordinary explosive . . . oh yes, their scientists were very close to producing a nuclear device of sufficient stability and manageable proportions which could be placed in just such a controlled delivery vehicle. Their problem was not in perfecting the warhead – it was perfecting a guidance system which would ensure accurate delivery of that warhead to its target. I agreed to work on their new V3 rocket. It was a monster of awesome proportions for those days. Unstable certainly, what prototype is not? But after re-designed gyroscopes were installed it flew like an arrow, straight and true. To my everlasting shame, I remember feeling a certain pride of achievement when that terrible weapon flew successfully the first time.

'But still the guidance system did not have the range to deliver the V3 as far as Hitler's chosen first target: Washington. And be assured that *was* his intention. In the same way as the Americans crushed the spirit of the Japanese at Hiroshima, so would Hitler have crushed the Americans – and after that he would have picked off the remaining Allies.

'Then we found the solution – and in the way of all scientific solutions it was so simple, so obvious, that we had totally overlooked it. We were working on a guidance system of radio control of course – but no *ordinary* radio waves. Our emissions were on a microwave frequency – what in this age of advanced technology we call *masers*. Yes, I did say masers.'

Chebrikov could have been God sitting in judgement, so complete was his hold on his audience.

'The solution was easy: if we could not guide the V3 all the way to its target we must guide it part of the way . . . then boost it onward. The rocket would be launched, then secret, silent stations would track it, lock onto its guidance mechanism as it flew over each sector, and pass it on at supersonic speed to its designated target – Washington. No one would hear it coming and no weapon could destroy it. It would kill so fast that its victims would hardly realize that they had ceased to live. There were some who believed they actually saw the passage of the earlier V2 – though of course that was impossible because of the speed of the vehicle – but the legend grew that as the rocket cleaved the air a strange sound could be heard – almost as if the gods were whispering in consternation. Predictably, Hitler named the V3 "*Der flüsternde Tod*" – the whispering death. He believed he had a weapon which terrified even the gods – so how could mere mortals stop him?'

Chebrikov pointed at the ground. 'Five booster stations were built – this was one of them. The others were either closer to Germany or in the icecap itself and beyond. All of them were utterly secret. The surface guards pretended to be fishermen – or in this case assumed the role of light-house keepers. All work was conducted below ground and *nobody* was allowed on the surface except the disguised guards. Do you know how I knew what this place had been? Smell! My nose told me the truth. The stench of old air, sweat, hot wiring and damp concrete still lingers even with your modern air-conditioning units and your filters. *Smell*. When I regained consciousness I thought I was dreaming – that I was back again in one of those dreadful places. But it was no dream.'

Weissleder's eyes were fixed like limpets on the frail old man.

'You were actually here?' Ledden exclaimed.

'Not here,' Chebrikov shook his head. 'My work was in the launching station in Germany, but I have *been* here – just as I have been in all the booster stations – even those under the icecap itself.'

Stracey lit up a cigarette. 'But all this was many years ago. Yet you said that you knew what is going on here now?'

Chebrikov looked up at the standing, lean-bodied American. 'Sir, forgive me, you are . . . ?'

'Stracey. Ed Stracey.'

'You too are a scientist?'

'Let's just say I am – or perhaps was – a US Government employee – but I know enough about science to understand everything you've said till now.'

'Ah!' Chebrikov murmured as if confirming something to himself. 'Well, Mr Stracey, my story is not yet finished – indeed it has not really begun. You see, even though we had found the solution to the guidance and tracking problems by building these stations, an extraordinary thing happened. Every time we launched one of the test vehicles it would travel as far as the booster stations, then – for no apparent reason – it would go out of control. We could find no solution whatsoever for many months, then, with the war almost at an end – and lost to Germany – Hitler decided that we scientists were sabotaging the V3 programme and ordered our liquidation.'

'But *you* survived,' said Stracey.

'I am alive, yes. But now I see the world I have survived into I wonder if I should not have died under the guns of the SS. You know they sent children to kill us? *Children!* Boys who could barely lift a machine pistol, let alone control one. Even the SS, the Chosen of the Führer, were reduced to using children to complete their final butchery. It was like a firestorm in that dreadful chamber as the Hitler Jugend tried to keep their weapons level. They sprayed bullets everywhere. I was hit by two ricochets from the walls and lay in my own blood begging God to make me look like a dead man.'

'You still haven't answered my question,' Stracey persisted, crushing out his cigarette. 'How do you know what work is being carried out here *now?*'

Chebrikov studied the American for a moment, then said, 'They sent me into the Arctic to look at the one rocket which had not exploded. It had broken up on the icecap but the fuel had not ignited. Inside, I discovered that virtually every scrap of electronic circuitry had been burnt out. But not by *flame,* you understand. Enormous heat – pure energy – had *fused* the circuitry. Such heat must have been of incredible temperature! I returned with my findings – but said nothing – and by then Hitler had already given his order to have us all shot. Years later I worked out exactly what had happened to the circuits, but by then Stalin had placed me in his own camps and I realized that I could not let him have the discovery I had made – even though it would certainly have ensured my release. Later, when I was considered "rehabilitated", I still said nothing. The world was not ready for such knowledge.'

Stracey leaned against the big steel cabinet and crossed his long legs. 'You had inadvertently produced a beam capable of being used as a weapon,' he stated. 'But the Soviets – and ourselves – are well into the development of beam weapons now. The information you have can be of no use now – it must be obsolete.'

Chebrikov smiled. 'Neither country has been able to reduce the physical size of these experimental beam weapons – and you must know that there are considerable problems with the power source. But what *we* had produced in 1945 was a weapon which was not a so-called "death ray" but a beam which could be produced from a relatively small unit and with no limitations as to its power source. The frequency we were working on had had the side effect of attacking the electronic circuitry of a rocket. Perfected, such a beam could render most modern weapons useless within seconds. If I had continued working on what I had found, the entire balance of power between East and West would have been disrupted. The risk was too great. Finally, when work began in earnest in the Soviet Union on the use of lasers and charged particle beams as weapons of war, I decided to defect to a neutral country and not get involved with either side. I considered that it would take decades before these new beam weapons could be reduced to manageable proportions and be made completely reliable. I thought, perhaps by that time nations would have come to their senses.'

'You were wrong,' said Ledden. 'We have already produced – and tested successfully – a beam weapon considerably smaller and more reliable than any others in existence. *Right here*. Our next phase was to perfect a tracking beam which would guide a disabled missile down harmlessly.'

'Yes,' Chebrikov said quietly. 'I guessed that. Now there is a great sadness in me.'

'Why?' Ledden asked. 'Because we have completed the work you could have done?'

'Ah! I wish it were a case of such simple vanity, but sadly it is far greater than that. I am no great believer in coincidence – and to be brought here, to this place and all that has gone before – is not a coincidence I can accept.' Chebrikov looked at Tavrin, his eyes filled with grief. 'Mikhail,' he said, 'You have betrayed me. Which piece am I in this game you have been playing?'

9

The Grandmaster stood up. 'Sometimes even betrayal is justified, Josef Andreyovich. No man can be greater than a cause. Gentlemen, I must tell you that this installation is no longer under your control. Your people are, at this moment, being held by the men from the submarine you believed destroyed, the *Admiral Grechko*. The vessel will arrive soon to take the necessary equipment and personnel off this island. I ask you to accept what has happened without resistance – these men are well armed and will not hesitate to kill. You should have taken the precaution of a complete body search, Sir Henry. But you can at least take solace in the fact that there has been no nuclear war.'

Ledden clutched his arm. 'But the nuclear explosion? The communications blackout? The news of the mutiny? The burns on those sailors' faces, for God's sake! Surely you couldn't have . . . .'

'Arranged them? Certainly. Radiation burns were the simplest of all – painful for the men, but you see they are not sailors but a specially trained KGB unit, quite used to a little suffering in the line of duty. The explosion? Yes, it was the *Brezhnev*. I "persuaded" Ulyanov to torpedo it. A great sacrifice, of course, but a necessary one. We chose the *Brezhnev* because we knew that an American Government agent was bound to be on the island and he would recognize the importance of that particular submarine. I knew, Mr Stracey, that you would be the hardest to convince – but the sacrifice of the *Brezhnev* ensured that you would finally succumb. The communications blackout? Simple, you are being jammed in a most sophisticated operation which covers all your wavelengths by both space satellites and vessels below the horizon.' He looked across at Ulyanov. 'Sergei, there was no other way. These people would have destroyed everything here if we had attempted to use force. We must have this weapon – surely you would not wish your country to be left defenceless, no matter how much you hate the system that rules it? Political establishments can be changed in time, but if our country is destroyed there will be no one left to bring about such change.'

But Ulyanov did not respond. He stood stunned by these revelations – his loyalties in disarray.

Ledden cut in. 'But you must understand that the device is purely defensive! It knocks down *missiles* – it does not destroy cities or kill people. I would never, *never,* have backed such a project.'

'It does not as *yet,*' Tavrin countered, then looked at Chebrikov. 'What would you say, old man? What limitations could be put on the use of such a device?'

Chebrikov shook his head. 'None,' he mumbled.

'I wouldn't allow the device to be developed for aggressive purposes!' Ledden snapped angrily. 'Any operational use of the device would be strictly controlled through the involvement of non-aligned, neutral countries. The whole purpose of the device . . . .'

'Like so many brilliant scientists, Sir Henry,' Tavrin interrupted, 'you are incredibly naive. We are all on a race to Doomsday and neither of our nations has had the sense to stop – so therefore, as always, it comes down to the survival of the strongest; and this weapon will ensure that the Soviet Union will be the strongest.'

Ulyanov seemed to regain his senses and placed a rough hand on the back of the Grandmaster's head, forcing it around to face him. 'One question,' he said, his voice a hoarse whisper. 'Is my child alive? Have you harmed her?'

'I do not harm children,' Tavrin replied, scornfully. 'Your child is alive. No harm has come to her. If you co-operate now, you and your men will all be pardoned when we return to Russia.'

'Do not believe him,' Chebrikov said, wearily. 'Truth has no meaning for him. Only the final outcome is important.'

Ulyanov tightened his grip and Tavrin winced under the pressure. The heavy-browed eyes bored deep into Tavrin's own, searching for truth. 'If she has been harmed, you know I shall kill you.'

'I said I do not hurt children. She is being cared for – you have my guarantee.'

'Do not believe him,' Chebrikov repeated.

Ulyanov released Tavrin's head. 'I have no choice. I care nothing for these great conspiracies. I care only for one child – the rest of the world can burn in Hell. Tell me what I must do so that we can leave this place.'

Weissleder stepped back to the door, locked it, then took out the silver Walther automatic. 'I can kill you very easily, Bolshevik,' he said.

Chebrikov looked hard at the gun and gave a harsh gasp.

Weissleder smiled with pleasure. 'You recognize it, Jew? But not my face – eh? That has been changed. But you remember *this*. In which camp did you see this silent beauty at work? Come, tell me, Jew?'

'Belsen,' Chebrikov whispered, cowed by old fear, but hatred grew in his eyes. 'Karl Muller. Yes, I remember you well. I will always remember you. I could never forget.'

'That is not good. You should remember from your past that silence can sometimes save your life.' He turned to Tavrin. 'Your men will not hear a thing – but you are luckier than the Jew. You are more use to me alive than dead.' He reached out and pulled Tavrin to the door. 'I know better than most how devoted men can be to a person they admire greatly. Your people will not harm me, I promise you. Now, everyone behind the desk!'

'Are you mad?' Ledden barked. 'There are people out there who could be killed!'

The former SS executioner moved his gun onto Jordan. 'Doctor, all the microfilm on the project. *Now!*' The silver silencer jerked toward the steel cabinet.

Jordan unlocked a chamber within the tall cabinet, then placed a heavy metal box on the desk.

'Everything!' Weissleder warned.

'That's all there is,' Jordan said woodenly. 'Anything else is in my head. What do you hope to gain? You can't get off the island – the only vessel coming here is a Soviet submarine. You think the Russians will wait around for the next chopper in a month's time?'

Weissleder tilted the gun at the box. 'Years ago I killed everyone on this island for what is in there – though of course I knew nothing of the potential weapon then. As far as I was concerned I was stealing information on a proto-type rocket which one day might be converted into hard currency. I was right – all INTERSAT launch vehicles in Africa are based on the V3 rocket. Then Sir Henry discov-ered the "fault" which would have turned us into billion-aires. You think I will let it go for nothing *now*? I let my own men rot *alive* for this secret – so you think I would let it be stolen from me? If the Bolsheviks want it then they must pay for it. Pay *me*. What do you say to that, Herr Grandmaster? The deal with the Americans is off and I am ready to re-open negotiations with other interested parties. Is your government still in the market?'

'Naturally,' Tavrin answered coolly. 'We want the weapon by whatever means. We would be prepared to negotiate a price.'

Weissleder smiled with satisfaction. He turned the gun on Ledden. 'Thank you, Sir Henry,' he said with mocking politeness. 'Only a true English *gentleman* would have been so honest as to tell me of your discovery. I am afraid that I cannot leave you alive or my product is worth nothing, is it?'

He shot Ledden dead instantly.

Stracey leaped forward and the silver barrel flicked sideways and spurted flame soundlessly, slamming him back against the wall, shot once, cleanly above the heart. Weissleder extended his arm and placed another bullet into his head.

Chebrikov lurched from his chair, snatching weakly at the German's hand. Weissleder pulled the trigger franti-cally, causing gaping wounds in the old man's back as the bullets exited.

Ulyanov launched himself at the off-balance German and crashed one meaty fist into the side of his face, but still Weissleder held the gun and fought back ferociously.

Then, inexplicably, there was a metallic rattling in the

ceiling and a section of tiles exploded downwards in a cloud of white dust. One arm appeared through the gaping hole, then the unmistakable impish face of Simon Howard hung down, his arm holding a black automatic.

'Drop it!' Howard called, his face reddening as the blood filled it.

Weissleder managed to raise his own weapon and Howard's fist bucked, once. The German screamed and crashed to the floor as if his legs had been kicked out from under him, his hands – still clutching the silver Walther – clasped to the gunshot wound in his stomach.

'Back off!' Howard called to Ulyanov, who lay close to the wounded German but was himself unhurt. 'I said back off!' Howard dropped down from the ceiling and retrieved the Walther from Weissleder's rigid fingers. The German continued to scream with the pain while Howard examined the superb weapon for a moment, then almost nonchalantly shot the man dead. 'Stand still!' he ordered the others.

Jordan started forward toward Ledden's prostrate form but Howard waved him back with the gun.

'Waste of time,' said Howard. His gun traversed the two Russians as he moved to the door and checked that the locking button on the door knob was pressed in. While he did this the door shook as a shoulder was thrown against it from outside. Howard said, 'Sergei, you tell 'em that if they do that just once more, I'll put a couple of rounds through the door right about here.' He tapped his genitals pointedly.

Ulyanov shouted out in Russian and the banging stopped immediately.

'Now,' said Howard, 'let's find out when we're going to get a visit from this submarine. Sergei?'

'I know nothing about –'

Howard's hand became blurred silver as the gun struck upwards with astonishing speed. Ulyanov hissed with the pain and brought his hands up to his forehead. The blood seeped through his fingers and dripped to the carpet. He cursed in Russian, his blazing eyes fixed on Howard despite the blood which flowed into them.

'Terrific,' Howard said. 'Now let's do it in English.'

Tavrin said, 'I do not know who you are, but your position is hopeless. Give this up before more people are killed.'

'No chance,' Howard stated, flatly.

Tavrin sighed, then called out quickly in Russian.

'What did he say?' Howard demanded, turning the gun on Ulyanov, but it was Tavrin who answered.

'I told the men to rape the American woman. Three of them. But being healthy Russians it might be difficult to restrain the rest.'

'You bastard!' Jordan exploded.

Jemma Elliot's voice came through the door, frightened. 'Matt! the Russians have taken over out here – they've got pistols from somewhere.' Then there was the sound of a struggle.

'Give it up, Howard!' Jordan ordered.

'You just stay still, Doc,' Howard insisted. 'The Ivans out there take their orders from the chess player here. While we got him there's no problem.'

From outside, the sounds of the struggle intensified and Jemma Elliot squealed, but Howard's dark face remained unmoved.

'Howard!' Jordan yelled. 'I order you to hand over those weapons!'

'*Order?* Order *me*! It was you idiots let the Ivans in here. If you want to spend your life in bloody Siberia that's your funeral, mate. I'm not getting chopped for your mistakes. They're only roughing her up a bit.' He ducked his head at Tavrin. 'He's lied all along. Still is.'

'No,' Ulyanov said heavily. 'He told them to rape her – and they will.'

The men of the KGB task force could hardly believe their ears. The Grandmaster had actually *ordered* them to rape the American woman.

The man posing as the petty officer pressed his pistol into Jemma Elliot's cheek, hard, so that she could feel the metal ring against her teeth through the soft flesh. He forced her downward with his free hand.

'No!' she gasped, seeing the greedy lust in his eyes. She

screamed and the man grabbed her hair, jerking her head back, then forced her down to the floor. Another of the men undid the flap of his naval-style trousers and drew himself out, his Mongolian features distorted and florid with lust. The petty officer held her down as the Mongolian unzipped her denims, then tugged them off her long legs. Underneath, she wore only frail black briefs. The Mongolian drew a big clasp knife, unlocked it and moved in closer.

Jemma lashed out wildly with both feet, but the man simply grabbed her legs and prised them apart, then slipped one finger under the elastic at her crotch and pulled the thin material away from her pubis. She gasped in horror as the blade moved across the tender flesh and slit through the flimsy material, leaving her exposed. Another man pushed forward and pulled her sweater up, baring her breasts, but the Mongolian pushed him away with a snarl, then using both hands lifted her buttocks and drew her up to him.

Jemma squealed as the brutal penetration was completed, then as the man began moving frantically she screamed, high and piercingly.

Howard pointed the silenced automatic at Tavrin's stomach. 'One word,' he warned. 'Just one word.' He covered the door knob with his body and made as if he was listening through the panel. Stealthily his finger released the button lock, then in one swift movement, jerked the door open and dropped. He shot the man holding Jemma down in the face with the silenced Walther, and simultaneously blasted with the Soviet-made automatic into the bunched group of leering men. All three crashed down to the floor, fatally body-shot in the confined space of the corridor. A head, then a hand holding a gun, snaked out from the corner at the end of the corridor, but Howard discouraged the man with two shots slammed into the wall.

The Mongolian had jerked himself out and squatted now on his haunches, his bared testicles dangling obscenely. He seemed mesmerized and stared at Howard as if he were a black mamba poised to strike. Then, suicidally, he snatched for the big knife.

The silenced bullet passed clean through the bones of the back of his hand, emitting sparks as it disintegrated on the haft of the knife. The Mongolian screamed and raised his shattered hand to his face, disbelievingly, as if it were no longer a part of his body. Howard glanced down the corridor quickly, then shot the Mongolian's testicles away. The man shrieked, his slant eyes as wide as his gaping mouth. Howard grabbed his lank black hair and snapped his head down between Jemma's naked, splayed legs, then pumped one silent bullet through the back of his cranium.

Jemma screamed and Ulyanov, who until that moment seemed unable – or reluctant – to react leaped forward and crashed his boot into the side of Howard's face. Howard lost consciousness immediately as his head crashed into the door frame, his cheek split to the bone and pouring blood.

Ulyanov saw Jordan shift quickly behind the desk, snatched the Russian automatic from the floor and swung around. 'Enough!' he said, almost wearily. 'Enough.'

'At least let me see to Jemma!' Jordan blurted furiously.

'She is unharmed,' said Tavrin. 'Get her dressed, then both of you come with me to the communications room.'

'What about Howard?' Jordan asked.

Tavrin spoke in Russian to Ulyanov. 'He is dangerous. Lock him in one of the small rooms and put a man on the door.'

'He is hurt badly,' Ulyanov observed. 'That bleeding must be stopped.'

The Grandmaster made a small shrug. 'Do whatever you want but waste no time. Time is running out for us very quickly – the Americans may be many things but they are not fools.'

Ulyanov hefted Howard over his shoulder as if he were a child and walked into the corridor, leaving a trail of blood behind him. He held his own automatic ready and pocketed the Walther.

'You evil bastard!' Jemma spat at him as he passed her. 'I *believed* you. Your *daughter*! Christ, what makes people like you?'

'I do what I have to do,' he replied.

'Don't blame him,' Jordan said, supporting her still. 'He's been suckered like the rest of us.'

'What is her position here?' Tavrin asked.

'Go to hell,' Jordan murmured.

'Then I must hand her back to my men – but this time they won't be stopped.'

'Guidance control!' Jemma said instantly. 'We use a laser tracking-beam to lock onto your missiles.'

'Very good,' said Tavrin. 'We shall need what is in your mind also – now that Sir Henry is dead. You, Dr Jordan, and perhaps some of your most important people, will save us much time in developing the weapon.'

Jemma's face blanched. 'You're not getting me to Russia – *no way!*'

Tavrin gave an ironic smile. 'I am not offering you an option,' he said. 'But you will find that scientists enjoy certain privileges in the Soviet Union. You will be treated well until the work is completed – we are not the ogres your propaganda machine makes us out to be. I am confident that you will not resist.'

'Try me!' she snapped.

'Let me put the facts of this situation to you very clearly,' Tavrin said mercilessly. 'You have been operating a secret military base in an offensive role against the Soviet Union – you have destroyed our missiles and you have monitored our test procedures from within Soviet waters. Now, at worst, all of you could be charged with committing an act of aggression – at best, espionage. If you were tried by our courts both these charges would automatically bring the death penalty. I am certain that you will co-operate.'

Ulyanov returned and faced Tavrin. He spoke in Russian: 'Tanya Chebrikova is stitching that small devil's wound – I had to tell her of Chebrikov's death.'

'What more have you told her?' Tavrin asked.

'The truth. She will kill you if you go near her.'

Tavrin shook his head impatiently. 'I have no time for these minor issues. She will have to be dealt with.'

Ulyanov stared at the Grandmaster stonily.

'Don't worry,' Tavrin reassured him. 'I will not have her killed.'

'It might be better for you if you did.'

'See that she is locked in with the Englishman. That way she will be no problem. Come, there is work to do.'

They entered the recreation area to find the base's personnel squatting on the floor under the threatening guns of the KGB task force. The atmosphere from both sides was ugly. One of the Russians was dealing with the man whom Howard had shot in the face. He raised his eyes to Tavrin and shook his head. Laid out next to him on the floor were the four dead bodies which had been collected from the corridor.

Ulyanov noticed for the first time that two of his own men lay against a wall – both seemed to be unmarked and he guessed that their wounds would be at their backs and almost certainly inflicted silently by knives. The young blond sailor sat beside them, his arms clutched to his knees and head down. Ulyanov could see he was weeping. He forced down his anger, knowing he had no other choice but to co-operate totally with Tavrin.

Now I know why he always wins, he thought. He calculates men's weaknesses while others are offering their sympathy.

Jemma Elliot glanced at his bearded face as they passed through the silent crowd and saw the anger flare and die in those dark, feeling eyes.

'You really knew *nothing*?' she whispered, sensing the inner battle within him.

'Quiet!' he answered sharply but gave a small shake of his head.

'At least you know your little girl is safe,' she whispered again.

A flush of happiness passed over Ulyanov's features and she saw that brief glimmer of gold at his mouth, then it was gone and his face became stony once more.

'Do not talk,' he ordered.

In the communications room Ray Peterson sat nursing a bruise on his head while an armed Russian stood behind him. Another of the KGB force sat at the control console familiarizing himself with the equipment. By his right hand he had a flat grey electronic unit with a digital read-out display and several buttons. It might have been an electronic calculator except that it was linked directly into the transmitter.

As they entered the room Tavrin said: 'Now, Dr Jordan, I will prove to you that the world you love so much is still very much alive and well.' He nodded at the man at the desk, who rapidly punched out a series of digits. Within the space of a few seconds the snarling hiss from the speakers died, then, as another sequence was punched in, it returned.

'The wonders of science, Doctor. How easy it is to deceive people – even scientists like yourselves – when other, human issues are brought into play. The old man, the young girl, genuine dissidents like Ulyanov and his men . . . all so easy, so predictable. The game was enjoyable – I am a little sad it is all over.'

Neither Jordan, nor Jemma, nor Ulyanov spoke.

'Sergei,' Tavrin said. 'Dr Jordan will unseal the entrance for a few moments while you go with two of the men to collect the automatic weapons from the surface. And please do not be foolish – remember you have everything to go back to in Russia.'

Ulyanov left without uttering a word.

Tavrin turned to Jordan. 'Tell me, Doctor, the Nazis called their ultimate weapon the whispering death . . . do you have a fitting name for yours?'

Jordan stared straight into the flat grey eyes. 'Sir Henry had a dream. He intended to create a device – an anti-weapon – which would cleanse the world of war. He named it Whitefire.'

'Ah!' said Tavrin. 'But dreamers can never look on the cold face of reality. Sir Henry, like his dream, is dead. That is reality. In the end it is the only reality.'

PART THREE

Counter

I

The crisis committee met in an inner room of the Pentagon and was chaired by the President of the United States. He sat facing down a long polished mahogany table, with the men he had chosen as his co-trustees of the Whitefire secret down either side.

Directly to his right sat the Secretary of State; next to him the Director of the Central Intelligence Agency; then two generals – Charles Macklin, the NATO Supremo, and Sam Walker of Strategic Air Command. Opposite these sat the Secretary for Defence; the Assistant to the President for Emergency Preparedness; the Director of Strategic Technology and the two Defence Secretaries responsible for Nuclear Weapons Command and Threat Assessment; then, finally, the Director of Intelligence for the Department of Defence.

The President knew that the two sides were, in effect, separate power blocs within his administration and normally he would have had to exercise his considerable personal charm and diplomatic skill to keep the meeting in order. But today there was no time for such niceties.

He placed both hands on the table palms down and began: 'There's too much to be said – and too little time left for positive action, so we'll deal with the facts with no interruptions.' He nodded down the table to his left.

The Director of Strategic Technology arose and coughed: 'Ah, some time ago we received a proposition from a consortium of European financiers and businessmen which ah . . . to put it in plain language . . . rather knocked the Department on its ass!'

The Secretary for Defence frowned and glared at the speaker, who continued: 'Essentially, the proposition was that they had developed a weapon for strategic defence which was cost-effective, manoeuvrable, but, more importantly, consumed a low ratio of energy – thereby creating a fuel surplus if introduced on the current usage of conventional weapons by ours and NATO forces.'

He cleared his throat and extracted a sheaf of paper from a folder. 'Naturally we were sceptical, but followed up anyway with a request for details of the weapon. The answer we received was curt to say the least. I quote: "The Consortium requires guarantees that *when*" – their terminology not mine – "*when* you acquire the weapon the United States Government shall divert the resulting energy surpluses into certain market areas which we shall designate." They added that the selling price of these surpluses should be – and again I quote – " . . . no higher than the original purchase price when the American and NATO military fuel reserves were laid down." '

General Macklin chuckled. 'What have they got – the hammer of God?'

'I said no interruption, General,' the President reminded. 'Carry on, Mr Director.'

'Thank you, sir. Well, obviously the Department could not begin to give such a guarantee. Nor for that matter could we consider their further conditions concerning initial up-front payments for the purchase of the technology and the subsequent granting of manufacturing licences to them. We replied again with a request for more details but got no further. The consortium was adamant. No guarantees . . . no deal . . . ah, no weapon. At this stage I went directly to the President.' He sat down quickly, avoiding the angry glare from the Secretary for Defence, and looked pleadingly to the President for help.

The President took over. 'The Director was afraid that the consortium might make the same approach . . . elsewhere. His decision to come directly to me was correct.' He shot a look at the Defence Secretary. 'The Soviets are already supplying Europe with a dangerously high level of energy via the new pipeline. They could easily make such a guarantee – whether they meant to honour it or not – *and* have the fastest method of delivering fuel direct to Europe. You get the point?' He watched the heads nodding around the table.

'So, in principle, I agreed.' He waved the protests down.

'I had no alternative. If the weapon was all it purported to be we could afford to sell off part of the military surpluses – and if it was some Mickey Mouse contraption out of a Buck Rogers movie then we were back to square one without losing a thing.

'The Chairman of this consortium is an Englishman – a highly respected scientist but also a powerful businessman. A clandestine meeting was arranged between us, and partial information on the weapon was handed over for our experts to look over. In that same room I might add – nothing was allowed out on Ledden's firm order.'

The President paused and passed a hand over his lined face. 'Then I was shown a video tape.' For a moment he seemed quite ill. 'You're all going to see that tape now – and perhaps then you might understand why the thought of it scares the hell out of me. Mr Director?'

The Director of Strategic Technology got up again and inserted a cassette into a video machine below an oversized TV screen. 'First sequence,' he intoned.

The film showed the launch, flight and eventual bringing down of three large missiles, all bearing the red Communist star of the Soviet Union.

'The NE-04,' the Director explained. 'The information we've gleaned from this tape alone is worth millions in intelligence terms.' He looked back at the faces around the table. They were utterly still.

'Jesus!' someone muttered.

'Second sequence.' After a momentary flicker of blankness a very dark sequence began. 'Shot from inside a Hercules transport aircraft,' the Director said quickly. 'There are large unloading doors in the rear of the aircraft. In a second you will see them open – there!' Bright white light filled the screen as the stark Arctic icecap leaped into view.

'What's that?' the NATO Supremo exclaimed as a white translucent dome filled the screen, blocking out the yawning exit of the aircraft.

He received no answer.

The dome moved down the wide body of the aircraft on a track, then fell through the doors into space, its plunging descent halted by triple white parachutes. The Hercules circled over the floating dome, monitoring the descent until the flat base flopped onto the icecap in a flurry of snow, sinking in deep. The parachutes trailed on the surface for a moment, before they appeared to be gobbled up by three slit apertures in the base of the dome.

'The next day,' said the President. 'Same area. Natural subsidence, weight and overnight snow have completely concealed the device.'

As if to give emphasis to his words the camera zoomed in on one area of snow, showing the completely unbroken surface.

'Ledden told me that that was a mock-up of the device, weighted accurately. It was merely a test to see if they could "seed" – as he put it – the icecap with real units.'

'If that was only a mock-up, where's the thing that downed those missiles?' General Macklin demanded aggressively. 'That's a pretty damn dangerous thing they did there! Or maybe they think the Russians don't object to their latest weapon being knocked clean out of the sky?'

'Oh, they object all right, General. And I believe that they have taken some equally dangerous steps to get the device for themselves. Steps which we have no option but to counter. That is why we are here today.'

'How was that sequence filmed?' asked the CIA Director.

'Orbital satellite,' the President replied. 'One of the major companies involved in the consortium is INTERSAT. I'm sure you've all heard of that particular corporation.'

The spymaster offered the information anyway. 'They operate out of Africa, South America . . . wherever they can lease a tract of land which gives them damn near sovereign rights in the area. Every emerging nation with enough spare money is having space satellites put up by them. INTERSAT is trouble as far as I'm concerned . . . it's damned risky having unscheduled hardware floating around up there in orbit.'

'So what's the wonder weapon?' said the Secretary for Defence. 'If it's as good as it looks why haven't we got it here already?'

'We should have,' the President answered, worriedly. 'I

authorized an evaluation trip by a man from ISS. We sent him up to their secret test station. Up till now he's failed to report in. We were expecting communication by satellite yesterday – it didn't happen.'

'Well, surely we can do something about that,' said the Defence Secretary with rising impatience. 'Where's the base?'

The President stood up and moved to a wall-sized map behind him. 'Right there,' he pointed.

'Jesus! Right up the Bear's snout!' General Walker proclaimed. 'What are they using for cover – invisibility?'

'Hardly.' The President gave a twisted smile. 'They even light themselves up. Someone open that packet on the table and pass the photographs around.'

'Ingenious,' Walker observed as the photographs of Beacon Island were dealt out. 'Everything below the surface. Just the lighthouse and these huts for cover. Clever.'

'Which country has jurisdiction over the island?' asked the Defence Secretary.

'Officially, it's neutral,' replied the President. 'Like all INTERSAT operations they negotiated a long-term lease. In this case, with the Russians.'

'What's this!' the CIA chief blurted suddenly.

'I wondered when someone would notice,' said the President. He held his hand out for the photograph, then turned it around for all to see. 'Taken from a satellite using heat-sensing techniques. The brighter areas show up the underground complex very well indeed from all the various heat sources . . . but this other heat source is from a submarine which appears to be circling the island. I'm afraid to say that it is a Soviet submarine.'

'Oh, my God!' breathed the Defence Secretary.

'I'm afraid He's not going to be much help right now,' the Secretary of State said. The silence was stunning. 'Tell them more about the weapon, Mr President,' he added.

The Secretary of Defence glanced with flaring anger at the figure opposite, realizing that the Secretary of State had already been briefed.

The President said: 'You take it from here.'

The Secretary of State raised his iron-grey eyebrows and

leaned forward, shoulders hunched, his head moving as he surveyed the faces around him. 'What we're discussing here is basically a beam weapon. But let me say this – a beam weapon which puts our SIPAPU laser particle beam project back into the Middle Ages.

'You all know the amount we've spent on research in that field. In the last decade $700,000,000 – and the defence industry has invested four times that amount in the same period. And all we've managed to do is to knock down some anti-tank missiles on the test range at San Juan Capistrano, California. But the Soviets aren't doing much better in their research complex at Semipalatinsk, Kazakhstan. We've all hit the same problem. *Size*. It's no damn good if you've got all the benefits of the laser – tremendous speed, accuracy, and rate of fire equal to the speed of light – if you can't reduce the weapon to a reasonable size.'

'And this consortium has done that?' General Walker put in.

'You saw it on the screen,' said the Secretary of State.

'And now the Russians have it,' the Defence Secretary said, cuttingly.

'Not quite,' came the steady answer. 'We might still beat them to the punch.' He got up and walked to the wall map. 'You all know about the nuclear alert exercise that went haywire yesterday. What you don't know is that there was no "faulty" computer tape, as was released to the press. An Air Force major deleted the exercise code from the programmed tape readied for the exercise. The major was a Soviet agent – a long-term penetration agent.' The Secretary of State ignored the uproar, studying his hands intently.

'Where's the son-of-a-bitch now!' General Macklin demanded.

'Dead. Died under interrogation. Hollow tooth the inquisitors missed. Cyanide. All he told us – rather proudly, I gather – was that it had been an order from the very highest level. An order, mind you, that blew a long-term spying career which penetrated our most sensitive defence area. The major's position at NORAD made him invaluable to the Kremlin – yet they gave him an order which was *certain* to blow him. Why? Because there was something else more valuable to be gained from such a sacrifice. The beam weapon.'

'Don't see the connection,' stated the Defence Secretary.

The Secretary of State rapped the map with a finger. 'The point where the Soviet submarine *Leonid Brezhnev* exploded yesterday.' He drew an imaginary circle around it. 'And the area designated hazardous by the Russians because of radiation fallout. *Nothing* is going into that area. No aircraft, no ships, *nothing*.' He rapped the map again within the imaginary circle he had drawn. 'Beacon Island.'

The Secretary for Defence objected instantly. 'But if they wanted to isolate the island there are a hundred ways they could do it – safer ways. Christ sakes, if they really needed a nuclear explosion, they've got enough bombs! You're not trying to tell us they'd destroy their newest sub *themselves*. That's beyond belief! Why?'

'The doctored tape was to get us panicked – and looking everywhere but at Beacon Island – which they probably knew from their other intelligence sources we were watching. The destruction of the *Brezhnev* – the *sacrifice* – of their newest and largest boat was to achieve precisely what you are expressing now – disbelief. Who in their right mind would sacrifice such an important vessel? The Russians would. Because they can easily build another *Brezhnev*, but without this new beam weapon they would be as far back as when we invented the atomic bomb. Any missiles the *Brezhnev* could put up we could knock down like skittles. You *saw* the film. Face it, the development of this weapon has made everything in their nuclear arsenal completely obsolete. *That* is why they sacrificed the *Leonid Brezhnev* and their mole.'

The Defence Secretary had not finished. 'So say that's the ploy. What are they doing now? Stripping the base? Hijacking the scientists? How did they get inside? A task force? What?'

The President shook his head and re-entered the argument. 'Sir Henry Ledden assured me that at the slightest hint of any emergency, the underground area can be sealed up tighter than a clam. He believed the base to be impregnable – it's built to the same standards as our deepest missile silos.'

'What about nerve gas?' General Walker suggested.

'No good. They've got a filtration system which would deal with that ... *and* fallout,' the President added pointedly.

'Well then, *how*?' the Defence Secretary demanded. 'The damned Russians can't be sitting around on their butts waiting to starve them out!'

'Two days ago,' said the Secretary of State, 'a Soviet submarine – crewed by mutineers according to our intelligence sources – was taken from its berth at their naval base at Severomorsk, near Murmansk. It was sailed to Norway and put in at a fjord. There it picked up three civilians, then disappeared. Prior to that incident, the CIA reported that the Soviet defector Josef Chebrikov and his grand-daughter also disappeared from their home outside Geneva. Chebrikov, in case you don't remember, is the Russian-Jewish scientist who escaped to the West, made his way to Switzerland and refused to talk terms with any country – including Israel. He's made his living since then by publishing books against the Soviet regime ... and maybe a bit of industrial work.'

'Right,' said the CIA Director, with the puzzled frown of a man who had answers to questions he did not understand.

'Also vanished,' the Secretary of State continued, 'is the Russian chess Grandmaster, Mikhail Tavrin – *right in the middle of the world championships. Also* in Geneva,' he added with emphasis.

'So?' said the Defence Secretary.

'So, a crew of mutineers – openly rebelling against the Soviet regime; an outspoken critic of the Kremlin – who happens to be a scientist; and a world-famous Russian who has spent a lot of time in the West and therefore could be construed to be sympathetic toward our system, have all vanished. And at roughly the same time. Coincidence, gentlemen?'

The faces of the crisis committee were blank.

The Secretary of State smiled. 'I doubt it. Tavrin we have suspected for some time to be a close advisor of the new Soviet leader. There are some Kremlin-watchers who believe that many years ago their paths crossed – well before either man came into prominence in his own right. This is unconfirmed, but the information comes from usually reliable sources. Now, Swiss intelligence report that the car which took Tavrin away so unexpectedly from the world championships contained the local KGB resident. It was pure luck that he was spotted. The car was driven to Geneva International Airport and Swiss intelligence tailed it. It drew up beside an Aeroflot airliner which had made an emergency landing for some obscure fault. The odd thing, the Swiss tell us, is that the entire aircraft appeared to be empty. They were using night-vision glasses and seem absolutely sure of this fact. The airliner, incidentally, was en route from Moscow, where, according to the filed flight plan, it returned immediately it was airborne again.' He paused and sipped water for a moment, then said: 'Now, in my opinion there is only one man in Russia who has the power to order a clandestine flight in an empty – *unofficial* – aircraft to perhaps *the* most capitalist country without being subject to the deepest suspicion. I mean, of course, the Soviet leader himself.'

The Defence Secretary leaned forward. 'All right. So say you're right. What does it mean? What's the connection with Beacon Island?'

The Secretary of State pressed his knuckles on the table and leaned forward. 'Where force may fail – sometimes passive persuasion may work. I feel – and the President agrees – that the only way that Sir Henry Ledden might allow people inside that secret underground base is if those people seem to be entirely helpless – and completely *genuine*. And by *that* I mean recognizable because of either events or reputation.

'If Tavrin set the whole thing up – and remember he's got the kind of mind to work it out – he would have landed on that isolated island with people who had witnessed a nuclear explosion on the horizon, and who were probably totally unaware of the *real* reason for their presence there – that being the infiltration of the base.

'What choice would Ledden have? He would be faced with people fleeing Soviet Russia who would almost certainly die from radiation poisoning if he left them on the surface.'

'But the *imponderables*!' the Secretary of Defence objected. 'How could he possibly plan – '

'There are no "imponderables" to a man like Tavrin. If he did indeed set this up you can be damn sure that every move was worked out in advance with precision and cover moves all the way.' The speaker was the Assistant to the President for Emergency Preparedness. 'I have met Tavrin on many occasions – I have even played chess with him. He is a master strategist. This type of deception – with such incredibly high stakes – would be irresistible to him. I can imagine his delight in being able to play human pieces – even countries – against each other while he controls the moves. It would be the ultimate game for him.'

'But Tavrin is an anti-communist!' the CIA Director protested. 'He's confirmed that openly. It's only his elevated position which keeps him alive. The man is a legend inside Russia – the State would not dare touch him.'

'I've never quite believed that,' replied the Assistant to the President. 'Anyone who could defect to the West as easily as Tavrin could – and still doesn't – has got to have his heart, or *mind* in his case, firmly in the East. And the Swiss intelligence service report proves my point.'

'Unconfirmed,' the Secretary for Defence reminded him, drily.

'We've talked enough,' the President said. 'We have only one course of action open to us and I believe we must take it.' He lifted the phone before him. 'Send in Colonel Shearer,' he ordered.

Joseph Shearer sat alone and very still outside the committee room, dressed in lightweight, starched summer tans – his discreet medal ribbons understating his valour.

Among his men at the 1st Battalion United States Rangers Headquarters in Fort Stewart, Georgia, he was known, affectionately, as 'The Arctic Fox', because of his survival against impossible odds after being cut off, alone, by a blizzard during an abortive Alaskan training exercise in 1974.

Joseph Shearer was one of those silent men whose very presence can be frightening. He sat perfectly still, his arms folded and his button-hard hazel eyes fixed on some point ahead of him, aware of every movement in the busy corridor but reacting to none. His ability to remain motionless for hours was akin to the hibernation of an animal – except that Shearer's eyes remained open.

There was a legend at Fort Stewart that Shearer had lain, utterly still, for thirty-six hours beside the Ho Chi Minh Trail in eastern Laos, noting the movement of supplies while Communist patrols prowled within inches of his prone body. When asked by the bored wife of a visiting three-star general at some dreadful duty dinner party if the famous story were true, Shearer replied, deadly serious: 'Not entirely, ma'am. I had to turn on my side once to piss.' His name was promptly struck off every guest list in the upper-echelon military social calendar. Nothing could have pleased him more. He suffered the rules of social convention with a cold indifference, and small-talking fools not at all.

Shearer was forty-three and his deeply tanned, almost cadaverous, creased and gaunt face showed his age. His pepper-and-salt cropped skull, too, gave away his years, but his whipcord-tough body belonged to a man ten years younger. He was proud of his physique and prouder still to be the man chosen to command what was arguably the elite of the elite in the grim world of rapid-strike-and-deployment warfare: the legendary Black Berets.

A hand touched his shoulder. 'Colonel? The President is ready for you now. Follow me, please.'

Shearer looked up. The speaker was young and dark, a presidential aide, with fluid deep eyes which hinted at a life holding back secrets. He turned and walked the few steps to the double doors of the committee room, knocked and held it open.

Shearer strode briskly to the foot of the long table and

snapped up a salute, his eyes fixed on his commander-in-chief.

'Please sit, Colonel,' said the President.

Shearer drew out the vacant chair before him and seated himself, facing down the length of the table. He took in the faces on either side without shifting his gaze. Tension as fierce as an electric charge filled the chill air-conditioned atmosphere.

The President lifted his phone. 'Bring it in,' he murmured, then replaced the receiver and folded his hands on the table. No one spoke, and every eye was on Shearer.

The shit's hit the fan, he thought shrewdly. And I'm the one who's going to have to put my hand in the blades to stop it flying.

The presidential aide came in backwards through the large double doors, carrying a large draped object. He placed it on the table before Shearer, then stripped off the cover. Beneath was a display model of an airliner in regular commercial use; the type of cross-sectioned model seen in thousands of airline offices.

Everyone looked at it except Shearer, who looked at the President.

'Boeing 727,' said the President, and Shearer nodded.

The presidential aide returned with a large sealed packet and placed it beside Shearer's chair.

'Colonel Shearer,' said the President. 'I must order you to carry out a mission the reason for which you cannot be told. Is that understood?'

'Perfectly, sir.'

The President glanced downwards briefly. 'Also – and I regret this very deeply – you and your men must go in without insignia or identification of any sort whatsoever. If you fail I will not help you. As far as this government is concerned you do not exist. It would be better if none of you survived if you are faced with capture. *Do you understand me, Colonel?*'

'Perfectly, sir,' Shearer repeated.

'The Black Berets are experts in the parachuting technique known as "stand-off"?' the President inquired.

Shearer's eyes flicked to the model airliner for the first time. 'That is correct, sir.'

The President floated a photograph down the table. Shearer picked it up and studied the hostile face of Beacon Island, recognizing the bright areas on the print as being heat sources.

'A sub-surface installation of some kind, sir?' he asked.

'Exactly,' replied the President, and sent down a second photograph. 'Same shot, wider focus. The heat source off the south face of the island is emitted from the reactor of a Soviet nuclear submarine. Its presence there is the greatest single factor for the disruption of world peace since perhaps the Cuban Missile Crisis. That is all I can tell you. Under no circumstances must that submarine be allowed to land and remove information – perhaps people – from that island. If you fail we would have to destroy the submarine ourselves and face the risk of retaliation by the Russians.' The President ignored the protests around him.

'How long since this photograph was taken?' Shearer asked.

'Don't worry – we have a minute-by-minute record of every move it makes. Up to now it has not approached the island. The gamble is to get you and your men there before it makes landfall, then leaves. If you are too late we shall destroy it – and probably the island too.'

'But the *risk* of such an action!' the Secretary for Defence exclaimed, as if the spectre of the appalling consequences was suddenly before him. 'We'd be faced by the threat of war!'

The President answered, seriously: 'Facing the threat of war now is infinitely better than the certain loss of one in the future.' He turned back to Shearer. 'The island has been isolated by the Soviets because of the explosion aboard their nuclear submarine, the *Leonid Brezhnev*. That entire area is reported by them to be contaminated by radioactivity.'

'I've heard the news, sir. Do we know what the radiation level stands at – right now?'

'Survivable,' the Secretary of State put in. 'Weather satellite pictures show an Arctic storm blowing south. Con-

167

tamination along your jump line and on the island should be minimal.'

Shearer nodded. 'You do realize, sir, that it would be virtually impossible to make this kind of jump with heavy protective clothing. Why the "stand-off" technique? That entails a far longer period in the air . . . and with a radiation hazard, however minimal . . .'

'No choice,' the President interrupted. 'The Russians have made that section of the ocean a "no-go" area. And they're enforcing it hard.'

'So we can't be dropped by military aircraft.'

'*Especially* not by military aircraft.'

Shearer dragged the model aircraft to him, flicked up a plastic section and pulled the exit steps under the tail of the 727 down. 'Well, D. B. Cooper did it!' he said, referring to the notorious hijacker of an American Airlines flight in 1971. 'With two parachutes, a million dollars and a drop into nowhere.'

'The stakes here are somewhat higher,' said the President grimly.

'How close can we get this bird in, sir?' Shearer queried.

'It will be an Icelandair scheduled flight – except of course that normal passengers and crew will not be on board. The Russians have got heavy surveillance on that area and made some very threatening noises when some of our Royal Air Force friends decided to get a bit closer. But if a civilian airliner has "instrument malfunction" – the pilot can blame the radiation – then drifted off course . . . ?'

'How close, Mr President?' Shearer repeated.

'Ten miles. And that's two miles into the no-go zone.'

Shearer's mouth tightened. '*Ten miles stand-off onto a small piece of rock in the Arctic Ocean?*'

'At night,' the Secretary of State interjected.

Shearer said: 'Sir, you said "no survivors" if the mission fails. If any of my men go down early – they won't even begin the mission. They won't last ten minutes in those waters!'

'I realize that,' the President said, quietly. 'But can it be done?'

Shearer looked at the plane, but only saw a cold black

ocean. 'I'll lose about one-sixth of my men in the sea, but the rest will get there. Yes sir, it can be done – with heavy losses. I'll need detailed plans of the island. Elevation, terrain . . . .'

'Everything is in the sealed packet,' said the President. 'Your orders are laid out clearly – but basically you must take and hold the island come what may.'

'And then – sir?'

'You wait.'

Shearer raised one eybrow but made no comment. Finally he said: 'Will there be any resistance on the island itself?'

The Secretary of State answered, heavily. 'We don't know. Anything we tell you would only be guesswork. Colonel, you take that island from *whoever* is holding it. That's your priority. *Any* resistance you meet with you counter and destroy. We've prepared as much as we can on the island. Some of the information dates back to World War II. It used to be some sort of experimental rocket station according to some captured Nazi records we have stored in the archives.'

The President stood and walked around the table to Shearer. He reached for the plane, swung the tail section to him and snapped off a section of plastic, then tossed it onto the table. 'The D. B. Cooper vane, colonel,' he said. 'Been fitted on every 727 since the hijack. In flight it works like a steel bar over the rear door. Make sure you do that to the real thing or you'll never get that rear exit open.' He stuck out his hand. 'Good luck, colonel – and may God help you.'

The corners of Shearer's eyes crinkled with amusement. 'I've got no influence on that level, Mr President. I'll rely on a following wind and a soft landing.' He turned, snapped a salute and walked from the room.

The President leaned forward in his chair. 'We have to give Shearer every chance we can – and that means making the Kremlin look the other way. Now, the last operation in the Middle East by the Rapid Deployment Force was a complete success – it had the Kremlin jittery for days, not knowing how far we would be prepared to go. Gentlemen, at this moment the RDP is awaiting my order to take off for Cairo. Except this time instead of landing and turning around they're going to sit on those runways in Cairo with their engines warm and their noses pointing toward Mecca.' He lifted the phone, but covered the mouthpiece. 'Last time it was called Operation Bright Star. I think that on this occasion Operation Eclipse would be more suitable.'

He gave the order to unleash the massive transports skyward.

2

Night was already closing in when a Lockheed C-141 Starlifter sank onto the runway at Keflavik USAF airbase, Iceland, its great swept-back wings drooping with the weight of the four big turbo-fan engines. It taxied past a row of Phantom fighter bombers before halting by a series of large hangars, its exits facing the entrance of one.

Colonel Shearer was the first man to step down onto the scarred tarmac. He stopped as the vast hangar doors were rolled back and studied the Icelandair 727 inside. Without turning he waved his men down from the Starlifter, then walked into the hangar.

With a rumbling moan the hangar doors were pulled shut behind the fifty Black Berets. Shearer stood on an ammunition box next to a blackboard and easel and clipped a map to it. This done, he pointed at the 727 with a leather-bound swagger stick.

He called out: 'If this bird were sticking to its normal flight schedule it would clear Icelandic airspace at 20.15 hours tonight. So will we.' He turned to the map. 'Target!' His voice rang against the metal wall of the hangar. 'One small island composed of rock. No vegetation to speak of – maybe some moss and lichen – but very barren and very hard. If you hit badly you get lunched! No second chances. Name, Beacon Island. Purpose of mission? None of our goddam business.' He allowed a spattering of laughter to spend itself before continuing.

He flipped the map over to reveal, a large aerial photograph of Beacon Island. He rapped the print with his stick.

'Cliffs! In the main, sheer. You come in too low and it's a cheese-grater ride straight down to the ocean.

'We have two objectives – both to be struck at the same time. One!' The stick rapped hard. 'The tower. Looks like a regular lighthouse? It isn't. It's a way in to the second objective. Strike Team One – designated Rooster – takes the tower and holds it . . . and I *mean* holds it. Strike Team Two – designated Gopher – will wait for Rooster's affirmative, then will move in and blow the doors concealed in the tower – that is, of course, unless the natives are friendly, in which case they'll welcome us with open arms. The doors lead onto a liftshaft which goes through two underground levels. Gopher will secure both underground levels and *eliminate* resistance, if any. Our orders – and I emphasize this – are to take the island and the underground base *whatever* the cost.' Shearer let his words sink in.

One of the Rangers stuck up an arm. Shearer nodded.

'Why the 727, sir?'

'I was coming to that. You've all heard the news of the explosion on board the Soviet nuclear sub, the *Brezhnev*? Well, right now they're touchy and have declared the area where the sub blew to be a radiation hazard. They've closed it off. A no-go zone which they're enforcing hard. Our target is within that zone. If we flew the Starlifter into the zone they wouldn't care too much about creating an international incident. They'd worry about that later – which wouldn't make much difference to us because we'd be just another form of sea pollution by then. The nearest we are ever going to get to that rock is ten miles – and that is already two miles within the no-go zone. Hopefully we can bluff our way out of trouble in those two miles because we will be in a civilian airliner on a scheduled flight . . . off course.'

One long whistle sounded clearly from the ranks of men.

'Ten miles,' Shearer repeated. 'We're going in with the

"stand-off" technique, ten thousand feet up and ten miles off target. The para-wing chutes will get us that far with sixty pounds of equipment. You've all done it before.'

'Not onto a piece of rock in the Arctic Ocean at night!' a voice complained, not softly enough.

'There's always a first time, soldier,' Shearer said, keeping the mood light. 'Any questions?'

'Any moon tonight?' a voice asked, cynically.

Shearer held up a night-vision vizor. 'We'll see enough – and we'll all have a receiver locked onto the leader's tracking beam. If the visibility is good enough we can use the lighthouse beacon as a marker. Now one final thing. We've brought with us a case of special black jumpsuits . . . and they're nothing to do with the fact that this is a night jump.' Shearer paused. 'This mission is totally deniable by the US Government. So we have to go in clean. No IDs, no dog tags, no insignia. I want to see everyone stripped naked before you put on the suits. No one must know who we are – so no one gets captured. We go in, we hold that rock – or we die on it.'

'What about weather, sir?' someone called.

'Met. reports have it good for the time of the drop. The storm that's been running up there will have blown itself out by then.'

'You mentioned radiation, colonel,' a deep, coloured voice spoke from the nearest rank of men. 'I don't see us flying ten miles in all that protective gear.'

'Washington says it got "blowed away", sergeant,' Shearer replied drily with a mock Southern accent. 'No protective clothing.'

'Sounds like they already figured that that's what's going to happen to us – sir!'

Shearer's eyes moved to the black face. He matched the tight, knowing grin.

'What happens when we take the rock, colonel?' a voice bawled from the back breaking the momentary silence.

'We wait for the Marines!' Shearer shouted back, then stepped down amid the following huge, derisory roar. One word which for the Black Berets said it all.

'Outstanding!'

While a USAF ground crew were making final checks on the Icelandair Boeing 727, the Egyptian desert outside Cairo was reverberating with the thunder of giant Lockheed C-5 Galaxy air cargo transports burdened with military vehicles and heavy weapons. Behind these came the smaller C-141 Starlifters, packed with paratroops. Operation Eclipse had begun.

In Cairo, a news blackout on the operation and the speedy preparations leading up to it had been ordered, and the perimeter of the airport and a wider area beyond it were now an armoured ring manned by Egyptian troops.

The Russians, thrown out of Egypt by a pro-Western President, waited impatiently in the Kremlin for intelligence from their wide circle of Egyptian agents. The suddenness of the operation and doubts as to its intentions had forced them to do exactly what the American President had intended. They were looking the wrong way.

All they really knew was that the huge aircraft had been refuelled and turned around, engines rumbling intermittently as they were kept warm, the tight-packed troops still aboard. And every one of the aircraft was pointed toward Mecca.

Rumours flew wildly within the ornate Kremlin walls.

'The United States,' said those who thrived on hysteria, 'has already started World War III.'

3

Simon Howard regained consciousness to the sound of heartbreaking sobbing. He raised his hand to the sudden sting at his cheek and realized that he could only see with one eye. The entire right side of his face felt like a fat, cold snowball.

Tanya Chebrikova drew his hand away, tears streaming from her reddened eyes.

'Sorry 'bout the old feller,' Howard mumbled, tentatively testing the torn flesh of his gums with his tongue. Right, Sergei, he promised silently, recalling the fleeting vision of the bearded figure and the boot striking at his head – got a score to settle with you, mate! 'Why's my face so cold?' he asked, through loosened teeth.

Tanya held up a can of spray anaesthetic and a needle. 'I stitch it. Five stitches, maybe you have a scar – later.'

Howard twisted his mouth, painfully. 'Got plenty of those, sweetheart.' He pushed her out of the way and got up from the bunk, his head swimming momentarily before his balance righted.

'Not good to get up yet,' Tanya objected. 'You have little concussion, I think.'

'You a nurse or something?'

'Nurse – yes.'

'Thanks then – for the face.'

She nodded and her tears began again. Howard began checking the small cabin. 'Won't bring him back, y'know,' he told her. 'We've got more problems than he has now. Whose side are you on in this fuck-up anyway?'

Tanya blushed. Howard glanced at her. 'A good Russian girl like you shouldn't know words like that.'

She shook her head. 'Not Russian. *Deutsch*. German. Mother German, father Russian. But now I am Swiss citizen.'

'I don't need your life story,' Howard grumbled. 'That sodding Commie chess player running the show now, is he?'

She lifted her head, her eyes blazing. 'Tavrin kill my grandfather – I kill him!'

'Not the chess player – the Kraut.' Howard threw up a stiff-armed salute to demonstrate. 'You know, Nazi? Your old boy recognized him from way back – that's why the Kraut gave it to him.'

'*Nazi*, here?'

'That's it. Take a look at this lot.' He handed her the yellowed papers he'd taken from the corpse at the table. 'Come on, you read German, what's it say?'

Tanya sifted slowly through the tattered script, her eyes widening in horror.

'Well?' Howard persisted.

She shook her head. 'Bad, very bad.'

'Read some of it, then!' He sat down beside her, his morbid curiosity completely taking him over.

She sniffed back her tears and concentrated on the writing.

'This man was Nazi Schutz-Staffel – that is, SS. His name is Gross, Otto, he is sergeant.'

'Was,' Howard cut in. 'Right now he's dead. Very.'

She turned more pages, then put her hand to her mouth in horror.

'This the best bit?' Howard asked, eagerly.

'He was – how do you say – buried . . . ?'

'Buried alive, yes. Then?'

'For some time there was food and some water, also some light and heat. They fight – he and his comrades – when all these things are finished . . . then . . . then he and another one they *eat* the ones they have killed. *They eat them!*'

'Yeah,' Howard confirmed. 'Then?'

Tanya shook her head in pity. 'I think now he is mad. His writings . . . they mean nothing.'

'But he did himself in – right?'

'I do not understand this.'

Howard mimed a gun in his mouth. 'Shot himself, blew his head off.'

She turned to the final page. 'Yes. He has tied himself so that he cannot move . . . then he writes he will . . . use the gun. Now he makes some promises for after he is dead. Bad promises, very bad. They are for the man who buried him and also for this island where he must die.'

'That all?'

'He makes one last saying: *Heil Hitler.* Then a very dirty word. He has much hate, this man.'

Howard took back the old papers and pocketed them. '*Had,*' he corrected. 'Right! They got a guard outside that door?'

'Commander Ulyanov he told me he must put one man outside. He told me also you are very dangerous – even if you are very small. I must be careful. But I tell him I am a nurse and I must help you.'

Howard mumbled something obscene, then said: 'Just the one guard? Is he armed? What with? Pistol – rifle?'

'Rifle. I hear metal sound, sharp.'

'Put one up the spout,' Howard muttered.

He looked straight at Tanya. 'You go tell the guard I'm very sick. Tell him *very* sick.'

Her face became wary, then she shook her head.

'You want to live in Russia?' he asked, the warning clear in his voice.

She shook her head again, this time frantically.

'Then do what I tell you and I'll get you out of here.'

'Not possible.'

'Bloody is!'

'How?'

He snatched the yellowed script from his pocket and held them in front of her frightened face. 'Through there! That's how. I've done it already, see!'

Tanya's face blanched. 'No!'

Howard stood up. 'Then go to fucking Russia!' He began examining the hinges on the door.

She got up and moved to him. 'What must I do?' she asked, her voice at once hopeless and fearful.

Howard turned to her, then looked her up and down. She was wearing denims, a shirt and a white overall coat – all obviously borrowed because of the size.

'Take off everything except that coat,' he told her.

'No! I cannot!'

''Course you bloody can. Just take them off.'

'But . . . .'

'For Christ's sake!' he exclaimed, and returned to his examination of the door hinges while patting his pockets in a vain search for his knife. Behind him, he could hear the crackling as her fingers worked on the buttons of the starched coat.

'All of it,' he said without turning. 'The lot.'

Her body was firm and almost boyish; she stood with the shirt clasped to her front. He turned and tugged it away and her face turned deep red as she tried vainly to cover her nakedness.

'Not a lot,' Howard observed, 'but it'll have to do.' He

handed her the white coat. 'Go on, put it on. Don't just stand there!'

Tanya frantically threw the garment on, her fingers scrabbling at the stiff material.

Howard sighed. 'Not *all* the buttons, love. Use your brains.'

'Why?' she pleaded, ashamed.

'Jesus! You tell the guard I'm sick. Get him to take a look at me, close – then you undo some more buttons and give him an eyeful. Got it? Simple enough?' Then I'll kill him, he thought.

'He must look at my body?'

'He'd bloody better – otherwise we'll all be down for the Siberian trip.' He climbed back into the lower bunk and drew the covers to his chin, his lethal hands passive, outside the blankets.

The sailor guarding the small cabin sat on a chair, tilted back against the wall, a foul-smelling cigarette between his lips and a lightweight automatic rifle across his thighs.

He heard Tanya call out in Russian and with a sullen frown crushed the cigarette out on the floor, then unlocked the door cautiously. She spoke rapidly, pointing desperately at Howard. The sailor made a face which displayed his lack of concern, then made to lock the door. As a last resort Tanya threated him with Tavrin and, reluctantly, he came inside and bent over the comatose figure on the bunk.

Howard smelt the coarse tobacco on the man's breath as he bent over him. Tanya, standing behind, her heart thudding like a gloved fist at her breast, undid more buttons, then leaned over to look at Howard. The coat gaped open but she kept her eyes on Howard as if unaware.

The Russian's eyes moved slyly to her exposed body. It was the last thing he ever saw. One of Howard's hands stiffened as the thumb was raised to harden the edge, then struck at the lowered throat. Then in the same explosive movement, he snatched at the man's head and jerked it sideways once.

Tanya heard the crack and saw the sailor's head flop

over backwards, the base of the skull resting on his severed spine. She stood, frozen with shock, her stomach beginning to heave. Howard leaped from the bunk and stowed the body under the blankets, then like an animal sensed the terror behind him. Turning, he saw Tanya's mouth and throat working and he knew she was one breath away from screaming. He hit her hard with a two-knuckle punch above the temple.

Howard caught her, lifted her easily onto the top bunk, and drew the blanket to her chin.

'Sorry, sweetheart,' he murmured, then grabbed the automatic rifle and checked the action of the unfamiliar weapon. Satisfied, he dug into the Russian's clothes until he found what he was looking for – a clasp knife. He breathed deeply three times to steady himself, then let himself out into the corridor.

He knew he was on Level One and that the lifts to the surface would certainly be heavily guarded. No-go that way, he decided: too risky. So it *had* to be through the old ventilation shaft. He had a choice: Jordan's office or the kitchen where he had emerged from Level Two. Kitchen first, he decided. It's closer.

He padded down the corridor, the butt of the rifle tucked into his ribs, ready, and the hefty clasp knife in his right hand held forward and low; his thumb on top, along the haft.

Complete silence, he told himself. Kill them without a sound or you'll end up fighting a running battle along the corridors and, sooner or later, your back will finish up against the wall. Then they'll cut you down in their own time. *No chance!* He wasn't going to finish up like a scurrying rat in the sewers. All right, knife first and the gun as the last resort.

He heard footsteps approaching, then voices. He tried the door nearest to him. Locked. Moving very fast now, he tried the next. It opened. He went in, snapped on the light and checked both bunks. Empty. The voices were nearer now. He tossed the rifle onto the top bunk, punched the light switch off and eased the door open a fraction.

'I want to check on Tanya,' he heard Jemma Elliot say.

'It's cruel to leave her to look after an injured man when she's so distraught. How can you go along with this?'

'You're wasting your time,' Jordan answered. 'He won't disobey Tavrin's orders.'

Ulyanov said: 'I have no choice. Tavrin controls all of us.'

Howard grinned evilly in the darkness. He let Jordan and Jemma Elliot pass, then threw an arm lock around Ulyanov's bearded throat, dragging him back and down to his own height. The knife flashed upward and settled in the beard; a bead of scarlet appeared on the blade, then trickled down it.

'Move,' Howard warned, 'and you get the lot.' He could feel Ulyanov's Adam's apple jerk under his forearm and applied the hold harder. 'The Kraut's gun,' he ordered, and Ulyanov passed back the silenced Walther. Howard tightened the hold again as his fingers grasped the weapon.

Jordan and Jemma Elliot stood hesitantly before the two locked figures.

'How did you get out?' Jordan exclaimed.

'Shut up!' Howard hissed.

'He's killed the guard,' said Jemma.

'You'd better believe it!' Howard growled and dragged Ulyanov back into the empty cabin. Jordan grabbed Jemma's arm and moved after him.

Howard had forced Ulyanov to the floor and was sitting on the lower bunk himself, the lock still applied and the knife drawing more blood.

'For God's sake!' Jordan said. 'You'll kill him.'

Howard let the silver Walther rest against his broken face. 'He bloody near killed me, didn't he? Doc, you make me puke! You think old Sergei gives two fucks about what happens to you? You people have had it if you don't get out of here.' He tightened his grip. Ulyanov's eyes bulged; his face darkened.

'He can't breathe!' Jemma cried.

Howard relaxed the pressure fractionally. 'Can't have that, can we? Got a use for old Sergei.'

'What are you planning?' Jordan asked.

'Planning? I'm not planning any bloody thing. I'm just

going to get off this rock before they throw me off – head first.'

'They've got no use for you – Tavrin told us that.'

Howard stuck out a leg. 'Pull that one too, Doc. I'll lay you six-to-one that when all you geniuses have been taken off, the people the chess player's got "no use for" will get a nice cold deep-six without the option. You go help the Ivans, mate. I'm doing my own thing.'

'You're crazy!' Jordan exclaimed. 'Where do you think you can go? This is the *Arctic Circle*!'

Howard smirked. 'Old Sergei got here in an open boat, didn't he? If he can do it, so can I. His boat's down by the jetty – I checked it out. There's a small island south of here – got stores on it, radio too. Saw it from the chopper. I'll make for that.'

'That's miles away,' said Jordan. 'You won't survive out there.'

'I won't survive down here,' said Howard flatly. 'I'm not going to sit on my ass waiting for the chop. I do it my way, Doc.'

'He's right, Matt!' Jemma said quickly. Then to Howard: 'Take me with you.' She saw the reluctance in his eyes. 'I helped *you*!' she exclaimed.

Howard sucked his teeth. 'OK – but you slow me down and I'll leave you. Got it?'

'Matt,' Jemma looked up. 'Come with us.'

'Not a chance!' Howard objected, harshly. 'He's too bloody big.'

'I don't understand?' said Jemma.

'You will.'

Jordan shook his head. 'I couldn't desert all my people. They took the risk before, I can't desert them now.'

'Terrific,' Howard muttered. 'Enjoy the Lubyanka, Doc.'

'You're an evil son-of-a-bitch,' said Jordan.

'I'm a realist,' Howard snapped.

Ulyanov had slipped into unconsciousness. Howard relaxed his hold again and watched the dark bearded face with interest.

'Is he dead?' Jemma gasped.

'Kipping,' answered Howard. 'Come on, Sergei, rise and shine.'

Jemma turned away in disgust. Jordan smiled wryly at her. 'Just the kind of man you need,' he said.

Howard grinned. 'Had, Doc. *Had*.'

Jemma's face coloured and she turned away – too quickly.

Jordan shrugged but his eyes gave away his hurt. 'How are you going to get out?' he asked. 'Through the same shaft you used to get in?'

'Why not?'

'You won't make it. There's a guard on my office.'

'Then I'll use the other hole.'

'Where?'

'In the kitchen.'

Jordan nodded. 'If you get to the surface, there's one thing you can do to help the rest of us.'

Howard looked at the big American warily. 'Oh yeah? What's that?'

'Washington have almost certainly got satellite surveillance on this island. Stracey was supposed to have reported in via our own satellite link yesterday. By now they'll be wondering why he hasn't.'

'So?'

'If they are watching us, we need to let them know that something is wrong here.'

'No way, Doc. No flares, no signals. I'm leaving with no fuss and I don't want that team out there gunning me down in a bleeding rubber boat. Sorry.'

'No. No flares – that would give you away completely. But if you get the chance, knock out the light – silently.' Jordan's eyes dropped to the silver Walther.

'What light?'

'The lighthouse, you idiot.' Jemma snapped.

Howard held her arm and she winced, though he had not seemed to apply any force. 'Easy, Doc,' he warned. 'I told her before, she's got an ugly mouth.'

Jordan's bunched fists uncurled as he brought both his fury and his jealousy under control. 'Will you do it?' he asked. 'Even if it's only for a few seconds. Just something to cast doubt in the watchers' minds. With no noise the guards up there might think the bulb blew.'

'I'll see,' Howard replied non-committally.

'It might be our only chance.'

'I said I'll see – don't push it.'

Ulyanov groaned, coming around. 'Come on, Sergei,' said Howard. 'On your feet.' He pushed the Russian away from him.

Ulyanov dragged himself upright, then crouched, glaring at the little dark figure before him – but the silenced gun was already pointing at his stomach.

'We're all going for a walk,' said Howard. He pointed at Jordan. 'You go in front with her and I'll stroll with old Sergei. One thing, Serg, I'm going to have this thing stuck in your side all the way. Now it's not far, just up the corridor and right, but if we meet any of your mates and you tip the wink, it's over. Got it?' He ejected the magazine from the automatic rifle, then pushed the cartridges out and replaced it. Finally he ejected the single round from the breech with a thin smile in Ulyanov's direction, then pushed the weapon at his chest. 'Hold that like you mean it,' Howard warned.

The corridor was deserted and they made their way to the kitchen without incident. Inside, Howard ordered Ulyanov to lean forward against the wall, then kicked the Russian's legs apart. Viciously, he cracked the butt of the rifle across the back of his head. Ulyanov collapsed.

Howard dumped the gun into a rubbish can and leaped onto the table. 'This one,' he said, prising one tile loose.

'I can't get in there!' Jemma croaked.

'Then don't,' Howard answered.

'She's claustrophobic,' Jordan explained.

'Tough shit,' Howard said. 'It's tight, but she'll make it if she keeps breathing in.' He leered at her breasts.

'I'll be all right,' Jemma said, shakily.

'I go first,' Howard warned. 'I'm not getting stuck behind you if you chicken out.' He pulled himself up smoothly into the aperture, then lay prone in the metallic tube. Reaching out into the darkness, his hand closed around the rubber-cased torch he had left when he exited the first time.

He backed up, crossing the open gap, then looked down to see Jemma facing Jordan, silently.

'Come on!' Howard snapped. 'I'm not hanging around. Doc, you heave her up when I move off, then shove that tile back into place. All right?'

Jordan nodded. 'Try for the light,' he urged.

'Maybe,' said Howard as his body crossed over the gap, then he was gone with a booming, shuffling sound.

'Get going,' said Jordan. 'That little swine won't wait. And try and persuade him to knock out that light in the tower. I love you.'

She looked at the ceiling and breathed in sharply, bracing herself. 'I can't stay,' she said. 'I'm sorry. Please lift me up.'

Ulyanov regained consciousness, dazed and nauseous from Howard's cruel blow. Immediately his mouth filled with saliva and he vomited, hunched over on his hands and knees. He forced himself to his feet and ducked his head under the tap in the sink. He turned around, his hair and beard streaming water.

Jordan tossed him a towel.

'That gun is empty, Doctor,' Ulyanov said thickly.

'I went back and refilled the magazine while you were unconscious,' Jordan replied.

Ulyanov rubbed his face and hair, gently dabbing at the split skin at the rear of his scalp. 'So?' he inquired. 'We wait here until Tavrin tells them – go find Ulyanov; then maybe you get yourself shot?'

'I'm not Howard,' said Jordan. 'I live by my brains – not blind violence.'

'Yet you let him take your woman?'

'He didn't take her – she went willingly.'

Ulyanov somehow found this shaming for he looked away, saying nothing. 'So what do your brains tell you to do?' he asked at last.

Jordan answered with a question: 'You've been promised a pardon for yourself and your men – and the safe return of your daughter?'

Ulyanov sighed. 'That I have been promised. But who knows what I will get?'

'If I told you that I could get you as much as Tavrin has promised – if you help me regain control of this station – what would you say?'

'I would say, Doctor, that you have been locked under the ground too long.'

'I'm serious.'

'So am I, Doctor.'

Jordan said: 'The one weak link in Tavrin's plan is that at all times he must have everyone who is involved completely under his control. Do you accept that?'

Ulyanov dabbed at his scalp, not bothering to answer the obvious.

Jordan continued: 'Basically he's been playing a game in which he has control of *both* sides. Us and you. Every move he has made has been easy till now because he knew exactly how such moves might be countered.'

Ulyanov chuckled. 'Doctor, you wish to take on the mind of the greatest chess strategist of all time?'

'He's dealing with human beings here, not inanimate objects.'

'Yes, and we have been performing tricks for him like Pavlov's dogs.'

'Not all of us. Howard is completely uncontrollable.'

'He is a killer. I have seen his face many times on many men. What difference can this killer make to Tavrin?'

'Probably none at all. But it proves my point. When one person didn't follow the predicted pattern, things began to go wrong. Tavrin's plan was to get us to offer, willingly, the information on the device we have developed here. If we had done that there could be no repercussions. No international incident could have resulted. The Soviet Union would have been given the Whitefire technology because we would have believed it to be useless under the circumstances Tavrin had fabricated. Chebrikov would have absorbed all the technology – he couldn't have helped it. Then of course your interrogators would have got it all out of him. Howard's action – also Weissleder's – changed that instantly. Now Tavrin has had to resort to force – and theft.'

Ulyanov protested. 'Chebrikov would never have divulged anything he learned to the Kremlin. He would have preferred to die under torture. He has withstood torture before.'

'Why do you think the girl was brought along?'

Ulyanov gazed steadily at the big American as though aware of him for the first time. 'You have much muscle, Doctor – but also you have much brain.'

'Commander, listen to me. I think I know a way in which we can apply our own leverage. It will mean a great sacrifice for my own country, but perhaps in the long term it may be a better solution all round. To do this I need to put one piece into play which would be impossible for the Grandmaster to control. His game is all to do with controlling the opposing sides – you agree?'

'Of course.'

'So, if one piece suddenly begins making moves for *both* sides the game begins to disintegrate.'

A half-smile touched Ulyanov's lips, and the piratical gleam which had disappeared from his eyes returned for a brief second. Then it faded. 'You are talking of me, of course. But I am one man. If the two of us tried to take over this place there would be considerable bloodshed – and I would never see my daughter again.'

'Ulyanov, forget violence! I am still talking about using our brains. All you must do is be ready to back me up when I decide to make my move.'

'But what can *you* do that will guarantee I get my daughter back – and live to keep her?'

Jordan told him.

When he had finished Ulyanov's eyes were alight again, but the cleft of a frown creased the skin between the black bushes of his eyebrows. 'It is a gamble, Doctor – a very big gamble. Have you played for so much before?'

'Never,' Jordan confessed. 'But then I've never had so much in my hand before.'

Ulyanov stuck out his gnarled palm. 'Give me the weapon,' he said.

Jordan passed it over.

Ulyanov worked the breech. 'Doctor,' he said slowly. 'You must never hold a gun on a man without first putting one round into the breech.'

'I'll remember next time,' Jordan said.

Jemma Elliot thought the journey along the old, disused ventilation shaft was a nightmare she would never wake from.

At times she felt that the metal walls were closing in on her, crushing the life from her body; at others she believed that she was within an endless coffin from which there was no escape. And when they had to enter the narrow, vertical, six-feet-deep connecting well between the two levels she almost screamed aloud, because she could see no way of making herself small enough to get back into the narrow horizontal shaft at her feet. She had stood, paralysed, the iron walls pressing against her all around, her arms stretched above her as Howard had directed. And if he had not kicked brutally at her ankles, forcing her to her knees, she would have stayed in that position until she had starved to death, and gone utterly insane first.

Sobbing hopelessly, she followed on in the darkness behind him, her only light an occasional glimpse of the beam from his torch. She kept so close to him, sometimes clutching desperately at his boots, that he lashed out angrily at her. She knew that her face and shoulders would be covered by bruises, but it was worth the suffering just to have physical contact with his body.

Finally, just when she was giving up all hope, an awful stench hit her. 'What's that smell?' she whimpered behind him.

'Not me,' Howard sniggered, still crawling forward.

Suddenly, he was gone. 'Simon!' she cried out.

'Shut up!' he spat angrily from somewhere, then, through an opened panel, she saw the dull glow of his torch.

The odour now was dreadful; she could not imagine anything that might smell so bad. She felt the gorge rising in her throat and held her breath to stop herself throwing up over her hands.

'Bleedin' come down!' Howard hissed from the darkness below. 'Your legs first for chrissake! That's it.'

She hung, dangling, in mid-air, her sweater snagging on the coarse edges of the metal tube. She lowered herself gingerly, then dropped, baring her breasts; but she did not care any more. She was out of the shaft and that was all that mattered in the entire world.

Howard tugged her sweater down. 'Not now, love,' he said, then turned away. 'Stay there. Don't move.'

The intense grave-like chill of the place seeped into her and she began shivering uncontrollably. Howard came back with one of the large fluorescent lamps he had left behind originally and switched it on.

She screamed piercingly.

The rotted corpse of SS Sergeant Otto Gross sat strapped to his chair beside her, his mouth wide to receive the full blast from the Schmeisser and the back of his skull blown away. Strands of hair still hung from the shattered skull and wisps of a beard sprouted where shrivelled remnants of skin still remained. On the table the huge bones seemed like the dreadful remnants of a meal laid for some terrible giant.

Howard slapped her hard three times before she stopped screaming. 'Oh God!' she gasped. 'What is it?'

'Friend of mine,' Howard said lightly. 'Gross, Otto – late of the SS. Very late!' He laughed, a little madly.

'What ate those bones?'

Howard jerked a thumb at the corpse.

'But what *are* they?'

He slapped his thigh.

'Oh Jesus, no!'

'You've got it.'

'I think I want to be sick.'

'OK, but do it in the corner. Old Otto doesn't want his dinner ruined – do you, Otto?' Howard patted the jagged top of the skull, then peered inside it. 'Anyone in there?' he asked, cackling stupidly.

'You're sick! *Sick!*' Jemma shouted, by now a little mad herself.

'Worse to come,' said Howard and grabbed her arm. 'Let's go.'

'I'm freezing,' she complained.

'Be warm soon, there's furs in one of the huts up top. Hang on a minute, I left my anorak down here before. Almost forgot. We came down in the wrong room. You'd have missed old Gross, Otto, if we'd come out where I went in.'

'Wait! There's no way I'm staying in here alone with that!'

'Better close your eyes then – like I said, there's worse to come.'

'Worse? What could be *worse* than that! What is this place for God's sake? It's like a hole in Hell.'

'This is where it started – that thing you geniuses have been working on. 'Cept everyone in here got the chop – like all those stupid bastards back there who believe in fairy stories will. Old Otto was one of the lads who did the chopping, then got stitched up by your mate Weissleder. Stitched up for good an' all. I'll tell you the rest in the boat. It'll keep you going for hours.'

He found the jacket and gave it to her. 'Now when we go out there,' he warned, 'you're really going to see something. Better than Madame Tussaud's this place.'

'Shut up! I'm not going to look, you can guide me.'

'Suit yourself, you don't know what you're missing. Won't see another sight like this for as long as you live.'

'You *are* sick.'

Smiling, Howard led her through the terrible chamber of death, holding the tube light in one hand, the torch in the other, her arm grasping his frantically. Finally, with Jemma's eyes still tightly shut, they reached the circular gas lock, then the low escape tunnel.

'All clear,' Howard announced. 'Just this tunnel, then we're out.'

At the end of the tunnel Howard stopped dead. 'Not a word,' he ordered. 'Not a fuckin' sound.' He switched off both lights.

'What's wrong?' she asked clutching him.

'Can't you smell it?'

'Smell what? I'll never be able to smell anything again after that place.'

'Cigarette, same as the guard smoked outside my room. There's a bleedin' Ivan out there.'

'Oh Christ,' Jemma wailed in the darkness. 'I can't go back in there. I can't!'

4

The Icelandair Boeing 727 plunged into the night, its main cabin dimly lit like any commercial airliner on a night flight.

Colonel Shearer made his way down the aisle, glancing down occasionally at the dye-smeared faces of his men. His own face, still white, caught the eye of a black NCO.

'Hey, colonel,' the man said, rubbing a pink palm against his cheek. 'You want to trade skins?'

Shearer smiled. 'I'll be as black as you, Thomson, by the time we make the leap.' He moved forward to the flight deck and, inside, surveyed the mass of glowing instruments over the shoulders of the volunteer USAF flight crew.

'Step aboard,' said the pilot in the left-hand seat, a baby-faced Air Force captain.

'Just watch the road, captain,' Shearer quipped, then turned to the flight engineer beside him. 'Getting anything on the radio?'

'Nothing, sir.'

Shearer faced forward. 'How long, captain?'

The pilot's shoulders lifted. 'If they're going to start squawking they should be doing it by now.'

Shearer frowned and began applying blacking to his hard, bony face, the deep drone of the three tail jets like the darker moments of a jungle fever which still struck at him. He opened the flight deck door and passed down an order; on each side of the aisle bulky figures stirred and loomed up over the high-backed seats, pulling on their black helmets and night vizors.

The flight engineer reached back, tapped Shearer's leg, then pointed at his headphones urgently.

The Captain turned around and said: 'Squawk!' Then he switched on his microphone. 'This is Icelandair Flight 324 from Reykjavik to Oslo. We are experiencing instrument malfunction and are off course. Please advise our present position?' He grinned widely, making chicken-like movements with his elbows, then turned away, a frown forming across his forehead. 'Yes, I understand radiation hazard . . . but we are off course . . . please advise our present position.' He reached forward and shifted the frequency control slightly. 'I am losing you, Murmansk . . . .' He turned, all humour gone. 'Get the hell out, colonel. We're not welcome any more.'

'How close are we?' Shearer asked calmly.

'Eleven miles and closing, but I have to turn now or they'll put those MIGs up. You've got thirty seconds before I depressurize.'

Shearer ran down the aisle towards the rear exit, catching the helmet the jump master threw at him. 'It's a go!' he yelled at the steel-helmeted men, their night vizors and oxygen tubes giving them a terrifying aspect.

'Depressurizing in ten seconds,' the captain warned through the tannoy.

His countdown was lost in the hiss of escaping air and, like rows of obscene tapeworms, the 727's emergency oxygen masks fell out of their overhead compartments. Behind Shearer, the jump master worked the release mechanism on the aircraft's rear exit and the door fell outward, then hung, its steps leading down into a black void.

The 727 started bucking, its smooth airstream broken by the protruding steps, and Shearer thought he heard the captain's voice shout 'Go!' But the blast of the three tail jets and the roar of the slipstream were deafening even with the helmet's ear protectors.

D. B. Cooper was a lunatic! he thought wildly, hauling himself down the hanging gangway, fighting all the way. At the last step he fell into a searing blast of air, tumbling over and over, then suddenly the world was quiet once more – even serene – and the oblong canopy of his para-wing was there, reassuringly, above him.

His descent was gentle, the brittle sharpness of the Arctic night sky above him and the leaden glint of the ocean far below as he skimmed along at an angle almost parallel to it.

At least we've got the altitude, he thought with relief, and forced his head around between the webbing to see his men behind him, floating as if on some ethereal ladder – fifty-one black angels under dark wings. He smiled at his own imagery.

Now he could feel his speed building – without wind he knew it could reach 30 miles per hour on a downward angle of four-in-one. So we've got plenty of time to think about meeting our Maker if we miss the island. He pushed the thought away and checked his heading on his wrist compass.

The swinging arc of the beacon light was mesmerizing and he tore his eyes away. He pulled down the night vizor, searching the ocean, and there in the artificial green day he saw two of the Primorye-class intelligence ships; he could even make out the whirling scanners on the closest of the two.

He checked his watch: eleven minutes gone. Not long now before the damn rock socks me in the butt! He raised the vizor again, preferring to see the stars as they really were.

In that split second – so unexpectedly that he could not believe his own eyes – the beacon light died.

He blinked and looked again, checking first the horizon and then his wrist compass. No change. They were on exactly the same course as before. The light had definitely gone out – or worse – had been switched off. Which meant they were blown!

He rammed the vizor back over his face and saw the jagged island plumb in front of him. All right, they would have to go in on the tracking beam alone – no problem – they had done that before. The tracking unit strapped to his chest would pass the warning to the display dial by his wrist compass if he strayed from a direct head-on path to the landmass. Behind him, every man was locked onto his leader's signal; it was a simple guidance device, and foolproof, if no one panicked.

A sudden downdraught of wind caught him, and he cursed the loss of height but guided the para-wing on course again, waiting for the sudden – and always unexpected – upward rush of the ground in the last moments of descent.

Then, the cliff was there in front of him and he was scrambling up his harness, his legs curled, praying to any God who could hear him for those last few desperate inches of height.

The Russian guarding the surface of the escape tunnel heard the deep hum of the 727, then it faded. For a moment he considered informing the Grandmaster that something might have penetrated the blockade but, sleepy from the cold and awed by the universe above, he drew the hood of his parka closer around his face and drew deeply on his cigarette.

Simon Howard eased the steel door open.

At first he did not see the Russian, but a cough gave the man's position away. Howard moved forward, silent as a shadow.

The man's automatic rifle lay at his feet. Howard planted his boot firmly on the butt as the Russian, realizing the danger, grasped for it, looking upwards into the dark elfin face. A hand lifted and struck.

Howard pushed the body off the rifle and picked up the weapon. 'Come on!' he whispered harshly. He grabbed Jemma Elliot's arm and virtually dragged her over the rocks toward the tower. He pulled up suddenly.

The man guarding the lighthouse came out and stood legs apart, staring up into the night sky.

'An aircraft!' Jemma whispered and Howard raised his eyebrows with mock surprise. She tugged at him. 'If you can knock out the light now maybe the plane will report it?'

'Too far away.'

'Try!'

Howard killed the Russian with two silent shots, then squeezed four more at the revolving beacon.

Jemma ducked involuntarily as the bulbs exploded, then felt iron-hard fingers grasp her wrist and pull her toward the cliff edge. 'Satisfied?' Howard muttered.

They scrambled onto a mossy ledge and Howard said: 'What's that?'

Straining her ears, Jemma heard an eerie sound – like a flock of huge birds slowly flapping their wings – and the stars were blotted out.

Colonel Shearer landed badly, his coccyx striking the rising promontory of rock as he lifted his legs over it.

Suppressing a cry of agony, he crashed to the ground, clasping a hand to the base of his spine and tangling himself in the webbing as the para-wing dragged him away from the cliff edge.

Struggling to free himself, he watched the dark, sinister shapes of his men gliding in – some, like himself, striking rock projections and others breaking rapidly into a short run, compensating for their approach speed before releasing their para-wings. Through his pain, he heard a number of solid thumps and knew they were some of his men hitting the sheer cliff face head-on. They had 'flown' well over the safe limit and any of the men caught badly by down-draughts had no hope.

Clenching his teeth, Shearer punched the quick release and the para-wing flowed over the rocks toward the cliff edge, then disappeared.

Simon Howard had almost had his head kicked off by Shearer's jump boots as the Black Beret colonel shot overhead. He clamped a hand over Jemma Elliot's mouth, then heard the first sickening *crunch* below their ledge. He counted four more parachutists who did not make it and only one had made a sound – and that was no more than a grunt, barely audible from the ledge. Then the dark shapes passing overhead ceased and only the sharp rush of the icy wind came to his straining ears. He removed his hand from Jemma's mouth.

'What – ?' she exclaimed, but he stifled her again.

'Paras,' he whispered. 'Don't know whose. Forty . . . maybe more. Some of the buggers went clean into the cliff. They were really shifting!'

'But where did they come from?'

'Must have been that plane we heard – but shit – that was miles away. Must have been free-falling from something higher up.'

'What are we going to do now?' she whispered frantically.

'Same as before – nothing's changed. Could be more Ivans for all we know. You want to find out? Do it on your own.'

She shook her head.

'Right, *move*. There's a path to the right which leads down to where the Ivans beached their boat the first time – and there isn't anywhere else the second team could have landed. Come on!'

The silence from above was eerie as they clambered downwards. Suddenly Jemma let out a gasp of pain.

'What's wrong?' Howard asked, impatiently.

'I've hit my shin on something.'

'Only the railing, you'll live.'

'I'm bleeding,' she said, holding a blood-smeared palm close to his face.

Howard bent to her leg, cursing, then his hand touched the railing and came away dark and sticky. 'Not you. One of the paras must have bounced off here after he hit.'

'Oh God! What are we going to find at the bottom?' She stared at him, sickly.

'Yeah,' Howard said and lifted her over the rusted railing.

At the bottom there were three inflatables, unguarded. In one lay the splayed body of one of the Black Berets, his vizor smashed, his face obliterated and almost every bone in his body broken by the impact and the fall. Howard turned him over, took one look at what was left of his face and pushed Jemma away. 'You don't want to see this,' he said.

She stood a few feet off, clutching herself around the

shoulders. '*Was* he a Russian?' she asked, her voice shaking, and not only from the cold.

'He could have been a bleedin' Martian.'

'What about his uniform?'

Howard shrugged and unzipped the front of the blood-stained combat jacket. His fingers sank into soft pliable flesh where ribs should have been. 'No dog tags, no badges,' he said, moving away. 'Come on, let's get going.' He tugged a boat down off the rocks.

'Where are we going?' she asked, looking at the ominous swell of the sea with apprehension. 'Which direction?'

The flat crack of an explosion came from the clifftop as Howard pushed her into the dinghy, jumping in himself as it gained bouyancy. 'Paddle,' he ordered. 'Paddle!'

Jemma shouted: 'I'm going back!' and jumped over the side, scrambling madly for the jetty, her breath rasping in shock from the freezing water.

'Stupid bloody woman!' she heard him call as he rowed away from the island. Then, shivering violently, she raced crazily back up the cliff path toward Whitefire One.

Two Black Berets formed a cradle with their arms, lifted Shearer and dashed across the rock plateau toward the darkened tower as the first charge blew on the sealed doors of the entrance to the lift shaft.

'OK, check it out,' he commanded as more dark figures broke from cover and made for the tower. 'Lay me down, damn it! Check that charge.'

He could see the top of the tower silhouetted against the stars, then heard the crunch of broken glass. The man remaining with him raised his silenced Ingram machine pistol as three figures came into view. 'Ours,' said Shearer, pushing the fat barrel of the weapon down.

The pain at the base of his spine was growing and he wondered how much damage had been done. He closed his eyes for a moment, then heard a voice speaking as if a mile away, yet inside his head.

'Colonel?'

He felt a light slap on his face and opened his eyes.

'You passed out, sir,' said the same concerned voice, and

Shearer recognized the black face of Sergeant Thomson, the NCO he had joked with on the plane.

'Hell!' Shearer swore.

Thomson pulled another man down beside Shearer. 'I got the medic here, colonel.'

The medic began probing gently at the base of Shearer's spine. 'How d'your legs feel, sir?' he asked, his face grave. 'Any numbness? Loss of sensation?'

'Forget all that,' Shearer snapped. 'Give me a shot.'

The medic frowned. 'You shouldn't be moved, sir.'

'The morphine,' Shearer demanded. 'And just enough, son – if I fall asleep you're in trouble.'

'It's your ass – sir.'

'That's right. It's *my* ass.'

The medic plunged the needle in, then turned to Thomson. 'Any more and he'll get drowsy.'

'Don't tell *him*,' Shearer growled. 'Tell *me* – I'm still here.'

'Yessir, but these guys got to carry you.'

The drug worked fast and Shearer dragged himself upright. 'Give me your arm, Sergeant. What about the tower?'

Thomson shook his head. 'Negative, it's armoured. The lieutenant's going to take another crack at it.'

'Let's take a look,' Shearer said, and hobbled off toward the tower.

The medic shrugged at the black face. 'He's your problem now.'

As Shearer approached the lighthouse a rangy figure came down the steps. 'Tower secured, colonel. We found one man shot dead. Soviet Navy. Right here, on the steps. Two rounds. None of us did it.'

'OK, so we know they're here. Now let's get that door down, lieutenant.'

They entered the lighthouse, then descended to the basement. Shearer whistled softly as the lieutenant switched on his torch. The surface of the door was blackened and scarred by the blast but was not otherwise damaged. He placed his fingertips near the metal, feeling the heat.

'Titanium armour,' the lieutenant said, then a gentle whirring sound caught their attention and they turned just as the closed-circuit TV camera came to rest on their blackened faces. Lights snapped on all around them.

Commander Ulyanov and Tavrin were talking together on Level Two when the blast triggered the alarm system. Jordan, working at the master console, oddly calm, stood up instantly.

'What is happening, Doctor?' Tavrin shouted over the blare.

'Emergency alarm – something must have triggered it.'

'Can you shut down that noise?' Tavrin asked sharply.

'Naturally.' Jordan moved to a red box on the wall, flipped up the glass cover and pressed a button.

Tavrin called over one of his men. 'Into the lift, Doctor. Let us find out what has occurred. How secure is the entrance?'

'Totally. The only way you can get in is by trickery,' Jordan replied coldly. 'You can't cut through the doors – and explosives will just be deflected.'

'What about the masonry?'

'No. The entire shaft is lined with titanium armour.'

They exited on Level One and made for the crowded recreation area. There Tavrin gave an order and the Russian guards began forming their captives into four separate groups.

'Observe how your people are being separated,' Tavrin said to Jordan. 'Now the communications room, please.' He led the way himself, as if he had spent months in the underground complex instead of hours.

Inside, Tavrin said: 'The surface cameras, please.'

Simpson glanced at Jordan.

'Do it,' Jordan ordered. 'Try the tower first.'

Simpson pressed buttons. 'The tower,' he said, flatly.

Two blackened faces stared out at them from the TV monitor. Tavrin's face did not flicker. Ulyanov shot a glance at Jordan.

'I wish to speak with them,' said Tavrin.

Simpson reached for a button, but the Grandmaster reached forward and stayed his hand. 'One moment,' he said and turned to face Jordan. 'Doctor, this is the situation. As you have seen, the personnel of this base are now separated into five groups, four on this level and one below on Level Two. With automatic weapons each group can be killed within seconds. Now, we take this in stages, and each mistake you make will cost the lives of one group. Is that understood?'

'It's understood.'

'Very well. Establish the identity of those men up there. For the moment, nothing more.' Tavrin released Simpson's hand.

A speaker crackled to life in the basement of the tower.

'Identify yourselves, please,' Jordan's voice said.

Colonel Shearer looked straight into the camera, ignoring the loudspeaker.

'We are a mercenary unit engaged by the INTERSAT Corporation,' Shearer lied calmly, using the prepared cover story in his orders. 'This installation has been out of contact with the Corporation's satellite network – we are here to establish why.'

There was a pause, then Jordan said: 'Why have you come armed? Why didn't the Corporation send the helicopter with technicians?'

Shearer felt his pain returning – and his patience ebbing.

'We believe you are being held under duress. May I speak with Sir Henry Ledden or Dr Matthew Jordan?'

'I am Jordan.'

Shearer sighed. 'All right, Doctor. My men have found a dead Russian sailor up here. We thought perhaps a terrorist group were attempting to extort a ransom from INTERSAT. Why the Russian?'

There was a long silence, then Tavrin spoke: 'The work that has been carried out on this island has constituted an aggressive act against the Peoples of the Soviet Union. A unit of the Soviet Navy is confiscating all material considered to be a danger to our national security. This island is within Soviet waters.'

Shearer shook his head firmly. 'Soviet coastal limits end miles *thataway*!' He stabbed a thumb over his shoulder. 'Now let's have this door open or I'll blow it off.'

Jordan cut in fast. 'You can't be employed by INTER-SAT – the first thing you would have been told is not to endanger the tower. Are you American troops? I *am* Dr Matthew Jordan and I am the head of this project. I must have this information.'

Damn him! thought Shearer. He's asking that question for *himself* – I know it. What the hell is he trying to pull?

He said: 'I repeat, I am a colonel in command of a mercen . . .'

'Colonel,' Jordan interrupted. 'It is imperative that I know if you are sent here by the United States Government. Many lives hang on your answer – please believe what I say.'

Shearer hesitated. What would be the consequences if he disobeyed the President's order to maintain the secrecy of their identity? Dare he risk the truth? Dare he risk lives? The element of surprise was gone and he saw little hope of blowing their way in through the titanium armour. And he was tired. God! he was tired. Then, Jordan took the decision away from him.

'Colonel,' Jordan said. 'You are here because a man named Ed Stracey who is employed by the Institute of Strategic Studies failed to report back to Washington yesterday on our satellite link. My guess is you are a Special Forces unit. An American Special Forces unit.'

Shearer's face was stony.

Jordan said: 'I know I am right, colonel. So, I must tell you that you are on neutral ground here and are as much in violation of our rights as are the Russians. I order you to do nothing.'

'I cannot do that, Doctor.'

'You must. For everyone's sake you must. Perhaps even for the sake of the world.'

He's crazy, Shearer thought. Clean crazy. 'Jordan,' he said harshly. 'I don't know what's going on here but I'll tell you this: this operation is on a timescale that can't be altered. There are things happening that I can't stop. I'm going to give those Russians down there thirty minutes before this escalates – after that everyone takes their chances. If you and your people are being held hostage –

that's tough – my orders are clear, right through to the end.'

'Yes,' said Jordan sombrely. 'I thought that might be the case. In thirty minutes I might be able to achieve something – if only a decision.'

The speaker clicked off.

Sergeant Thomson stood on the circular staircase, out of camera shot. He curled a pink palm at Shearer, who moved to him.

'Got one of 'em,' Thomson murmured. 'A woman. Almost hysterical. American. She's in one of the huts outside. You better talk with her, colonel – she can open this place up for us!'

Shearer's eyes brightened. 'Let's go,' he breathed, then swayed, the lower half of his body growing more numb by the minute.

'Sergeant,' he said. 'You're going to have to carry me.'

'I know it, colonel,' said Thomson.

The Grandmaster watched Jordan carefully, a quizzical look in his pale eyes. 'Doctor, I understand you are something of an idealist – but I still felt there was a patriot hidden under the skin. You've nullified your own people – you do realize that.'

'That was my intention,' said Jordan. He looked at Ulyanov. 'It's time,' he said. 'Now – or never. Lock the door.'

Ulyanov hesitated only for a second, then pressed in the locking button. Tavrin – for probably the first time in his life – was a fraction too slow to understand. Jordan drove an elbow under his ribs, then hit the guard below the belt in the lower abdomen, following up with a crashing blow to the side of the doubled-over man's jaw. The guard collapsed and lay still. Ulyanov turned his gun on the KGB man at the communications console.

Tavrin sucked in deep draughts of air, the thick vein on his forehead more prominent now. 'Sergei,' he wheezed, 'you will never see your daughter again.'

'Don't listen to him,' said Jordan. 'Trust me. You know damn well you can't trust *him*.'

'He is right,' Ulyanov told Tavrin.

'You are both committing suicide,' Tavrin warned, rubbing his stomach muscles.

'Maybe,' said Jordan. He laid a hand on Simpson's shoulder. 'If we lose that jamming can we still use the satellite telephone link?'

'Of course. I can patch straight into the British or German telecom systems.'

Jordan laid a notebook on the desk. 'There's a list of numbers at the back. One of them is for the President of the United States.'

Simpson flipped pages, frowning. Tavrin's face had regained its former inscrutability but behind it his icy brain was turning fast – though he still could not see which option Jordan might have chosen to use.

'202-456-2414,' Simpson read out. 'Where'd you get the book?'

'Stracey,' Jordan answered. 'I guessed – as Washington's man – he was bound to have direct access to the President in case of an emergency here. This project worried Washington sick – I saw that in his face.' He turned his head to Tavrin. 'You realize that this is a game which neither side can afford to lose?'

'I don't intend to lose, Doctor.'

'For God's sake, it's no longer a matter of *you* losing or winning – the issue is too big now, too dangerous. Listen to me, Tavrin, if you don't co-operate *now* we will *both* lose . . . and what might happen out there in the world doesn't bear thinking about. I guarantee that the colonel up there is on a suicide mission. You saw his expression when I told him this island is still considered neutral by me. But that won't make any difference to him . . . he's been sent to take us over and he'll die trying. He knows very well that in something this big he and his men are all expendable.'

Tavrin smiled wryly. 'Surely your Government has not told mere soldiers what is really on this island?'

'No. But the fact that they are here means that a decision – a dangerous decision – has been taken at the very highest level. Only the President would be able to order in troops so close to the Soviet Union. Tavrin, you have *got* to have that jamming stopped!'

'To what end? So that you can tell your President to send more troops?'

'Listen to me,' Jordan urged. 'You and I are holding destiny in our hands, and neither one of us is qualified to do that – I don't believe that Presidents are, either. We must act now to stop a *real* catastrophe. Your clever "game" has probably caused a genuine crisis and unless we stop it escalating we *will* be trapped down here until the nuclear dust blows away. And that will take a long, long time, I promise you. You *have* to co-operate. There is no other choice.'

'Very well,' said Tavrin. 'What is your solution?'

'There is only one solution. America and Russia must *both* be given the Whitefire technology.'

Tavrin threw his head back and laughed, then, totally unexpectedly, clasped Jordan by both arms. 'Doctor! You wish to force me to a draw? Excellent play. We must sit at the board some time together!' He gave an order to the Russian communications officer still under Ulyanov's gun beside Simpson.

Ulyanov moved forward and placed his automatic against the man's neck. He said to Jordan: 'There is a coded sequence to clear the jamming – Tavrin told him to use it. Did you see which numbers he used before?'

Jordan shook his head. 'Ray?' he asked Simpson.

'Sorry, Doctor.'

'Trust,' said Tavrin with irony. 'If we must work together then you must trust me.'

'Too many sides to your head,' Jordan murmured.

Tavrin reached for Simpson's notepad and quickly wrote a number. 'This too will ring on the desk of a world leader. Let us speak with these two men and settle the outcome.'

Jordan tried to read what lay in the brain behind the dead eyes, knowing that it was impossible. 'All right,' he said finally. 'Have your man make his signal.'

Tavrin gave a nod and the Russian stabbed out a complicated sequence on the electronic keyboard. Within a minute the equipment was working normally.

'Get both those phone numbers,' Jordan snapped to Simpson. 'Fast!'

'Says her name's Elliot,' Sergeant Thomson told Shearer, easing him into a chair in the main hut.

Jemma Elliot had shed her clothes and sat huddled on her chair wearing two oversized sweaters and thick trousers she had taken from one of the weathermen's lockers. 'Christ,' she breathed, 'they've sent a cripple to help us.'

Thomson gave her a baleful glare.

Shearer said: 'I understand you escaped from the underground facility?'

She nodded warily.

'You've got to help us.'

'Why? I don't know who the hell you are.'

'Americans – like you.'

'Sure, you've got the accents – but right now I don't believe anybody. OK?'

'Tell us what's been happening. It's very important.'

'Happening? Oh! Nothing really. Just one set of lies after the other. First we get Russian defectors . . . then we get shipwrecked sailors . . . .'

'Russian sailors?'

'They said they were Russians like you say you're Americans . . . .'

'Go on.'

Jemma laughed, still shivering. 'You *really* want to hear it? We were told there had been a nuclear war and that we were the last people alive . . . and we *believed* it! Doesn't that make you laugh?'

'No. Under these circumstances – cut off as you are – it could be quite believable. Especially with the nuclear explosion after the Russian sub blew.'

'Oh! You mean that part was *true*?'

'You must have seen the blast from here.'

'Saw it – and felt it,' Jemma said remembering, as if in another lifetime, Jordan leaping off her as they had made love.

'Then what?' Shearer urged, feeling his strength ebbing.

'A second party of survivors reached the island.'

'From the submarine – the *Leonid Brezhnev*?'

'No . . . oh God, I don't know anything any more. They

said they were from another submarine. I don't believe any of this.'

'I don't blame you, Miss Elliot.'

'Have you come for Whitefire too?' she asked, sick of conspiracy.

'I know nothing about that,' Shearer said warily. 'And I don't want to know.'

'Then you must be genuine,' she said sarcastically. 'That was all the Russians wanted to know.'

'All I know is what you told my sergeant here – that you got out. I don't want to know what work has been carried out here. Our job is to secure this island until we can get some heavier units up here.'

'More parachutists? Haven't you lost enough of your men already? I saw some of them down on the rocks.'

'Navy,' Shearer said. 'There's a back-up force on the way.'

'The Russians won't stand for that.'

'Not my problem. I need to know how you got out from underground without being stopped. You didn't use the elevator.'

Jemma shook her head. 'There's an underground section – an older one – built by the Germans during the war. We got out through an old ventilation shaft.'

'We?' Shearer questioned.

'Simon Howard and me. He's one of the people from the base. He brought me out.'

Shearer glanced at Thomson.

'No one else around,' said Thomson.

'You won't find *him*,' said Jemma, sticking out her arm. 'He's out there on the sea. Took one of the Russian inflatable boats. Making for some small island he'd seen. He's crazy! So was I for going with him.'

Thomson said: 'He hasn't got a hope in Hell.'

'Tell *him* that!' Jemma snapped.

Shearer persisted. 'Will you show us how to get in?'

'No way! I'm not going back down there again. Forget it.'

'Why?'

She laughed, slightly hysterically. 'You'll find out.'

'Any Russians down there?'

Again she laughed and Shearer looked at her with concern. She seemed very near cracking completely and he needed someone very composed indeed.

'Germans,' she grinned. 'Very, very dead Germans.'

Shearer frowned. 'You'll have to show me.'

She stood up. 'Listen, I'll take you to the entrance – but I'm not going in. You'll have to drag me.'

'Can we get in through the same ventilation shaft?'

'Not a hope. You're all too big.' She shuddered. 'I was almost trapped. It was the worst thing I've ever had to do. I'll never lock another door again – ever!'

'What are the walls like down there?'

'The walls? I don't know. Old, I suppose. I didn't exactly make a survey of the place!'

'You mean they're not part of the new complex?'

'You have got to be joking! That place has been sealed up since the war. I told you . . . you'll see what I mean if you go in there.'

'Bring her,' Shearer snapped, and two Black Berets grabbed her and pulled her up.

'I'm not going back!' she screamed.

'I'm afraid you are, Miss Elliot,' said Shearer as Thomson lifted him.

'No! I won't!'

'Bring her,' Shearer ordered.

5

The Soviet leader left the War Command Centre buried deep in the heart of the Kremlin at a pace faster than he had moved for years. Inside the Centre he had left behind him the commanders of his combined military services – all in the mood for war and perplexed by the strange reticence of their leader to commit the Soviet Union to anything more than a low state of readiness after the provocative action by the United States in the Middle East.

'Saudi Arabia,' they had insisted. 'That is the target.

The Americans are going to take the oilfields.' Then their own invasion plans had been spread before him enthusiastically; all prepared months in advance and constantly updated in line with Soviet political and military thinking. Their strategic rocket forces, ground forces, national air defence forces and their mighty navy could be unleashed against the West within seconds of his decision to strike.

But he had simply smiled gently – even a little secretly – and played down the situation, though he knew that the mood in the Kremlin was uneasy and his enemies within the Politburo were shaping up for a major power struggle.

But still he had waited.

Then, at last, came the news of the call from Mikhail Tavrin. Now, he thought as he walked quickly through the deep corridors, he could grind his enemies to dust.

In the Pentagon, too, an air of hesitancy hung over the Satellite Control Centre. The massive screen which dominated the Centre showed the black clawed fist of Beacon Island illuminated only by the smudges of light which were the underground heat sources.

The President sat in the long control booth, looking down through the expanse of plate glass at the rows of operators at their consoles. 'Can we maintain the connection?' he asked his aide.

'No reason why not, sir,' said the young man. 'The call came through to the White House direct. I've instructed them to re-route it here. You realize there is no way we can guarantee how secure the line will be. This end, OK, but . . . ?'

'We've no choice but to take it. What do we know about this man Jordan?'

The aide had the information already in his head. 'Graduate of Cornell, doctorate in advanced electronics, specialized in laser and maser technology . . . something of a college football star but a brilliant student. Politically liberal – though not active. Been out of the States for four years.'

The President frowned. 'Why can't we speak with Ledden? He's the man we should be dealing with. Something must have happened to him.'

His aide shook his head. 'It's Stracey we need – at least he'll be able to deal with an insecure line.'

The President's temper flared momentarily. 'Why the hell aren't these people patching in through the military satellites! At least that way we'd have some cover against leaks.'

'Only Stracey would know how to go about that link-up.'

'Then Stracey's dead. There can be no other reason.'

The aide made a face. 'Seems likely.'

The President gazed out at the screen. 'Hell, I wish we could contact Shearer.'

'Sir, you insisted in his orders that no contact whatsoever was to be made until the navy arrived.'

'I know what I said! But right now we need information.'

One telephone in a battery of instruments pinged. The aide lifted it, listened, then passed it to the President. 'Jordan,' he said.

'Mr President,' Jordan said into the microphone on the console. 'This is Matthew Jordan, Operations Head of the INTERSAT Corporation's Whitefire Project on Beacon Island.'

'Dr Jordan,' the President's voice came through a speaker after a brief delay. 'This line is insecure – please be very careful in what you say. Do you understand me?'

'Mr President,' Jordan repeated, ignoring his words. 'I understand you have some kind of Special Forces unit on the surface of Beacon Island. Will you confirm this?'

A brief silence followed, then: 'I have no idea what you are talking about.'

Jordan came back quickly, guessing the President might consider cutting the connection. 'Sir, we have on another line the Soviet leader. In effect, this is a four-way conversation.'

'What do you mean? You have no right to put me in such a precarious position. Jordan, do you *realize* how dangerous this present situation is?'

'Completely. That is why I am talking with you. Don't hang up, sir – this is vital: the Soviet leader is talking with Grandmaster Mikhail Tavrin of the Soviet Union. Do you know that name?'

'Of course,' the President replied, warily. 'He disappeared from the world chess championships a few days ago.'

'He is here – right here in this room. Tavrin formulated a complex plan to infiltrate this base and gain control of the Whitefire device and its technology for the Soviet Union. They have succeeded in doing that.'

'What! Jordan, understand me . . . .'

'No, Mr President, *you* must understand *me*. The situation here is at stalemate. Your troops are above us but have no hope at all of getting in here. This installation is impregnable.'

'But the Russians got in, damn it!'

'They infiltrated the station, sir. By deception. But to be blunt that hardly matters now. They are in and they're here to stay. They won't come out as long as your men are out there . . . and as I said there is no way your men can get down here. It is as simple as that. We are sealed in.'

'*Sealed in?* Can't you get to the controls to open the exits?'

'I have the controls in front of me, sir.'

'Then *open* them. You'll have to take your chances. This is too important, Jordan. *Open up the underground levels!*'

'No, sir.'

'What do you mean – *no!*' the President exploded. 'You're an American – I order you to do it.'

'No, sir,' Jordan repeated patiently. 'This island is registered as neutral territory. You must be aware of that. Your men are in violation of that neutrality.'

'Well, so are the damn Russians!'

'No. We let them in. We welcomed them.'

'*Deception!* You said so yourself.'

'That is correct, sir. But I'm afraid that the facts are that they are inside and have the information they came for – while your troops are outside and do not.'

The President paused for so long that Jordan thought he

had gone off the line. Finally, he said: 'So where do we go from here, Doctor?'

'We negotiate an exchange.'

'An exchange of people?'

'Yes, sir.'

'But you say that they already have the Whitefire technology. That is hardly a realistic exchange.'

'They don't exactly have the technology, Mr President. They have *me*.'

'What do you mean – they have *you*?'

'Sir Henry Ledden is dead. Your man Stracey is dead. Josef Chebrikov, the scientist who was here with the Russians, is also dead. He was the man who would have absorbed the Whitefire technology. It has always been Sir Henry Ledden's policy to treat the secrets of the Whitefire device on a need-to-know basis. *He* knew everything – as I do – but what is on the computer programs or on microfilm are the results, not the *essence* of the original idea. If Sir Henry could have known what sort of crisis would have resulted from the development of Whitefire he would never have gone ahead with the project.'

'That's absurd, Jordan. Of course Ledden knew what would result from the emergence of such a weapon. He was no fool.'

'No sir, he was no fool. He was an idealist.' Jordan glanced at Tavrin who stood beside him, a telephone in his hand, translating for the Soviet leader every word that was spoken.

Jordan continued: 'Sir Henry believed the world could be freed of the threat of nuclear war. If the Whitefire device – and it was not a weapon, sir, but an *anti*-weapon – proved to be completely efficient he intended to leak the technology to the Soviet Union. That way, *both* sides could – very cheaply in comparative terms – destroy each other's ridiculously – no, criminally – expensive nuclear weapons before they hit their targets. Whitefire would have made nuclear war a non-viable proposition. Sir Henry's dream, Mr President, was that in the end all the money saved by not building more nuclear weapons would be put to more humanitarian uses. I intend to give that dream a chance to become reality.'

'This is lunacy!' the President fumed. 'You're jeopardizing the security of your own nation. You could be classed as a traitor, Jordan.'

'You might class me as that, sir. I certainly don't. I have found myself placed in this position by chance – and I intend to use this opportunity ruthlessly.'

'Jordan,' the President pleaded. 'All this is pure idealism and has no place in modern society. You are playing into the hands of the Communists. Can't you see that? They will be the only ones to benefit.'

'Not true. They will gain – and lose – exactly what America will. They will gain a cheap deterrent against war and a large surplus of funds to be put to far better use than building more means of total destruction. They will lose the economic drain of nuclear weapons and their suicidal potential for mass destruction. Can't you see, sir, how ridiculous nuclear strategy has become?'

'I'm not on this line to discuss nuclear strategy. Hear this, Jordan: Sir Henry Ledden was a capitalist whose only concern was making money. You must be aware that the consortium which backed the Whitefire project demanded we sell them our military fuel reserves as part of the deal. Fuel saved if we bought Whitefire. *And* at the lowest possible price, I might add. Now *that*, Dr Jordan, is *not* the way of an *idealistic dreamer*, I can assure you!'

'Those were the consortium's terms – not Sir Henry's. In the end he would have leaked the secrets and got his way.'

Tavrin was watching Jordan's face with a new understanding. It was as if his opponent had been transformed into another – much more dangerous – person before his eyes. He cupped his hand over the mouthpiece of his telephone and indicated that Jordan should close his microphone. He said: 'Are you speaking the truth?'

'I am.'

'And Ledden? These were his beliefs?'

'Ledden is dead,' Jordan stated. 'Only *now* matters.' He flicked a switch to open the microphone. 'This is how we shall break this stalemate, Mr President. The only way which will guarantee good faith on both sides—'

The deep thump of an explosion rocked the room. Jordan's eyes locked with Tavrin's.

Tavrin said: 'If those are the American troops I cannot stop what he might do.' His pale eyes flicked to the covered mouthpiece of his telephone, still connected to the Soviet leader.

Jordan said to Ulyanov: 'No one comes through that door.' The rattle of machine-gun fire sounded below their feet. Jordan spoke into the microphone: 'Mr President – if you can't stop your men, believe me you'd better get into that flying war room of yours and take off, because you'll be facing Doomsday very soon.'

Colonel Shearer had done what Jemma Elliot had warned him he would have to do. His men dragged her, screaming, down the dark low tunnel, their flashlights lancing into the darkness of the old Nazi installation.

In the dreadful main chamber they were shocked to a standstill by the sight of the piled-up decomposed corpses. Sergeant Thomson breathed a profanity, then pushed the men onwards, forcing directions from Jemma. They halted outside the room where Otto Gross still sat as he had done for decades. Jemma crouched on the seeping concrete, her head down and covered by her arms.

'You bastards,' she whispered, over and over.

Thomson put Shearer down beside her.

'Miss Elliot,' Shearer said. 'How close are we to the new section? You *must* help us.'

She might not have heard him, then she threw out an arm and raised her head. 'We came out of the ventilation shaft from that room . . . where that . . . *thing* is. Howard told me he first went in from the room next door. That's where he heard voices coming from the new complex through the shaft.'

Shearer looked up. 'All right, absolute silence. No one even breathe. Someone check those shafts.'

Thomson mounted the table in front of Otto Gross's hideous corpse and pulled himself up by his arms into the square aperture of the inspection panel Howard had removed on their return journey. He lowered himself down. 'She's right, I can hear voices.'

Shearer ordered: 'Fix charges against the back walls in both the rooms. Time them for simultaneous detonation – one of them has to lead us through to the other side. Everyone get back.' He called Thomson over. 'Get one of the men to take the girl out of here. Put her back in the hut. Then he can back up the men on the surface.'

'Charges placed, colonel,' said the lieutenant as Jemma was led away.

'Everyone down!' Shearer shouted and the charges blew almost instantly, showering masonry out into the main chamber. Thomson found himself crouching beside the grinning skull of SS Sergeant Otto Gross.

'*Jeesus!*' he hissed and kicked it away. '*Go!*' he yelled, and dashed forward over the pile of smashed concrete and twisted steel reinforcements, then through the gap, his silenced Ingram machine pistol jerking soundlessly in his hands as two of the stunned Russians made to fire. Both men crashed backwards, spurting blood from a dozen wounds. Beside him, the incredibly rapid, soft *phrutt-phrutt* of more Ingrams firing lashed the remaining Russians with their silent whips of lead. One of the Black Berets fell from a jagged burst by a Kalashnikov assault rifle and dropped to the rubble; behind him another cried out and crumpled over, almost cut in two.

'Don't shoot!' a voice screamed, and the advancing Black Berets swung around, their Ingrams still ready to hack down anything that moved. Then, slowly, white faces began to appear from behind the banks of equipment. Thomson surveyed the room, marvelling at the array of electronics around him.

'You people work here?' he yelled harshly.

'Yes!' a number of voices answered quickly from behind the array of electronic equipment.

'Everyone up!' Thomson shouted. 'Keep your hands on your heads. We'll shoot anyone who drops them. Come on – all of you – up!'

Terrified, the shocked figures rose to their feet, some of

their faces badly cut from flying stone chips and glass smashed by the murderous fire fight.

'Anyone in charge here?' Shearer called, forcing himself forwards unaided, though his legs no longer seemed to belong to him.

One man eased himself forward. 'You Americans?'

'Never mind that,' said Shearer. 'How many Russians were there down here?'

The man looked around, dazed. 'You've killed them all. There's probably another ten or more on Level One.'

'How do we get there?' Shearer demanded.

The man pointed. 'The lifts.'

'Right, show us.'

At the lifts the man touched the sensor control but nothing happened.

'What's wrong?' Shearer asked.

'Your explosion probably activated the automatic seals. Electromagnets. Very powerful. They cut in as soon as any concussion is picked up by the sensors.'

'So how else do we get to Level One?'

'You can't – there's no other way. They'll have to deactivate the magnets from the communications room.'

'And more Russians are guarding that?'

The man nodded.

Shearer swore.

The lieutenant pushed forward. 'Your life-support systems must be run by computer. Where is it?'

The man shook his head stubbornly. 'No. Some of our people are still up there. You're not getting my co-operation so that you can kill them.'

'I didn't mean that,' said the lieutenant. 'If your life support is linked to a computer then so must all your other operational functions be. Maybe we can re-programme the mechanism for those doors.'

'Not my field,' said the man.

'No,' said the lieutenant. 'It's mine.'

The American President held the phone away from his ear; his ageing face seemed to have sagged as if the flesh beneath

213

the skin had dissolved. He stared, eyes wide, as if he had seen the reality of a vision he had long dreaded.

'Mr President?' said his aide, very concerned.

The President lifted another telephone and spoke one word: 'Springboard.' Then he replaced the receiver. In his mind's eye he could see the huge Lockheed Galaxies thundering over the runway, then lifting ponderously into the humid desert air, heading for Saudi Arabia.

The aide's lips parted. 'You're going to take the oilfields?' he murmured.

The President sucked in breath. 'Not unless we have to. But at least the Rapid Deployment Force is airborne. If the Soviets decide to move they will strike into Europe first – and you know damn well we can't hold them there. We must secure our fuel lines. Get me the Kremlin.'

The aide moved fast to a phone, feeling the sweat breaking out over his body. He waited, the instrument in his hand, then turned to the President. 'He won't talk with you. They say he's unavailable.'

'Dear Lord,' the President exclaimed. 'That Jordan must have gone crazy! They always warned me that it would only need one lunatic to start the holocaust. Is the line to Beacon Island still open?'

'Yessir. We kept the connection open but no one has come through.'

The President flopped down into a chair. 'Shearer has got to take that installation. He's simply got to.'

'Tavrin,' said Jordan. 'What did your man tell you?'

'No more than I expected, Doctor. If the American soldiers take this place his options are closed.'

'What does he mean? A pre-emptive strike?'

Tavrin lifted his high shoulders a fraction. 'Perhaps. Depending on the factors involved. Surprise is out of the question now. More likely he will try to take as much territory as he can without resorting to nuclear weapons.'

'It's bound to escalate,' Jordan said, looking into the dark eyes of Ulyanov.

'It is taken away from us now,' Ulyanov said, hopelessly.

'We can no longer make decisions. Mikhail, even you are just a pawn now.'

Tavrin rubbed the side of his hooked nose with a long finger, his heavy eyelids lowered slightly. 'Perhaps not,' he replied quietly. 'Nothing has changed. Doctor, you say that the soldiers cannot reach us here?'

'Right. The controls to break the contacts on the electromagnets on the lift doors are situated in here. But how does that matter? The Whitefire control area is their target – and they're in it.'

'But the real secrets are in your head – as you said – not in the electronics below.'

Jordan shook his head. 'Right, but there's bound to be a back-up force waiting to follow them in. Soon this place will be crawling with more soldiers, and scientists, eager to pick it – and me – clean.'

Tavrin waggled his finger. 'Not so. Our leader will certainly have given an order for this area to be blockaded. Without having to engage in a full-scale naval battle, no American force will get through. You and I still hold the pieces in our hands. All we have to do is decide where to place them on the board.'

Jordan raised his eyebrows. 'So what is our next move, Grandmaster?'

'You can contact the level below?'

'Yes, through the PA system.'

'Then do so. Inform the commander of the strike force that if he does not withdraw immediately the consequences are certain to be terrible.'

'He won't believe me.'

'Then let him hear the voice of someone he will believe. Give your President the option.'

'Simpson,' Jordan said, decisively. 'Open the line to Washington again and relay the call over the PA system.'

'The line's still open,' Simpson said.

Jordan pushed the switch on the microphone. 'Mr President, are you there?'

'Yes,' a voice replied tersely through the speaker.

'Sir, every word of this conversation is being relayed

through to your strike force, who have been halted by our own protective mechanisms on the level below this one.'

'I understand, Dr Jordan. Have you come to your senses at last? Perhaps you don't realize how far-reaching the effects of the situation on Beacon Island are? The United States and the Soviet Union are escalating by the second to a state of war.'

'I am still prepared to offer a solution, sir.'

'This so-called exchange?'

'Yes.'

'But what will it achieve?'

'Sir, Grandmaster Tavrin will agree to try and persuade the Soviet leader that I am genuine in my offer to go with him to the Soviet Union and pass to their scientists, over a graduated period, the Whitefire technology. Let me finish, please. Also, he will insist that if I do offer my complete co-operation then *your* scientists will be allowed onto Beacon Island to study our work on the device.'

'And the device itself? I understand that you have one operational unit actually on the island.'

'That is correct, sir. But I could not allow one side to have an operational device in their hands before the other. The only way to solve this dangerous situation is by both sides having to develop their own systems in tandem. Later, neutral countries could be brought in to produce and oversee its distribution.'

'Jordan, I cannot make this sort of decision within minutes. It takes time to get agreement from the various . . .'

'You *have* to,' Jordan cut in. 'You must make the decision yourself and stand by it.'

'And if I don't?'

'Only *you* know how the crisis is developing, Mr President. It's up to you to balance the price of keeping the peace against the cost of waging war.'

'Give me a few moments.'

'Don't be too long, Mr President. Before you leave the line will you please instruct the commander of your forces to make no attempt to enter Level One of this installation.'

'Very well. Colonel Shearer, I understand you can hear me. Operation Gopher is to cease for the moment. However, if you are attacked by Soviet forces I shall expect you to defend your position at all costs both above and below ground.'

Jordan jumped in fast. 'One moment! Colonel Shearer, I must warn you that I have closed-circuit TV cameras in the tower. If your men attempt to tamper with the White-fire device I will have no alternative but to engage the self-destruct mechanism. Any attempt to blind or disconnect the cameras will result in the same course of action.'

'The colonel will have understood that, I'm sure,' said the President. 'Shearer, hold your position and do nothing – for the present. Jordan, I'll come back to you.'

The line hissed and Jordan sat staring at the speaker. 'Poor bastard,' he said. 'I wouldn't have his job even if it meant my life.'

Tavrin gave a sharp grunt. 'It may mean your life in any case, Doctor. You have placed yourself in a very precarious position. Both sides want you alive for themselves – and dead if the other gets you.'

Jordan gave a rueful grin. 'I hadn't looked at it that way.'

'Then you should,' Tavrin replied, and reached for one of Simpson's cigarettes off the console. He lit it and inhaled deeply.

'I didn't think you smoked,' said Jordan with surprise. 'Strange habit for a man so disciplined.'

Tavrin's grey eyes smiled. 'Always one – when the game is nearing its end.'

'It's not over yet,' Jordan reminded him.

'A few more moves,' said Tavrin. 'Then it will be over.'

PART FOUR

Endgame

Jemma Elliot stood on the clifftop wrapped in furs, the binoculars she held in her mittened hands pressed to her eyes. The grey dawn was like a shroud slowly lifting off the inert sea.

'You still searching for your man?' said Sergeant Thomson, coming up behind her.

She kept the glasses to her eyes. 'Not *my* man,' she answered, a little rudely. 'Simon Howard is *nobody*'s man.'

Thomson kicked at the rocks lightly with the thick sole of his paratrooper's boot. 'Not much chance for one man in a small boat out there. Maybe the ships spotted him?'

She shifted the glasses in the direction of the American warships settled on the horizon like grey plastic toys, their silhouettes blurred by the haze.

'He'll survive,' she said. 'You don't know him.'

'From what you told us, he sounds a little crazy.'

She turned to Thomson sharply. 'You call what you did sane?' She pointed down at a row of black plastic bags on the cracked jetty below. They resembled seals, long and shiny, and bulky from the bodies zipped within them, their feet splayed outwards within the wrapping like tail flippers, completing the illusion.

'It's the risk we take, ma'am. The job we do.' Thomson kicked a ball of black rock over the edge. It hit a steel hand rail low down and fragmented like shrapnel. 'You want to come back inside? It's not exactly Miami Beach out here.'

'What's going to happen?' she asked him, returning to her searching.

'Out there? Who knows?' He pointed to the horizon to their left and a flotilla of warships. 'There's the Russkies, and over there's the US Navy. They got every kind of device on board to tell what the other is doing. They know what's going on in the air, under the sea and maybe – God knows – what we're rappin' about up here. That's how they fight wars nowadays. Me? I'm an anachronism. I jump out of airplanes, land on my butt and kill any guy who's wearing the wrong uniform. And I kill with my bare hands.' He jerked his stubbled chin at the horizon. 'Those guys, they kill at a distance – but they watch and they listen very carefully first because, lady, when they get to killing each other all us other people are gonna get it too. You going to come inside – or watch the war?'

She smiled below the glasses but did not turn. 'I'm going to watch the war, sergeant. I'm not going to miss the real thing.'

'Suit yourself, lady,' Thomson said and loped back to the tower.

Shearer raised his head to the lens of the TV camera. He sat ashen-faced on a chair at a small window cut in the brickwork of the tower like an arrow position in a castle rampart.

'Jordan?' he said. 'This is Shearer.'

'I hear you, Shearer,' Jordan answered. 'You look terrible. What's the matter?'

Shearer glanced down involuntarily at his lifeless legs. His spine was damaged – he could not hide from that any longer. The medic had tried every method he knew to test for sensation but the flesh was dead.

'Jordan,' he said. 'You got any decisions yet? It's getting damn cold up here waiting for you people to solve your problems.'

'You should be here in winter, colonel. We're setting up a deal. You'll have to freeze a little longer.'

Shearer raised his binoculars to tiny flickerings of light, like silent gunfire, between the opposing warships on the horizon.

'Jordan, the navy is getting impatient out there. Maybe they won't wait for Washington to decide when to begin World War III.'

'Or the Kremlin,' Jordan reminded him.

'Sure.' Shearer lowered the glasses to the fur-clad figure on the clifftop. 'That female who works for you? She's had a rough time. Seems to have cut herself off from the situation.'

'She'll be OK. Just make sure she gets off this rock.'

Shearer grunted and tried to shift position, but the lower half of his body refused to respond to the commands of his brain.

You can't jump from a wheelchair, he told himself. You can't do anything from a wheelchair except roll yourself around and pretend it never happened. He looked again at the camera. 'This thing you've got in the tower – what does it do?'

'Stops people from dying.'

'How?'

'It neutralizes missiles right now, but anything with electronic wiring can be stopped dead by it. The beam destroys the circuits.'

'But most *everything* has got electric wiring – even my old Chevy Corvette.'

'That's right.'

'So missiles, tanks, planes, ships . . . .'

'Everything.'

'And you want to give it to the Russians?'

'I want to give it to anyone scared shitless by the thought of nuclear war. It's the only way.'

'It's the only way as *you* see it, Jordan. Could be they knock out every weapon we have before we switch on our own units, from space or something. You're the scientist, you work it out – then they hit us with their nukes while we sit there turning our keys in a dead ignition?'

'That's the risk we'll have to take. But it's better than living under the constant threat of being vapourized.'

'Is it?' Shearer said earnestly, staring deep into the camera lens. 'Jordan, that's the risk we will have to take because *you* are *making* us take it.'

'I don't believe there is any other choice.'

Shearer watched some of his men dash to the cliff edge, then saw, far out, the sudden rearing black hump of a nuclear submarine. It wallowed like a whale for a brief moment before submerging again, leaving only a bubbling white froth on the surface as evidence that it had been there. The red star on the conning tower remained printed on Shearer's retina as he lowered the glasses.

'Jordan? This the only gizmo of its kind? Hear me, Jordan? No others hidden somewhere else for the crazies to steal?'

'Just the one,' Jordan replied. 'Why?'

'Just wanted to make sure. Let me know when you decide to come out of there.'

'Just as soon as I hear what Washington and the Kremlin have decided. You going to stay in the tower, Shearer?'

Shearer stared out to sea again. 'Doctor, I'm not going anywhere.'

The survivors of the KGB task force had given up trying to make sense of the situation. One man had gone to the door of the communications room to ask what their position was, but Tavrin had sent him away with orders to stay with the hostages. So they stood, weapons ready, and obeyed blindly, knowing that whatever was going on was now out of their hands and therefore beyond their control.

In the communications room, Ulyanov had slumped dejectedly into a chair, his head bowed and his eyes fixed to a spot which in reality he did not see.

Matthew Jordan stared at his large hands, avoiding in his mind the momentous action he had precipitated and, instead, thinking about Jemma and wondering *how* he had failed so completely to hold her.

He glanced at Tavrin who stood absolutely still, arms folded and one long leg crossed over the other, his large head tucked into his chin like a great bird asleep. And what are you thinking, Grandmaster? Jordan wondered. Is that brilliant, devious mind at this very moment plotting the move for my destruction. Trust? I trust you as I do a computer – with the hope that I have programmed sufficient cut-outs to stop it taking over.

An angry buzz sounded at Tavrin's hip and he reached down for the telephone. He answered, speaking entirely in Russian. Jordan gave Ulyanov an interrogative glance but the bearded submariner raised a hand reassuringly.

Tavrin replaced the telephone, then announced: 'There is agreement on these points. Ulyanov will receive a pardon for his actions and will also receive recognition for his co-

224

operation in this matter. He will be posted to Moscow in an administrative position where he will benefit by having a privileged status with special consideration for the education and wellbeing of his child. I regret there can be no seagoing command. As to the surviving members of the mutiny, they will not be charged either, but they cannot be trusted with active positions. They too must be shore-based. Sergei? This is agreeable?'

'Do I have any choice?' Ulyanov answered drily. 'But it is better than the camps – or a quick bullet.'

'Remember what I have told you,' Tavrin reminded him. 'Change from within is more effective than reaction from without.'

'And Whitefire?' Jordan urged, bewildered by Tavrin's dealing with the lesser matter first.

Tavrin raised an eyebrow. 'But Doctor? Our Leader was always prepared to accept your offer. It is *your* President who cannot make up his mind.'

Jordan exploded. 'Why can't these people deal together like civilized human beings? What the hell is the problem?'

'The problem', said Tavrin, 'is that when two men are facing each other with loaded guns conversation is – should we say – difficult?'

'Then they must lower the guns!' Jordan answered angrily.

'Surely. But who will take the risk of doing it first?'

In the Pentagon, the presidential aide lifted a ringing telephone and passed it to the waiting President.

'It is time for decisions,' said the Soviet leader. 'You cannot hope to hold the oilfields. Your military action is against the will of the people of Saudi Arabia – whose revolutionary struggle we shall continue to support – with our own forces if necessary.'

'Mr Secretary,' the President said, his tone resolute. 'Shall we face some facts of life? What is the greatest fear of the Soviet Union – and its greatest priority if war threatens? The security of your frontiers of course – history has proved it so. We both know that in the event of direct confrontation between our two nations your first act will be to make a massive armoured strike across Europe, thereby securing your frontiers. Even at this moment our satellites confirm that your armies are poised at the borders.

'The West's greatest fear – in *peace* and in war because of your damaging foreign policy – is to secure our fuel lines from the Middle East. The Soviet Union has forced us into this conflict.'

The Soviet leader's voice came back confidently. 'Some other facts of life, Mr President. The Warsaw Pact has 150 tank divisions against 45 NATO; 27,000 artillery pieces against 900; 1,240,000 soldiers against 1,200,000. And although the manpower of both sides is almost equal, our capacity for rapid mobilization would give us a three-to-one superiority in fighting troops after only three weeks. NATO could only close that gap after a further three weeks had elapsed. By that time, Mr President, it would be too late. An *inescapable* fact of life.'

'*If* you could rely totally on Hungary, Poland, Romania . . . ?' the President countered. 'Perhaps, with the possibility of NATO troops fighting near their borders, they might be tempted to rethink their allegiances . . . even their political ideology? Hungary and Czechoslovakia are not such distant memories, Mr Secretary . . . and Poland is still in crisis.'

'In which case,' came the heavy reply, 'we would be forced to use our nuclear weapons.'

'Without a doubt,' said the President. 'So when both our nations are reduced to rubble the remnants of our armies will fight over what is left of Europe and any other still habitable pieces of land?'

There seemed to be a sigh down the line, then the Soviet leader said, impatiently: 'The issue of the Whitefire device. This exchange must be carried out immediately.'

The President said: 'Oh, I think that when certain guarantees are laid down regarding our oil supplies we could meet together with the consortium who developed the device. Also I feel that your considerable naval presence near the island – which far outweighs ours – should be recalled so as not to prejudice any further negotiations . . . .'

The Soviet leader's voice lashed out from the earpiece. 'I am not interested in this capitalist consortium! We are prepared only to deal directly with Dr Jordan on the island. He is ready to make this exchange – so are we. You are pushing too hard, Mr President. Be very sure of what you are doing here.'

The President breathed out slowly. 'Very well,' he said. 'I agree to the terms of the exchange. You take Jordan and we will move onto the island.'

There seemed to be little relief in the Soviet leader's voice. 'Then it is agreed. I shall inform Grandmaster Tavrin, and also remind him that the existing device must be destroyed utterly. A Soviet nuclear submarine is ready to bring Dr Jordan to us. He will work at the Lebedev Institute here in Moscow. He will be treated well.' The phone went dead.

The President replaced the receiver gently.

'That's it?' said the aide.

'That's it,' the President replied, but inside he said: Do it, Shearer. Do it.

'You're lucky. Damn lucky,' said the captain of the missile cruiser USS *Pittsburgh*. 'If our lookouts hadn't spotted you, you'd have been chilled meat for the birds by now.'

The *Pittsburgh*'s radar room was very warm and kept darkened for the reading of the instruments. Simon Howard let his quick eyes traverse the kaleidoscopic patterns of flashing, coloured lights which somehow the operators of the equipment translated into hard information crucial to the survival and attack capability of the ship.

Howard grunted. 'I'd have made it to the island if you hadn't sent that boat after me.'

'I doubt that, mister,' the captain replied. 'You were in bad shape when they got you back here. You weren't going anywhere – except maybe in circles.'

Howard glanced up at the tall officer, taking in the ruddy face under the white hood of his flash protector – the *Pittsburgh*, like every other vessel standing off Beacon Island, both American and Russian, was on full alert. 'I was

OK,' Howard retorted. 'Told you everything you wanted to know, didn't I?'

'Right. *After* the medics worked on you.' The captain glanced down pointedly at Howard's bandaged hands. 'A couple of months later in the year and nothing would have saved your fingers. Take my word for it, you're lucky.'

A seaman placed a signal in the captain's hand. 'Washington, sir,' he said.

The captain held the signal under the dull glow of a shaded lamp. 'They've pulled off some kind of deal,' he told Howard, his eyes still on the signal, his voice relieved. He pulled the white hood off his head, letting it lie on his shoulders. His hair was wavy and dark, and quite suddenly he appeared to be too young for the enormous responsibility of his command. 'Just what have they *got* on that island?' he demanded in frustration, crushing the signal. 'What's so damned important that we're caught in a Mexican stand-off with the Soviet Navy?'

Howard said: 'Ask those geniuses when you get them on board. I'm saying nothing. It's in my contract.'

The captain stared at him. '*Contract!* After the crisis your people have caused I don't think they'll be in any position to keep you on the payroll.' He tossed the balled signal to Howard. 'Not after Washington gets through with them.'

Howard smirked and let the paper fall to the carpeted deck.

'Do you want to come up to the bridge?' the captain asked.

'Sure. What's going on?'

'They've agreed on some kind of exchange. One man from the island is leaving with the Russians. We go in after that's been done.'

'Who's the man?'

'His name's Jordan. That's all I know. Know him?'

'Yeah, one of you lot. Yank. Bloody idiot, the Ivans will take him apart.'

They stepped out from the gloom of the radar room.

'Probably,' said the captain. 'But there's nothing we can do about it.'

Jordan's voice spoke through the speaker in the tower: 'Shearer? They've made the deal.'

'I want to hear that direct from the President,' said Shearer.

'I have him for you.'

Another voice came through the speaker over a squeal of feedback, and Shearer guessed that Jordan was holding his microphone to another speaker.

The President said: 'Colonel Shearer, this is the President. An agreement has been concluded between myself and the Soviet Secretary-General. It is this: Dr Matthew Jordan will accompany the Russian party to one of their submarines which will surface three miles from the island. Boats will be sent to take them off the island and back to the submarine, then on to the Soviet Union. At this moment a back-up force of Marines is leaving the American warships you must be able to see on your horizon. It will take some time for them to get to you. I can do no more from this end, colonel.' The President hesitated fractionally. 'Shearer, I trust you to carry out my final order. Goodbye – and thank you, colonel.'

'You hear all that?' Jordan inquired.

'Got it.'

'What did he mean by that last remark?'

'To hold the island against enemy attack,' Shearer lied. 'Maybe he doesn't trust the Russians not to have some force ready to pounce once you take the ride to Moscow.'

'He needn't worry. Tavrin and I have hammered out the most sensible agreement possible under the circumstances. I told you before. There's no other way.'

Shearer said nothing.

Jordan went on: 'The next thing to do is to destroy the Whitefire device.'

'You going to blow it? Give me time to get out of this tower.'

'No need. Explosives can be made harmless. That's why our self-destruct mechanism doesn't incorporate them.'

'So how are you going to do it?'

'Simple, the device destroys itself in the same way it destroys anything else. It turns upon itself.'

'Very poetic,' Shearer said drily. 'Am I safe in here?'

'Perfectly. You might find the smell a little acrid but it won't last long.'

Shearer's eyes moved to the horizon. 'Your transport just surfaced. Do what you have to do, then get out of there.'

Above his head Shearer thought he could hear a sharp crackling sound, then the acrid stench of scorched metal reached him. 'Jordan, your thing just fried,' he said. 'Just make damn sure you don't give the Russians any short cuts, OK?'

'There are no short cuts, colonel. We're coming out, so keep your men's fingers away from their triggers. See the boats yet?'

'On their way,' said Shearer, and the speaker shut off.

He opened the small window and watched his men deploying themselves along the clifftop, the marksmen wedging themselves into the rocks, nestling their high-powered scoped rifles to their chins. Three light machine gun positions had already been set up, but Shearer knew that if a concerted attack was made before the Marines landed, his men would be hard pushed to defend the island for any length of time. 'You might trust them, Jordan,' he murmured. 'But I don't.'

He thought about the President's words and re-read in his mind the final order he had received at the Pentagon. It had been written – added – by hand. It read: 'Colonel Shearer, in the event of things going wrong – if your mission fails – I trust you to carry out the ultimate sanction on my behalf. This rests on your judgement alone and you cannot – must not – count the cost. I know you will understand.' The President's personal signature completed the handwritten message.

Below the tower, Thomson cupped his gloved hands to his face and shouted up. 'You see 'em, colonel?'

Shearer leaned outwards. 'I see them. Have the men deployed so that there's a clear path through for the Russians. Jordan and his people will be out in a moment. Let him go with the Russians. The others we'll take off when the Marines get here.'

'Let them take *Jordan*?' Thomson yelled. 'You gone crazy, sir? That woman says he's the brains here!'

'Those are my orders, sergeant. Just carry them out.'

'OK, sir, if they're your orders . . . !' Thomson loped off, his head shaking from side to side.

'Sergeant!' Shearer shouted and pointed at the marksmen. 'Get me a rifle. I'm staying up here.'

Thomson walked on and thumped one of the marksmen in the side with his boot. 'Get that weapon up to the old man,' he ordered, tossing the man his own machine pistol. He walked off muttering: 'He got a bump on the head – not the ass!'

There was no wind as Jordan emerged from the tower with Tavrin. Ulyanov followed with the remnants of his men, then came the hostages and finally the armed KGB task force. The chill morning lanced through their warmed bodies as they walked across the sloping rock plateau.

Jemma Elliot ran from the cliff edge towards him.

Jordan stopped. 'They told you?'

'Yes! I don't understand? Why are you doing this?'

Jordan's face was set. 'This is the only solution. We were fooled into believing there was a nuclear war – well, there almost was. My going with them has stopped the lunacy. Maybe even stopped it for good.'

'You and Ledden!' she snapped. 'You both belong in a cage. You're too dangerous to be let out with normal people. You don't really believe that *they* are going to take any notice of what you say or do?'

'I'll take that chance.'

'And what about me?'

'Do you want to join me?'

She glanced down.

'You don't need to answer that. You get off this rock as soon as you can. Look after Chebrikov's grand-daughter – make sure she's treated well by our people. What happened to Howard – any news?'

'Nothing.'

'Why Howard?' he asked, though he knew he should not.

She looked into his face. 'Because he was there. Because he was the only one who was doing anything positive – the only one who hadn't given up. He *made* me believe him. And he was *right*. I didn't *give* myself to him – he took me. But right then that was what I needed.'

'But in the end he dumped you – just like he said he would.'

'No, I jumped overboard. I left him.'

Jordan grinned. 'That was one hell of a way to change your mind. But you never could do anything by half, could you?'

Jemma gave a small shrug and looked at him.

'I'll see you,' Jordan said.

She jerked her head furiously, still looking at him defiantly. Tears lay on her furs like dew on an animal's coat. Jordan walked on. She called out: 'I love you! Matt?'

He stopped and turned toward her. 'No, you don't. You love that coat you're wearing because it keeps you warm. But if something else could keep you warmer, you'd discard it.' He walked on, then descended the steps to the jetty.

She ran to the cliff. An American voice rang out from the rocks: 'Hey, lady! You're too close to the edge.'

'Go to Hell!' she shouted back, not turning.

Below her Jordan was in a black inflatable fitted with a big outboard motor. With a rasping roar its stern dug deep into the freezing water and began the long journey to the black hump in the distance. She could see him clearly, facing her, seated; the biggest man by far in the boat. Beside him the gangly figure of Mikhail Tavrin was hunched forward, long legs drawn to his chin, arms clasped around them and head down as if avoiding the spray. Tavrin lifted his head, and perhaps he said something to Ulyanov because the bearded face, too, turned her way. Jordan raised one arm, then both, waving. The single shot was so close that she toppled momentarily but saved herself from plunging over the edge. She swung around hard, towards the tower.

Through the telescopic sights of the rifle Shearer saw Jordan snatch with both hands at the wind, then he was over the side and the boat was circling around. He brought the binoculars to his eyes and now Jordan's face was resting by the side of the boat. Then he seemed to topple back into the sea, and when he was tugged up again the water had still not washed away the blood.

The other figures in the boat were crouched low, and the tiller man's arm and the hand which had dragged up Jordan's smashed head were the only limbs visible on the rounded sides.

The boat circled on its own axis then, as if on a command, sped away, leaving Jordan's body thrashing in its wake. Shearer realized he was holding his breath. From below he heard a desperate shout and leaned forward through the gap. Jemma Elliot stood screaming up at him, and when he raised his eyes from her he saw that every face was turned up toward him. His own men, the bewildered technicians, all of them.

'*Why?*' Jemma screamed up at him, but he had no answer for her that she would understand.

His stomach and chest felt strange – like a nausea that couldn't reach his throat. It was not from the killing; he knew that. He had killed too many times before. He looked down again. The girl had dropped to her knees and he supposed she was crying, though for all he knew she could have been praying. But for whom? For Jordan? Herself? But not for him.

He saw the noiseless flickering again on the superstructure of the warship, then, lower down, a deep orange flash and a pure circle of black smoke. The flat report rolled over the island like a thunderclap, then was gone. A waterspout rose close to the Russian submarine, and even without the glasses Shearer could see that she was blowing her tanks. Her bows wallowed and her stern lifted as she plunged for her life to the comparative safety of the depths.

The sound of a chain of explosions swept over the island, and a vast pink and orange ball appeared on the horizon.

Shearer felt desperately ill now and was not really aware of the distant sea battle. He could see the whitewashed granite too close to his face, and he felt the sting in his cheek where the forward iron sight of his weapon dug in cruelly.

Didn't feel it slip, he told himself. When did I fall forward? He pulled himself up, his hands scrabbling at the stone ledge of the window. He managed to get his head through, and now the girl was rising from her praying, beseeching him for an explanation. Though he might have had one for her now, his throat would not work.

He saw the multiple flashes as eight missiles broke the surface and ignited, then they were away. The black inflatable had turned and was coming at full speed back to the island.

Must stop them, he thought. But he knew he could never lift the rifle again. The light in his hard hazel eyes brightened, then died. Shearer crashed backwards to the circular staircase and plunged downwards to the stone basement.

On the bridge of the USS *Pittsburgh,* her captain's fists tightened on his big high-powered binoculars. 'Someone overboard!' he snapped. 'Went over like he'd been shot.'

Around him, his officers had their own glasses trained on the same spot in the distance.

The captain thrust the binoculars at Howard, hard. 'Tell me if you can see Jordan in that boat. Quickly!' He turned away and rapped out orders. The harsh rasp of a klaxon horn echoed through the big missile cruiser.

The binoculars seemed huge in Howard's hands. He moved them in quick, jerking movements, searching. Then the black inflatable was in his sights, arcing around and splashing heavily through its own bow wave. The men inside had dropped flat and all seemed confusion. The boat swung around again and an arm struck out over the rounded rubber sides towards something in the water. For a moment the arm went rigid, straining to keep its grip, and Howard could see the raised, smashed head with its blond crew-cut, now blood red.

'Jordan,' he said. 'They shot him.'

'*Who?*' the captain demanded. '*Who* shot him?'

Howard pushed the glasses back at him. '*Your* people. From the island. The Russian sub's too far away for that sort of shot. Anyway, they wanted him alive. It's you lot who would prefer him dead.'

The bellow of the klaxon died, leaving only the deep throb of the cruiser's powerful engines to fill the ominous silence.

The shriek of the first shell came before the sound of thunder in the distance, and everyone was moving fast. Howard already down on the deck both hands pressed to his ears to save his ear drums.

The sound of the explosion seemed to take an eternity before it reached his ears, and then only after he felt the steel below him shudder and reverberate as if some gigantic hammer had struck the cruiser's hull. You hear the bang and you've made it, he thought. You just used up one more life. He realized they were moving and uncurled himself from the deck, pulling himself shakily to the armoured glass of the bridge just as the steel battle shutters clanged down. One of the men pushed him roughly aside, and Howard came up against a vision slit on the port side of the bridge. Through this he could see the black fist of Beacon Island and the sluglike hump of the Russian submarine. Under his feet he felt the slam of the cruiser's heavy guns and the tilt of the deck as the ship slewed sideways with the recoil. He saw a waterspout appear close to the submarine as, almost instantaneously, the black hull plunged below the surface, leaving the sea boiling in its wake.

Howard turned around and saw the *Pittsburgh*'s captain sitting in his raised command seat, stony-faced but utterly calm as he absorbed data being fed to him from a panel at his side.

Again the great ship shuddered as its guns were fired.

Howard looked out through the slit towards the island and could just make out the black dot of the inflatable as it sped towards land. He saw eight missiles smash through the surface of the waves, appearing to hesitate as they hit the air, their exhausts flaming fiery red against the grey morning. Then they were gone, climbing at supersonic speed, and though Howard crouched low, his face jammed to the glass, he could not follow their progress.

'Enemy ICMBs launched, sir,' a voice intoned, flat and controlled.

'Confirmed?' the captain queried, apparently unmoved.

'Affirmative, sir.'

Simon Howard felt the prickle of terror – and a strange excitement – course through his body. This is it, he thought. No fucking around! It's *happening*. *Now*. *Right now!* He felt absurdly detached – almost as if he were watching each event from some other, safer, place. He could have been watching a film.

An envelope, heavily sealed, had appeared in the captain's hands.

'Enemy missile to port,' said an officer. 'Ship-to-ship. Ten miles and closing.'

The captain unsealed the envelope. 'Scatter decoy,' he ordered.

Port, thought Howard. Left. I'm left! He turned his eyes back to the vision slit.

At first he did not see the missile because he was looking upwards for it, but the sharp flicker of scarlet behind a black speck just above the waves caught his eye and held it. He was mesmerized.

'Decoy scattered,' the officer confirmed.

The speck was now a black blob, and still Howard's eyes were onto it like limpets.

'Missile still closing on primary target. No deviation,' said the officer, and now his voice held a faint tremor of anxiety.

'Second enemy missile launched,' said a man whose face was buried in a radarscope.

'Bring her around,' the captain ordered. 'Full ahead both. Scatter decoy!'

'Decoy scattered, sir.'

Howard clutched at a safety rail as the cruiser swung hard to port, the deck tilting crazily under his feet. Through the vision slit he could see a great glittering cloud of what might have been tinsel as the missile decoy exploded its millions of fine strips of metal foil, forming a false, alternative target for the oncoming missiles. He hauled himself forwards, just reaching a forward vision slit as the first

Soviet missile thundered past the *Pittsburgh* no more than fifty feet to port of the bridge.

The rolling thunderball of the first missile's detonation amid the shimmering foil cloud was lost in the shockwave that followed. The flash, viewed through the vision slit, was like looking bare-eyed into a white-hot furnace. Simon Howard gasped and fell back onto his knees, blinded. He never saw the second missile career over the bows and stab deep into the heart of the great ship.

The USS *Pittsburgh* exploded twice. First from the detonation of the missile's warhead, then from her own magazine igniting – but viewed from afar she blew up once only, turning instantly into a new orange sun on the Arctic horizon. A sun which would never rise and could only die, leaving little or nothing to testify to its existence.

The motorized inflatable sped up to the jetty, facing the guns of the Black Berets. Tavrin stepped out first, then Ulyanov, and the rest followed arms aloft. Ulyanov looked down at himself, then at Tavrin's clothes. They were both splattered by Jordan's blood.

Jemma Elliot ran wildly down the cliff path towards them, uncaring whether she fell. She stopped, winded, in front of Tavrin.

'He was right!' she screamed. '*He was right!* Why is it that men like him can never win? Why do they always have to kill them?'

The Grandmaster lowered his arms and turned his arrogant head toward the growing clouds on the horizon. 'Because there was too much to lose if he had won. He thought, on the board, there was room for compromise. He forgot that when the game is this important there is no place for compromise. Only reality. And reality is winning. Jordan was wrong. So he lost.'

The skies had turned a strange murky yellow and the air seemed charged with electricity. Jemma Elliot snatched at a lock of her hair as it blew sharply across her face.

'And you think you won?' she asked, then turned away, not really wanting to see any more.

THE TORCH

Glover Wright

The Wolf needs you . . .

Each had served under him and knew his power. He was a force, a law unto himself. Now he had summoned them – and the pack had come.

They were all ex-SAS men, seasoned survivors trained in distant hells who owed their allegiance to one man and one man only. His name was Colonel John Fraser. But they knew him as the Wolf.

Fraser was assembling a private army for a very private war – a war not to be fought in the bloodied jungles of a third world nation but in the cosmopolitan streets of London itself. It was a personal war of honour and revenge – waged by men who were never paid to lose and who finally had an even bigger reason to want to win.

'With *The Torch* Glover Wright jumps straight into the first rank of thriller writers' Jack Higgins

BESTSELLING FICTION FROM ARROW

All these books are available from your bookshop or newsagent or you can order them direct. Just tick the titles you want and complete the form below.

☐	ALBATROSS	Evelyn Anthony	£1.75
☐	1985	Anthony Burgess	£1.75
☐	THE BILLION DOLLAR KILLING	Paul Erdman	£1.75
☐	THE YEAR OF THE FRENCH	Thomas Flanagan	£2.50
☐	EMMA SPARROW	Marie Joseph	£1.75
☐	COCKPIT	Jerzy Kosinski	£1.60
☐	CITY OF THE DEAD	Herbert Lieberman	£1.75
☐	STRUMPET CITY	James Plunkett	£2.50
☐	TO GLORY WE STEER	Alexander Kent	£1.75
☐	TORPEDO RUN	Douglas Reeman	£1.50
☐	THE BEST MAN TO DIE	Ruth Rendell	£1.75
☐	SCENT OF FEAR	Margaret Yorke	£1.25
☐	2001: A SPACE ODYSSEY	Arthur C. Clarke	£1.75
☐	THE RUNNING YEARS	Claire Rayner	£2.50
		Postage	____
		Total	____

ARROW BOOKS, BOOKSERVICE BY POST, PO BOX 29, DOUGLAS, ISLE OF MAN, BRITISH ISLES

Please enclose a cheque or postal order made out to Arrow Books Limited for the amount due including 15p per book for postage and packing for orders both within the UK and overseas.

Please print clearly

NAME ....

ADDRESS ....

....

Whilst every effort is made to keep prices down and to keep popular books in print, Arrow Books cannot guarantee that prices will be the same as those advertised here or that the books will be available.